LITTLE CREEPING THINGS

D0171915

LITTLE CREEPING THINGS

LITTLE CREEPING THINGS

CHELSEA ICHASO

sourcebooks
fire

Published by Sourcebooks Fire, an imprint of Sourcebooks
P.O. Box 4410, Naperville, Illinois 60567-4410
(630) 961-3900
sourcebooks.com

Library of Congress Cataloging-in-Publication Data

Names: Ichaso, Chelsea, author.
Title: Little creeping things / Chelsea Ichaso.
Description: Naperville, Illinois : Sourcebooks Fire, [2020] | Audience:
  Ages 14-18. | Audience: Grades 7-9.
Identifiers: LCCN 2019045289 | (trade paperback)
Subjects: CYAC: Murder--Fiction. | Best friends--Fiction. |
  Friendship--Fiction. | Brothers and sisters--Fiction. | High
  schools--Fiction. | Schools--Fiction. | Mystery and detective stories.
Classification: LCC PZ7.1.I1158 Lit 2020 | DDC [Fic]--dc23
LC record available at https://lccn.loc.gov/2019045289

Printed and bound in the United States of America.
VP 10 9 8 7 6 5 4 3 2 1

For Kaylie, Jude, and Camryn,
with love.

1

"Kill it, Cass!" Tina Robbins yells over the pulsing music. My tank top clad teammates scramble into position, shoes squeaking across the gym floor.

The ball is a high lob. I take three running steps to the net, inhaling the scent of sweat and deodorant. Adrenaline hums in my ears as I swing my arms, jumping. My palm slices through the air, pounding the ball.

Straight into the net.

I grind my teeth, biting back a curse.

Ever since Coach started trying out new girls in my spot, I've been training day and night. But I'm jittery; this practice is my only shot at tomorrow's starting lineup. Coach's hand is plastered over her forehead. I'm one screwup away from my new friend, the bench.

Laura Gellman, our setter, crouches in the back row, ready for the next serve. She sneers and murmurs, "You can't say the *K* word around Cass. It's like a trigger. It'll give her ideas."

As I find my position, a memory coats my thoughts in a smoky haze. I turn to glare at Laura, but her eyes aren't small and hazel anymore.

They are massive, like a doll's. And bluer than the sky.

Not now.

I blink hard, trying to clear my vision.

Stephanie Reed squats beside Laura, up at the net. But her eyes have gone impossibly cerulean too. Long, spidery lashes line her unblinking lids. The smell of smoke tickles my nose, and a swell of heat crawls up my skin.

"Cassidy, pay attention!" shouts Coach. I pivot, wrenching my mind from the hallucination to focus on the ball spinning over the net. Stephanie dives for it and sends a crisp pass to Laura, who sets it up my way again. I skitter into place, my steps timed to the beat of this über-inspirational '80s song from our practice playlist.

Three, two, one. I jump again.

But the phantom smoke swirls around me, filling my eyes, my lungs. Its tendrils expand into a thick black curtain as I soar through the air. Every voice drowns beneath crackling fire and the groan of the buckling gym ceiling. I search for the ball in the thick darkness, but my face collides with something real, and I fall backward. All around me, flames dance and leap and ash rains down.

I land flat on my back, face stinging. Gasps trickle through the buzzing white noise. I rub my eyes to find everyone hovering over me. Laura is in the middle, pink lips tugging at the corners like she's holding back a smile.

But her irises are back to small and hazel. The smoke has cleared. Not a single flake of white ash clings to my T-shirt or sprinkles the wooden floor.

I get up—much too fast—and shove my way through the swarm of volleyball players. I spot Gideon at the back of the gymnasium, clothed in football practice gear, and rush toward him. The panic starts to fade with each step closer.

Laura scurries ahead of me, flinging her chestnut-colored ponytail and impeding my path. "Cass, are you okay? Do you want me to call the nurse?" Her sugary voice brings on a wave of nausea.

I brush past her, my legs wobbly. *Do not lose it.* "I'm great." Other than the total-humiliation thing. In front of the whole team and the boy of my dreams.

When I reach Gideon, my voice barely emerges over the lump in my throat. "Can we get out of here?"

He studies me for a moment, his olive skin flushed, dark eyes concerned. Then he nods and slings an arm around me.

We exit the gym, the chatter behind us fading, and stop at our lockers to grab our backpacks. "What were you doing in there?" I whisper.

"I knew today's practice was important, so I skipped warm-ups to watch."

My face ignites. "Pretty impressive, wasn't I? You know, I'm the only volleyball player to nail the triple-axel double backflip mid-spike." I tilt my head. "Minus the spike part."

Gideon squints down at me. "Cass, what happened back there? You can hit that ball with your eyes closed."

"Nothing. Let's just go." Technically, this counts as skipping school because we both have sports for the last period of the day. We sneak down the hall and out the double doors to our bikes. We don't need to exchange a single word about where we're going—we're headed to the underground hideout we built as kids, our one escape.

Any trip to the hideout includes a quick stop at my house for snacks; Gideon is always hungry. My mom's car isn't in the driveway, but we park our bikes against the back gate just in case. The fact that my brother Asher's car is out front doesn't worry me. Before he graduated last year, Asher would have ditched school with us. He was an accomplice in all of our shenanigans.

Asher was accepted to UCLA and NYU but turned them down to start a property management company. My parents were skeptical. *Everyone* was skeptical. It's difficult to imagine someone with only a high school diploma telling grown-ups how to run their investments. But Asher's not most people. My parents said he could live and work from home until he got his company up and running.

We reach the kitchen, where the burnt-toast smell of breakfast lingers. My eyes still sting. How did I let that shiny-haired attention fiend get to me again? I browse the contents of the pantry, tossing bags of chips into my backpack.

"Are we ever going to talk about this?" Gideon's voice is low and gentle. "I couldn't hear what Laura said, but I can imagine." He reaches for my shoulder, and I spin into him, a few tears leaking onto his green hoodie. I look up, and his deep brown eyes wear me down.

I can tell him. He's the one person I can trust with anything. I just don't exactly know *how* to tell him. *Gideon, I hallucinated flaming doll people.* Not quite right.

"Gideon, I think…I might be…" New tactic. "I think I have 'the shine.'" Gideon arches a brow. "You know how Jack in *The Shining* sees creepy stuff around every corner, and he's not sure if it's really there or if he's hallucinating?" I take a deep breath and spit it out. "I had a similar premonition in the gym."

Gideon shoots me a wry look. "You saw demonic twins in the school gymnasium."

"More like I saw the gym go up in flames," I say somberly.

"Wait a minute," he starts, leaning toward me, but the wooden hallway floor creaks and we jerk apart.

Asher saunters in, wearing dark jeans and a crisp gray polo. He stops when he sees us, eyebrows cocked, and gives a curt wave. "I thought I heard voices." His gaze travels to the wall clock above the counter. "Shouldn't you two criminals be somewhere?"

"Uh," I stammer, "yeah. We were—"

"Cass had a rough day," Gideon cuts in.

"What happened?" Asher's skin is paler than Gideon's, but their furrowed brows match.

My face burns as I draw in a slow breath. "Fire stuff."

Both boys bristle, and Asher's fingers graze the jagged pink scars on his left hand. He steps closer. "Who was it? Laura?"

"Calm down. I'm fine."

Asher's shoulders slacken. He steps closer, peering down at me with those crystal blue eyes we share. "I know what you need. A movie night. Tonight?"

I force a smile. "That sounds good." As long as it's not *Firestarter*.

"Great. Maybe Brandon will stop by."

A week ago, the thought of sharing a sofa with Brandon Alvarez would've sent me deeper into depression. Asher's former best friend hasn't been around much since he decided to date Laura Gellman freshman year. Out of loyalty to me, Asher stopped hanging out with him. Then last spring, Brandon and Laura broke up, and Asher got the deluded notion that I'd magically forgive and forget.

It doesn't help that Asher spied Brandon and me getting on swimmingly together at a party last week. I told my brother the truth about my moment with Brandon: we'd discovered we had something in common.

I'll never tell a soul exactly what it was. When the buzz wore off, I tried to go back to despising everything about Brandon, down to that stupid dimple. But I couldn't. Everything's weird now.

Asher's head tilts toward Gideon. "Cass, give us a sec, okay?" I nod. They duck into the hall, and I can't make out a word over the hum of the air-conditioning.

I stand alone in the cold kitchen, backpack heavy in my hands. The whispers floating through the air send pangs into my gut. I hate their guy talk.

Moments later, they slink back in, smiling.

"Okay." Asher checks his back pocket for his wallet. "I ran out of printer ink, so I'm off to see if Carver's has anything remotely compatible. If not, I'll be back in three hours." He's exaggerating, but not by much. Maribel, Oregon, is a tiny former lumber town in the rural depths of the state. We have one drugstore, one diner, one dive bar, and one ice cream parlor. If that doesn't cut it, the nearest shopping center is an hour drive. Though Maribel boasts breathtaking scenery, boredom is the leading cause of death. I don't plan on sticking around long enough to challenge that statistic.

Asher grabs his keys from the hook by the door. "See you tonight." He tosses me one last concerned look before the door clanks behind him.

I turn to Gideon. "What was that about?"

He sighs. "What do you think? He tried to pump me for more information. I honored your wishes and kept quiet. He just told me to watch out for you."

My heart surges and falls. Of course. My brother, the hero. He has a way of making me immensely grateful and astoundingly irritated all at once. "You always watch out for me, Giddy."

Gideon zips my backpack and takes it from me, shoulders rolling as he hefts it on. "Tell your brother that. And tell me we're going to exact some sort of vengeance on Laura."

I follow him out the back door. "Why is she such a terrible person?"

"Please remember she's not really a person. Laura—demon spawn, alien, whatever she is—is jealous of you."

"Sure," I mutter dryly. But we both know why Laura really targets me.

We begin walking through the forested area behind my house. The fragrance of my mom's perfectly pruned jasmines fades, replaced by fresh pine and earth. A cool wind whips through the trees, and I wrap my arms around myself. Gideon stops suddenly, and grumbles, "I forgot about Dave's thing tonight."

Right. Dave Halper's big party. Gideon and the rest of the football players are supposed to go, which means he wants me to go and keep him company while our schoolmates grope one another until they puke.

I pick at a fingernail. "We already met our quota of *things* for the year. Wouldn't you rather stay in tonight and watch movies?"

"Of course. I just promised I'd stop by. But I can text Dave that something came up."

He starts walking again and I tag along after him. "Gid—"

"Cass, I'm supposed to be making *you* feel better. Forget the party. Forget Laura. Let's talk about life's big questions. Like…what are you going to study in college that combines your academic prowess with your volleyball abilities?" Gideon scratches his head as if in genuine, deep thought. "What sort of profession entails working equations while cramming a ball into someone's face?" His smile is contagious.

"I'm sure we can think of something," I joke.

"We'll have to make a list of those prerequisites and you can give them to the guidance counselor, Whatshername, at your next appointment."

"Whatshername was always my favorite counselor."

"Definitely beats out my counselor, Whatshisname, a.k.a. Haymitch, when it comes to counsel." Gideon's steps pause. "Though I'm starting to wonder if the Haymitch thing applies to more than his uncanny resemblance to Woody Harrelson."

"Ahhh, you think there's a flask behind the desk?"

"His cheeks are so gosh-darn rosy." He passes me a silly, knowing look, and I punch him in the arm.

We reach the small creek that runs through my family's property. At this hour in the afternoon, the creek becomes enchanted by the sunlight that bursts through the spaces in the trees, making the water shimmer. We carefully hop over a few stones blanketed in green moss to cross to the other side.

Gideon and I approach the barricade of trees that shelters our sanctuary. We crouch down like forest animals and push through the bases of the tree trunks where the leaves thin out. The grass and weeds itch all the way up to our faces.

Once inside the clearing, we kick aside the woven cover of twigs that camouflages the opening. We tug off the large blue tarp, setting it to one side, and use a wooden crate to step down into the roofless, bunker-style hideout. A crumpled math test and a few empty soda cans litter the floorboards. Gideon shoos a stowaway lizard up the wall and brushes aside some cobwebs while I pull out the snacks. Then, using my backpack as a cushion, I settle into a corner, breathing in the musty scent.

This place had been Gideon's idea. When we were ten years old, I read *The Lord of the Rings: Part 1.* Gideon, on the other hand, didn't have the attention span for it. But one day, he appeared before me beaming.

"I saw *The Fellowship of the Ring,*" he said, his words dripping with excitement and mischief. "My parents were watching it last night. I snuck out of my room and sat behind them in the hallway."

"You watched a three-hour movie sitting on the hallway floor?" I struggled to imagine Gideon staying silent and still for anything for three hours.

"Mm-hmm." His eyes had a vacant look that let me know he was somewhere else—in this case, Middle-earth. "Gave me an idea."

I thought for sure we were in for an afternoon of sword fighting and arguing over who would get to be Aragorn when he simply said, "We're going to build a hobbit house."

"A hobbit house?"

"It'll be our *secret hideout*. No one will know about it except us."

It was our first secret.

Now, Gideon digs a hand into a chip bag. "And if Whatshername and Haymitch can't help—you know who'd *love* to help you find your true calling? Peter. He can't stop asking about you when he's supposed to be helping with my math homework. He's a smart guy. I'm sure he'll have some ideas about your *unique future*." Gideon is smiling, but his eyes aren't.

Peter McCallum is Gideon's tutor. "He's probably trying a lot harder on your math homework than you are," I mumble. It's an old argument, that Gideon could easily get out of the remedial class if he applied himself.

He munches noisily on a handful of chips, reclining against the wooden boards that make up the underground walls. We'd done a decent job for two ten-year-olds, but our hobbit house ended up more of a glorified six-by-six-foot hole. Dirt seeps through the cracks in places, and we have to be careful to avoid loose nails. Rain sometimes trickles beneath the tarp, leaving a perpetual smell of damp wood.

Leaves rustle above us, and the snap of a twig echoes through the woods. "Shh," I whisper, swatting my hand to silence his munching. "I heard something."

A female voice floats into our haven, followed by giggling. I roll my eyes at Gideon, and through the scattered rays, he rolls his back. Some kids at the log. Years back, my dad set up an idyllic sitting spot beneath the pines. Occasionally, kids discover it, sneaking over during the summer or on weekends to have a smoke or a beer, even though this part of the creek is on my family's property. When we were little, Gideon and I used to play spies, camouflaging ourselves within the coniferous trees and trying not to get caught.

We aren't kids now, though, and it's just annoying. I figured we'd have this area to ourselves, at least until school lets out. I want to talk to Gideon, the person who's known me since second grade and never once whispered about my homicidal tendencies in the school halls. The person who's always known just what to say to cheer me up. But now we have to keep our voices down, so no one discovers this place.

Even after Asher became the third member of our trio, back when he and Gideon became football buddies freshman year, I refused to let him in on our secret. Asher has lots of things—the adoration of the town and our parents, for starters. The hideout is *mine*. The one thing I've kept between my best friend and me.

Gideon exhales, his breath warm on my bare arm, and my pulse quickens. A rogue strand of dark hair has fallen over his eyes, and I resist the urge to push it back. When we were kids and built this place, he had the wiry body and static-stricken hair of a primate. Now he's tall, with the muscular body of an athlete. It doesn't leave much space between us in the tiny, underground hovel.

"Come on, you really brought me *here*?" asks the girl. I cringe, recognizing the chirpy voice and distinctive kooka-burra cackle. Melody Davenport. She was in my brother's class at school, and we used to play volleyball together. She's Laura Gellman's best friend and basically an older, blond version of her. After high school, Melody started working at Gina's Diner in town.

"Ooh," I whisper, grinning slyly. "Who's she talking to?"

Gideon listens, chin resting on his palm. "Herself. She has to invent friends while Laura's at school."

"Is that so?" Melody asks coyly, her perky voice trans-forming into something softer. The rest of her words are partially drowned by the gentle whooshing of the stream.

Silence follows, broken only by the occasional giggle and moan. I dig around quietly in my backpack, searching for a distraction as I mentally will Melody and whoever she's with out of the vicinity.

Gideon leans in. "What if she's up there with Seth?" he whispers, laughing into the sleeve of his sweatshirt.

"No way!" I sputter, scrunching my nose. "Melody would never." Seth Greer graduated with Melody and Asher, but before that he was our school's token creep, who loitered behind the bleachers, spying on girls.

Gideon's eyes twinkle with amusement. "They looked pretty heated this morning."

Gideon had tutoring at Gina's Diner in town this morning. When I stopped by to bike with him to school, we saw Seth and Melody arguing outside. We did a double take since Seth never speaks to anyone, much less a girl like Melody Davenport.

"Not *that* kind of heated," I say. There's no way it's Seth up there with her. Still, I plant my hands firmly over my ears, just in case. I make a gagging face at Gideon. He bends closer, using my shoulder to stifle his laughter, and the vibrations rumble against me. Then he scoots closer to the backpack, yanking out his phone.

He nudges me with an elbow and I lower my hands. "I've got to text Dave before Coach calls my mom looking for me."

This part of the forest is a notorious dead zone. The

closest place to get a signal is back toward my house, but Gideon would pass right by the log. Thanks to Melody, he'll have to trek in the opposite direction until he reaches the next cluster of homes.

"Are you sure you want to go up there *now*?" I whisper, my eyes widening dramatically. "What if she's only one of a thousand homecoming-queen-demon-temptresses hiding in the woods? What if she lures you over there with her blond hair and that seductive witchy laugh and then it's a feeding frenzy?"

He shakes his head. "And Asher thinks you need to watch more horror movies." Gideon climbs stealthily onto the crate. "But jot Melody down for the part of blond female vampire in *Dracula*."

"Never," I spit out. Gideon and I like to recast our favorite horror movies with people from our real lives. Whenever we come up with a genius new casting, we jot it down in my mini spiral-bound notebook, which gets passed back and forth during classes and between classes. Or anytime, really. "The day Melody gets a part bigger than *background zombie with insides on the outside* is the day the game dies."

Gideon nods. "So true. That was wildly irresponsible of me." He drags himself up and out of the hole. "I'll be right back."

His footsteps soon fade as he wanders deeper into the woods. I shut my eyes and lean against the boards. I should be doing chemistry homework; instead, I daydream about filming Melody and her invisible stranger. And showing everyone in school. Documented footage of her up there with Seth would be gold—Maribel's queen kissing the town freak. Maybe I can channel the spy days of my childhood and sneak a couple photos. Just to even the score. I reach for my phone, but stop short when a second voice surfaces, deeper than hers and muffled by the conversation of the forest.

My hand freezes. I decipher the words *we're alone*, but a raven's raucous call erupts overhead. An unsettling thought prickles in the back of my mind.

Then, nothing. Only the wind whistling through the pines and the water slapping the rocks. Even the raven sounds like it dropped dead. *Good.* Maybe they're gone. I heft the backpack onto my lap and scrounge up my chemistry book. I flip it open and attempt to focus.

From above, Melody's voice rises. The other person must've already managed to piss her off. She's shouting, words too jumbled to decode, and my irritation climbs. I fumble for the backpack, wondering if I left my earbuds inside.

But then a new noise—a shrill squeal—tears through the trees, stopping my heart. "Hel—" Melody cuts off abruptly, the shriek ending in silence.

A thread of panic spirals through my head, making its way down my spine and out to each limb. *Was that a scream for help?* Over by the log, the other voice speaks quietly. I can barely make it out over the trickling water, but it sounds like "Shh, it's okay now."

My heart spasms. I swing my head around, searching frantically for Gideon. But he's still off trying to send that text.

Maybe he heard the call for help and he's rushing back. I listen for footsteps, for the voices, but the raven's caw—ominous and piercing—starts up again.

Gideon's too far away. I should scream at the top of my lungs. But my jaw is bolted shut, throat obstructed. My heart is working again, pulsing faster than ever before and sounding like gunfire in this tiny space. But the rest of me is paralyzed.

My thoughts and vision blur. Everything darkens. *Breathe*. Lifting my chin, I suck in a deafening breath. Then I grab my phone, remembering with a sickening sense of dread that I won't have a signal.

I have to find Gideon. I have to get help. But one thought punches through the others, drowning all reason:

I have to get out of here.

Because I know the other person up there, the one whose hushed voice drifted over from the log and into our sanctuary.

He and I planned this murder together.

2

My heart jolts. Someone's up there, branches cracking underfoot.

"Cass?" Gideon. I exhale. It's been hours since he left. Or maybe minutes? I have no idea. When I look down, the heavy textbook still rests on my lap, its pages now mangled between my fingers. Gideon drops into the hideout, looking the same as when he left. Like he has no clue the world just flipped itself over on us. But his eyes widen as he takes in my crouched, frozen figure. "What's going on?"

I release the book and grab his bare wrist, fingernails digging into his flesh. "I don't know." But it's a lie. "Did you hear that?"

"Hear what?" Gideon stares at me like I've lost my mind,

which would be better than the alternative—that I drank a couple beers, spouted off an angry fantasy to a guy I barely knew, and then it all came true.

It's not *possible*.

But those sounds Melody made—that scream for help— were as real as my trembling hands and chattering teeth. My mind flashes to the little silver notebook with the gold trim. To the conversation scribbled in its pages, half in my handwriting, half in Brandon Alvarez's. Like an instinct, I slide my hand inside the unzipped pouch of my backpack, feeling around for it. But my fingers don't find its smooth cover.

A new wave of panic surges through me. I rifle around in the backpack as silently as possible, dumping half its contents into the dirt.

My notebook isn't nestled beneath the textbooks like usual.

Gideon places his hand over mine. "Cass," he whispers, voice hoarse with worry, "talk to me." His phone drops to the splintery ground and he pulls me to my feet.

"Melody." My voice barely rises above my heartbeat. I point in the direction of the creek, beyond this wall of trees. Gideon came from the opposite direction; he wouldn't have seen anything. "She might be in trouble up there." We have to get to her. Now. "She needs help." And we can't call 911 from this useless place. I shove my phone into my back pocket. "Come on."

He rubs at the marks I just made on his wrist. "Cass, I don't hear anything." He's right. There's only lapping water. Maybe Gideon's voice scared the guy off.

Or maybe it was nothing. I heard Melody in some sort of lover's spat. That's all.

But my mind spirals back to the notebook. *Get her to the abandoned sawmill.* What if they're quiet because he's taking her somewhere else to finish the job? I climb onto the crate with shaky feet, motioning for Gideon to follow. "Hurry."

He sighs, his breath riffling my T-shirt. I heft myself out of the hole and he clambers up next. "Wait," he says, his voice resigned as he skirts past me. "I'll go first."

I practically push him through the trees. When I see the log, with its scabrous bark that sloughs off in patches, my mind floods with the sound of voices, talking and laughing one moment and silent the next. *Snap out of it.* The ground is heaped with broken twigs, brown crumbling leaves, and dirt, like the rest of the forest.

And Melody's gone.

"What exactly are we looking for?" Gideon asks, brows skewed.

"I don't know." Proof she's in trouble. Proof I imagined everything. "Maybe there's..." Not blood. There wouldn't be blood.

Gideon points at some indentations in the dirt. "These marks could be fresh, but I don't get it, Cass. What did you hear?"

The sound of my darkest desire materializing.

I tug anxiously on the hem of my T-shirt. "She screamed for help. And then it got really quiet." My eyes well up. I keep reliving those sounds Melody made, and my mind flashes to that party with Brandon. To the words I wrote in the notebook.

The notebook that isn't tucked inside my backpack anymore.

Gideon lays a gentle hand over my arm. "We could barely hear anything from the hideout. Are you sure she wasn't laughing?"

"I don't think so." But there's no proof. I look over the dead leaves and endless rows of trees, powerless.

Then something snags my eye. Behind the log, strewn amid the pine needles. A glass bottle. Normally, this wouldn't seem out of place. Except this one is raspberry flavored. More words flash in my head. *Load her up on raspberry wine coolers flavored with a little something extra.* My stomach turns. He couldn't have actually gone through with it.

But there's the bottle. At the exact location I scribbled down. It's all line for line so far, minus the scream. Something must've gone wrong. Maybe Melody caught him slipping something into the bottle. I clutch my abdomen and take a staggering step back. "We have to call the sheriff," I say, and Gideon frowns.

I ignore him and rush in the direction of my house,

pulling my phone out, checking my screen every few yards for a signal. Gideon follows, crunching leaves in my wake. When the sun cascades through the last lines of trees, a tiny bar lights up at the top of the screen. I locate the number to the sheriff's station and dial. It rings over and over again, and a panicked thought hits me like a bullet. *What am I going to say?* The only way to save Melody would be to mention the sawmill. And I can't.

The ringing never stops, and I slam the phone against my thigh, muttering, "Stupid small-town joke of a station." But a twisted sense of relief swoops through me.

Nearby, there's a *snap* and I jump, gripping Gideon's arm. "What was that?" I hiss.

He scans the forest and then turns back, staring at me like I need medical attention. Carefully, he places a hand on my shoulder. "A squirrel, I guess. Cass, maybe there's another explanation. Maybe this guy was hurt, and Melody screamed for help. It could've been an accident."

Maybe. After all, we didn't *see* anything. Still, my voice quavers when I say, "You're probably right. I just have to make sure."

Gideon's eyes dart toward the edge of the woods. "Melody's house isn't far. We could grab our bikes and swing by. Maybe we'll see her and Seth on the way, and it'll set your mind at ease."

"It wasn't Seth," I say before I can stop myself.

Gideon's forehead creases. "Who do you think it was?"

Brandon. "I don't know. But we're wasting time standing here." He could already be taking her into the hills. And if someone finds that notebook, he could try to pin it on me; his word against mine. No one wanted Melody gone more than I did.

And he knows it.

Maybe that was his plan all along. An image flickers in my head. My face silhouetted by flames. Melody's laughter resounding in the background.

I wipe the sweat from my forehead and start in the direction of my backyard. "Let's get the bikes."

As we speed-walk to my house, I rack my brain for where that notebook could be. I meant to tear out the pages Brandon and I used before Gideon saw them. But by the time morning came around and the hangover had kicked me in the face, I'd forgotten all about it.

I inhale, trying to talk some sense into myself. It probably fell out of my backpack when we were getting snacks. Or maybe even in my room while I was doing homework last night.

Suddenly, I remember with a gush of relief: the notebook is still in my purse. I never took it out after the party. At least, I don't think I did. But this cloudy vision and jet-speed heart rate are making it impossible to remember clearly.

We brush through the last line of trees, finding our bikes

propped against my back fence. The wooden slats covering the back of the house, the shrubs framing the yard—everything looks distorted, like I'm stuck in a nightmare. I'm scrounging for an excuse to duck inside when a car door slams around the front of the house.

"I think Asher's home," I call to Gideon, hurrying through the back gate. "If Melody walked or drove back from the woods, he might've passed her."

"Good idea," Gideon says, the lines around his mouth softening.

"But…" I pause on the back porch. "Don't tell him what happened." If I give my brother one more reason to worry about me, he'll probably lock me up or call our parents. "Make something up."

Gideon shoves his hands inside his pockets and follows me without answering.

I slide open the glass door to the house and continue into the kitchen. Scanning the floor with each step, I find no trace of the notebook. I leave Gideon in the kitchen, calling out to Asher down the hall. But he must still be unloading the car out front.

I yank open my bedroom door and rush to the desk, scrambling for the small faux-leather saddlebag I took to the party on Saturday. I dump it out, frantically combing through the lipstick and tissues.

But the notebook isn't there.

Slumping to the floor, I search under the bed, but there's no sign of its shiny silver cover. Could I have dropped it in the diner that night? My heartbeat quickens as I imagine the people who could have picked it up. Especially if something bad really did happen to Melody. I scrounge through my drawers, mentally flipping through the events of the last couple of days.

A thought makes my heart skid.

I went to the restroom that night before leaving the diner. And I left my purse on the seat of the booth. It was only for a minute, but I never should have trusted someone sketchy enough to be seduced by Laura Gellman.

Still, is Brandon really capable of killing a person and stealing my notebook to...to what? Frame me for it? Blackmail me into keeping my mouth shut?

I speed back into the kitchen, where Gideon pushes a glass of water into my hand. "Still no Asher?" I take a quick sip and set the glass down on the counter.

Gideon shakes his head. "Cass, what aren't you telling me?" His eyes narrow as I clamber for words.

I gave someone the perfect plan for murder, and he might be carrying it out. If I say it, I'm involved. The thought shrivels and rots as guilt moves in; I'm already involved.

But if I say anything about the plan—if anyone finds out—it's over for me. This town will assume Fire Girl found another victim.

I try to meet Gideon's eyes, but smoke fills my mind as the memory slips in. I blink, just like I did that day when I found myself coated in ash, attempting to cough out the dry, burning sensation in my lungs. "Giddy, someone…"

He reaches for me, lowering his head to make eye contact. My gaze sinks to my gray trainers. "Cass, what?"

I inhale a slow breath. "I think—"

The front door squeaks, jolting us apart. Asher walks in, carrying a small plastic bag. He stops when he sees us, like he did earlier, brows hoisted. "Wow. You guys haven't moved much, have you?" He doesn't wait for an answer, but strolls past, chuckling softly. We remain huddled together, unable to budge.

Gideon glances to where Asher disappeared behind the wall. When he looks at me again, lines mar his features. "You were saying?"

I shake my head, feeling the separation between us like a fog, cold and thick. I've spent the past ten years trying to erase this image. Fire Girl. Trying to convince everyone— trying to convince myself—I'm not a killer. And the only person who bought into my efforts was Gideon. He's always seen a better version of me. Now, that version is about to shatter into pieces on my kitchen floor.

This is the one thing I can't tell him.

"Nothing. Let me ask Asher about Melody."

Hope wiggles its way into my mind. Maybe Brandon

doesn't have my notebook. Maybe I dropped it somewhere in the house, and Asher picked it up.

I knock, my thoughts jumbled as he opens the door. He wears a smile, but it wavers as I stand in the doorway like a mannequin. "Everything okay?" he asks.

"Uh, yeah. Hi." I scan the items scattered on the desk. The crumpled plastic bag is weighed down by a pack of gel pens, some stationery, and a printer ink cartridge. No spiral notebook. "Looks like you got lucky," I say, putting on my best casual voice.

He nods. "Who would've guessed Carver's actually carries something real people use?"

"Hey." I lean against his door frame for support. "I use the cat jewelry, every time I dress up like an eccentric cat lady for Halloween."

He grins, but it fades quickly. "Actually, Cass, I have to print up these documents by three. Did you need something?"

"Oh. I—yeah, sorry. I was just wondering if you'd seen Melody when you were in town. Or on your way back here. I'm going to lose my spot on the team if I don't get some extra help with my hitting."

Asher's eyes widen. "You want *Melody* to help you? She calls you a cousin killer every time she sees you."

Okay, maybe I could've come up with a better reason. "I really want to keep my spot, and she's still the best outside hitter in town. You didn't see her?"

"No, sorry."

"It's fine." But a tiny fragment of hope tears away, leaving an ache in my chest. "Also," I add, trying to act casual, "I was wondering if you'd seen my notebook. The little silver one? I think I dropped it somewhere in the house."

Asher looks up in thought, then shakes his head. "Nope, haven't seen your *diary*," he says with a smirk. "But I'll let you know if it turns up. We wouldn't want the world finding out about your crush on *you know who*." He winks, and I can't even manage a sisterly quip. "I'm sure it's in your locker at school or something, Cass. It'll turn up. Remember, classic horror will wash away all of your troubles tonight."

I sigh through my fake smile and back into the hallway. "I'll let you get back to work." I shut the door, standing there for a long beat.

Back in the kitchen, I find Gideon exactly where I left him, his foot tapping on the tile. "Well?"

"He hasn't seen her. Let's go." I rush out the back door again, stooping to pick up my bike. If Melody's not home, I have to get to the sawmill before it's too late.

Gideon looks worried that whatever happened in the gym today isn't over. That Fire Girl is having an episode.

Maybe he's right. I can't deny seeing the school gym burning down one minute, and blinking to find it perfectly fine the next. But if this isn't an episode—if I really heard Melody scream for help until she couldn't scream anymore, this is time I can't afford to waste. I clench my teeth and start pedaling.

We went to Melody's house once for a party at the end of sophomore year, when all of the volleyball players, even junior varsity girls, were invited. She asked me to go down to the basement to grab more beer, and when I obeyed, she locked me inside and turned up the music. It was an hour before anyone heard me pounding on the door.

The houses in her neighborhood aren't quite as spread out as they are in mine. Large trees drape over the narrow road, creating a tunnel of false serenity for us. It feels like we could ride through and end up on the other side of all this.

When we reach the quaint white-paneled home with mocha trim, I slow down and drop my bike onto the lawn. Gideon trails me up the porch steps and I ring the doorbell.

A flash of blond emerges in the doorway, and my heart soars. But it sinks again when I realize it isn't Melody. It's her younger sister, Gracie, who's a year behind Gideon and me at school. She's on the tennis team. I went to a match last year. When Gracie returned the ball straight into her opponent's face, knocking her to the ground, Gracie nearly burst into tears. Before the girl knew what had happened, Gracie was over the net, helping her up.

"Hey, Gracie," Gideon says.

Gracie blushes and her mouth quirks to one side. The Gideon Hollander Effect. "Hey, guys. What's up?"

My hands are numb. I rub my fingers together to get some feeling back.

"Is Melody home?" Gideon asks, pushing the hair off his forehead.

Gracie shakes her head softly. "She was supposed to be working, but the diner just called looking for her. Apparently, she didn't show up for her shift." My heart sinks to the cement porch, but Gracie flashes a cherubic smile. "My sister's not exactly a star employee, though. What'd you need her for?"

"Just some help with my hitting," I say, using the lie that didn't work on Asher.

Gracie lifts a brow. She doesn't share her sister's hatred of me, but she knows Melody and I don't exactly hang out. "I can pass on a message, if you'd like."

I'm suddenly mute, my foot tapping on the porch.

"That's okay," Gideon cuts in. He sounds cheery, but I feel him deflate at my side. "We'll catch her later. Thanks, Gracie." He musters a half smile, and Gracie's cheeks flush crimson as she closes the door.

"Let's go back to your place and call around," Gideon says to me, descending the steps. "Someone must've seen her."

I follow him to the curb, but my legs slow. *This can't be happening.* I reach the bike and pick it up with Jell-O hands. I slip a flaccid leg over the seat, but I can't lift my feet to place them on the pedals. Everything—the sounds Melody made, the muffled voice in the woods—is swirling around in my head. My bike is too heavy resting against my legs. *It's okay now* repeats in my mind, gluing my feet to the asphalt.

Those words never mean anything is okay. Those were the words a paramedic cooed to me while wheeling me away on a stretcher. The firefighters still worked, their heavy yellow coats fading into the distance as my world crumbled. Those were the words my mom whispered to me after I woke up from a particularly gruesome fire dream a few years back. Only Asher was finally able to help by pulling *Fox in Socks*, my favorite childhood book, from the shelf and reading until his voice became croaky.

The ashes may have sunk into the soil years before, the smoke long since dispersed, but I'd never escape that fire.

Now Melody may be beyond saving too.

I blink again to see Gideon take off down the street. I get my bike moving, but the pedals are leaden. I'll never catch up to him. I huff and wheeze and drip sweat until finally, I give up. I can't catch my breath. I can't call out to Gideon. The words, the notebook, wisps of my giggling conversation with Brandon have landed on my chest and filled my throat, suffocating me.

Gideon's figure becomes speckled with tiny grayish-white flecks. More white dots appear, like he's biking straight into a snowstorm despite the tepid feel of the air.

Overhead, the sun vanishes behind an ink-dark cloud. I

glance down at a snowflake that's fallen on my bare arm. It doesn't melt against the warmth of my skin.

Because it's ash. When I look up again, the horizon is a blazing display of neon orange and red, the sky is black with smoke, and Gideon keeps biking straight into a cloud of ash.

My head feels tight. Too tight. And the silver cloud swallows him up.

3

"Cass." Gideon's voice. Slowly, I blink his blurred face into focus.

"What happened?" I slur.

"You crashed your bike into a trash can. I think you hit your head on the pavement."

I attempt to stand, but my vision fogs. We're on the sidewalk, but it looks like we're floating on a stormy sky. Gideon must have dragged me and my bike off the road before any cars managed to squash me. I wince. The entire right side of my body stings. I'm bleeding from my knee and elbow. I clearly hit the asphalt hard.

Gideon pulls me to my feet and steadies me, brushing gravel off my arm. "We need to get you home."

I want to agree, to head home and watch a movie, safe and snug on my couch with Gideon. But instead I say, "I'm fine. Just some scrapes. I have to get to the sawmill. I have to find Melody." Too shaky to ride, I grip the handlebars of my bike and roll it.

"The sawmill?" Gideon asks, eyeing me. My body sways until he grabs my waist. "Why the sawmill? Cass, you're bleeding and you might have a concussion. I'll find Melody. After I take you home."

I shake my head. "I have to do it."

"Why? What are you not telling me? Why don't you trust me to take care of this?" He leans in close enough for me to breathe in his familiar scent—sweat, pine from biking through the woods, and a hint of citrus from his shampoo.

His face falls. I know what he's thinking. We don't keep secrets from each other.

My gaze drifts to the oak trees lining the road. "I trust you. It's just…" I want to tell him. I do. So he can fix this, the way he fixes everything.

But I can't ever tell him the truth about that night with Brandon. He'd never see me the same way again; he'd see me the way everyone else does. I don't respond, and Gideon growls under his breath, rolling his bike a yard ahead of mine. My eyes sting and my chest wrenches.

"Look, someone took my notebook!" I force out. The words hang in the air as Gideon turns to stare at me, mouth and eyes wide open. I double over, breathing in the grass-scented air with my chest pressed into the handlebars.

"I'm lost."

"I wrote something in there about Melody. Something bad. And now the notebook is gone, and…"

"Cass, this is what I was afraid of. I think someone's messing with you."

"That's not it." But my stomach flips. Or is that exactly it? Melody and Brandon could be doing this together. They could've seen me head into the woods and decided it would be fun to mess with Fire Girl.

The horrible feeling wrapped around my chest squeezes tighter. I blink back the tears. "I'm just afraid if I tell you—" The tears escape, running down my face. I wipe them, smearing the back of my hand with mascara.

"Cass…" Gideon softens, gently pushing a strand of hair behind my ear. "Melody's not at work because she ditched her shift to stay with that guy from the woods. I don't know what you heard, but I know you're not going to get in trouble."

Considering my history, that's the last thing he should claim to know with any certainty. Everyone in this town knows I'm trouble. Or *troubled*. Add that notebook with the detailed murder plan; it seems I've laid out the evidence, nice and neat, right in front of them.

But I can't tell Gideon about any of that.

"Sit down," he says. "I'll call Asher to come with the car. In the meantime, I'll bike to the diner and grab you some ice."

I nod and lower onto the curb. "You're right," I say, touching my head and finding my fingertips sticky with blood. "I probably have a concussion. I'm sorry for acting so weird."

Gideon smiles weakly. "I'll be right back." He places a gentle hand on my arm, and guilt churns in my chest. Then he hops onto his bike, tossing me one last concerned glance over his shoulder.

The second he disappears around the corner, I'm on my feet and slipping a wobbly leg over my bike. I start pedaling in the opposite direction, up the street with manicured lawns and picket fences, and onto the narrow road that weaves through the hills.

To the abandoned sawmill.

I pedal as fast as my weak legs will allow, my head pounding. I might've lied to Gideon about staying put, but I very well could be concussed. A trickle of sweat or blood drips into my eye and I rub at it with a sleeve, keeping one hand on the handlebars. Ahead, a hare hops through the tall grass off the path, pausing on his haunches, muzzle twitching, black eyes wide. I swerve to avoid him as he springs back into the trees.

When I reach the fork in the trail, I brake and dismount. Off to the left, trees line a dirt road that is just large enough to fit a vehicle. If Brandon drove Melody up here, where would he hide his car? I drag my bike through the tall grass a few yards to the right, then I take off running up the windy trail.

Water gurgles in the distance, and I push through the weeds and brambles until the mill bursts into view, its roof partially caved in and the door missing. This place hasn't run since the late 1800s. The mill owner, Tom Garrison, used this place to dispose of his wife, Maribel, our town's namesake. Tom was executed for the murder, but, according to town legend, his spirit haunts the place to this day. If he sees you, the mill starts up and running of its own accord, sawing you into tiny bits that no one will ever find.

Which explains why not even the drug addicts come up here. I near the old building, which looks empty, like always.

But I have to make sure. I can't let someone else die because of me.

My breathing is ragged as I head past the rusted wheel half-buried beneath overgrown weeds and twigs. Knee-high in rubble and vines, I duck under a fallen beam.

I'm not worrying about the ghost of Tom or even about stepping on something sharp and tetanus-inducing. I need to figure out what to do if I discover Brandon inside with Melody, ready to enact part two of our plan.

Or worse, finished with part two.

I tiptoe around the back of the mill. Some swallows dive through the blackberry bushes beside the wheel, startling me.

This side of the building is completely eroded, with parts of the wall missing. Black mold and oxidized paint splotches mingle over the remaining bricks, but there's a tiny stone window for me to peek through.

I reach up, loose mortar crumbling beneath my hand as I push onto my tiptoes and hold my breath. The ruined brick building is empty inside.

I exhale, relief flooding my body.

But then I see a glint. Beneath a rotted wooden bench, tangled up in the dirt and rubble.

I press my face closer, scraping my chin against the stone. My stomach twists. It's a gold necklace with a charm of a musical note. Melody's—she always wears it. The chain is coiled like a bronze snake, its broken clasp shimmering in a slanted ray of sunlight. I lower onto the gravel.

I'm too late. I struggle to take a breath, bending over with my hands on my knees.

Or maybe Brandon heard me coming and took Melody somewhere else.

I pull myself up and skirt the building, searching for any signs she could still be alive. I should get back on my bike and away from the mill. If someone has my notebook and Melody really turns up dead, I can't be seen here.

But if I run away now, I'd be letting this happen.

Back near my bike, I whip out my phone and dial the sheriff's station again. I'll deal with the repercussions later.

Please pick up. It rings, rings again. And then, miraculously, a woman's voice answers.

"Maribel sheriff's station. This is Pam speaking."

"Hello," I whisper, my voice hoarse. "Someone's in trouble."

"Just a minute," she says casually, like I called to schedule a routine dental appointment.

"We don't have a minute!" I hiss, my fingers quivering around the phone.

A *crack* sounds behind me, and I freeze, dropping the phone into the tall grass, the voice on the other end still chattering into the air.

I spin around, ready to face Brandon or even the blade-wielding ghost of Tom Garrison, himself. Instead, Gideon is standing beside an oak tree, ankle-deep in weeds, betrayal etched on his face.

4

"What are you doing up here?" Gideon asks, gaping like I took a swing at him.

"Gideon, I told you we needed to hurry!" I point back to the mill, frantic. "Melody's necklace is in there."

"What?" he asks skeptically. Maybe this is why I was too afraid to tell him. Deep down, I knew even my best friend wouldn't believe me.

"We don't have time," I say, realizing the phone at my feet has gone quiet.

Gideon takes a cautious step toward me. "Cass, Melody's fine. She updated her Instagram ten minutes ago."

"No, she was—" I crane my neck to look back at the

ruins. "But her necklace." I reach down to snatch my phone and then sprint back to the mill. Gideon's steps pound the earth behind me, but I keep running, this time straight through the glaring hole that used to be a door. I barrel through the cobwebs and overgrown vines, kicking over the rotted bench.

But my heart lunges, knowing before my eyes do. The necklace is no longer coiled on the stone.

It's gone.

"How..." I kneel, pushing aside the leaves and trash in desperation.

"Cass, what are you doing?" I stand to face Gideon, who delicately presses his fingers to my cheek. A hint of sweat mixes with the pine scent of the air. "You shouldn't be up here. You're not well."

I pull back, torn between laughing and crying. Maybe I am unwell. Was the necklace an unfortunate effect of my concussion? Another hallucination? Maybe Gideon was right all along, and this was a massive prank.

Or he came back. Brandon could've ducked back into the moss-covered ruins and taken it. He could've cleaned up the evidence.

Gideon tugs out his phone, scrolling through before handing it to me. It's Melody's Instagram account. There's a photo of a deflated tire with a caption: Sooo frustrating when you get a flat and miss your shift 😣. I swipe to a second photo of Melody wearing her Gina's Diner uniform and a big frown. "I checked her social media accounts while I was waiting for the ice."

I reread the words, hearing Melody's loud, whiny voice through the post, clear as day. "She's really fine," I say, barely believing the words.

"She's really fine," he echoes, like a parent trying to convince his toddler there's no monster in the closet. "What were you doing up here?"

My head sags. "I'm sorry I ditched you."

"But what made you—"

My phone rings in my hand, and I jump. It's the sheriff's station. I want to ignore it, but I have to deal with this. "Hi, ma'am, I was mistaken. Everyone's fine."

"What?"

"So sorry to bother you."

"Okay, then," the secretary, Pam, says slowly, like I'm another stupid kid wasting the sheriff's valuable time. Which is exactly what I am. And Gideon knew it.

Stupid. The raspberry wine cooler was so specific. Too specific. Brandon decided to mess with me because he's exactly the kind of guy I always suspected. First, he pulled my darkest secrets out of me like a magician with those never-ending handkerchiefs, then dragged me around all day like a fool.

And now, for the first time, Gideon's watching me in that guarded way people do.

People who know I have secrets.

"Let's go," I say, taking one last look at the ruins before heading to my bike.

Twenty minutes later, I stumble into my house and Gideon helps me to the sofa. "Don't say anything about Melody to Asher," I whisper. I can't deal with my big brother worrying about me right now.

"Fine." He heads to the kitchen for more ice. My mom is in there, prepping for dinner. She rushes out to the living room, carrying the pungent smell of freshly cut onions with her.

"Cassidy, you fell off your bike?"

"Yeah, Mom," I mumble as Gideon stoops beside me, pressing ice to my head.

Asher hears the commotion and wanders in. My mom takes over ice duty, lowering onto the sofa. Her figure blocks Gideon's as he and my brother exchange hushed words I can't make out.

"Do you need something for the pain?" Mom asks.

I nod, which only magnifies the ache. She stands up, lips pinched as she studies me. "Any nausea? What did you have for breakfast?"

"No, and burnt toast with grape jelly," I answer. Satisfied, she hurries off down the hall.

Asher nears the sofa, smiling gently. "Sounds like you've had quite a day."

My face falls. I can't help it.

He sits down on the edge of the sofa, but Gideon hovers at the edge of the living room. "I'm going," he says, his gaze veering to the rug; he can't even look at me.

"You sure?" Asher asks. "My mom always makes enough dinner for you. I thought we were going to sit around and watch movies tonight."

"I'm supposed to go to that party," Gideon says, running a hand over the back of his neck. "I'll text you later, Cass." Then he and his comforting scent walk through the foyer and out the front door.

Asher scoots closer. "What's up with him?"

I fight the aching, stinging sensation in my eyes. "He's mad at me."

"For not going to the party? You're injured."

"No, it's not—it's fine. I'll talk to him in the morning."

Concern floods Asher's face, but he shrugs.

"Asher, do not talk to him about me."

He peers at me for another moment. "Okay." Then he bends closer, gingerly lifting the ice from my head and squinting at my wound. "You've looked better, Cass."

I smile, but it's false and makes my head sting.

Later in the evening, I learn Brandon can't make movie night. Which figures. He's had quite the day, after all. Hasn't he? He's probably afraid I'll call him out in front of Asher for messing with me. But the last thing I want is for my brother to know about today.

Even without Brandon, it swiftly becomes the worst movie night ever. When Gideon's over, we usually watch classic horror. Really, we're all big scaredy-cats. We scream, laugh until we cry, and then find the most inappropriate times to quote ridiculous lines. Since Gideon's not here, we're watching some old, boring movie Asher says is important because it's on the American Film Institute's top 100 list. But my attention drifts. I check my phone every two minutes for a text from Gideon that never comes. I think about that muffled voice in the woods. My notebook, the page smeared with drops of strawberry milkshake. The look on Gideon's face at the sawmill. It wasn't the first time I've seen that look in my life. But it was the first time I've seen it from him.

Growing up as the girl who survived the fire has merited that look from family, friends, and strangers alike. Mostly because another little girl, a neighbor, wasn't so lucky.

Also, because I started the fire.

5

When I arrive at school the next day, Gideon's not in Hathaway Hall, by the lockers where we always meet. The warning bell sounds. Still no sign of him. I sit down in English, finally spotting him in his usual place at the front, where teachers put the ones they need to keep an eye on. His jaw is scruffy and his hair is rumpled. He barely greets my nervous smile.

After class, I try to catch him, but I'm swarmed by Laura Gellman and a few other girls.

"So, did you and Gideon accidentally bump heads while you were making out?" asks Emily Greer, indicating the bandage on my forehead. She leans in with a mischievous grin, her red corkscrew curls bouncing. Emily Greer is the polar opposite of her skulking, raven-haired brother, Seth.

Smiley-faced, bouncy-haired Emily probably should've demanded to see a DNA test before sharing a roof with that guy. She's the kind of sweet that still passes out Valentine cards with little chocolate hearts taped inside to every kid in our grade. But at our tiny school, she gets teased almost as much as I do, just for being related to him. I feel bad for her.

I roll my eyes. Time to go bury my head in a locker.

Laura Gellman glides into the huddle now, smelling like she doused herself in a bucket of floral perfume. "Oh, she had a small encounter with a volleyball yesterday. Right, Cass?" She winks in an exaggerated way, then glances at her phone. "So annoying. Melody isn't answering my texts. I swear, if she doesn't respond in, like, five minutes, she's dead to me."

The word *dead* rolls at me like a slow moving, noxious gas.

I back up, ready to lock myself in a bathroom stall. But Peter McCallum spots me from the lockers and flags me down. "Hey, Cass," he says, tucking a notebook under his arm. "Have you seen Gideon? I need to reschedule tomorrow's session." His green eyes narrow pensively. "Are you okay?"

"Yeah, fine," I say, managing a smile. "Sorry, haven't seen him. But I'll let him know you're looking for him."

If he ever speaks to me again.

At morning break, Brandon's sturdy figure trudges through the hall. He high-fives a teammate before guzzling a bright blue Gatorade. How can he prance around this place after what he did? At the very least, he put me through hell.

At the very worst... I swallow back the sick feeling, watching from behind my locker door as he spins his combination.

I'm done staring at Brandon's back. I need to look him in the eye.

When he finally zips up his backpack, I slam my locker door. "Hey, Brandon!" I call out, hurrying over with two books tucked under my arm.

He looks up with a confused grin. "M'lady," he says, tipping a hand to me. That ridiculous dimple looks like an asteroid crashed into his face. "Cass, what happened to your head?"

His fingers dart toward my bandage, and I jerk back, out of his reach. "Nothing, just fell off my bike." I chew the inside of my mouth. "Hey, do you think Gideon's going to be in trouble for missing practice yesterday? He says he doesn't care, but it was my fault he missed, and I feel bad, is all." I'm rambling, but it doesn't matter as long as he gives something away. Anything.

Brandon reddens. "Sorry, Cass, couldn't tell you. I wasn't there either."

Shocker. "I hope everything's okay."

He shrugs. "Just personal stuff." His brown eyes dart in the direction of his open locker door.

Anger needles into my veins. I tuck my hair behind an ear. "Personal, huh?"

Brandon nods, pressing his lips together tightly. Watching me. He leans in closer and the adrenaline I felt with him at the diner surges in my chest. "I don't know why you're so worried about Hollander. Not even Coach can get mad at that dreamy face." He backs up, laughing, and I suppress the urge to claw at him.

"Besides, Coach has been distracted lately. Marital problems or something. He probably didn't even notice who was there." He shrugs on his backpack and shuts the locker door.

What do you have in there? Did he have the nerve to stash the notebook in there? Or worse—is Melody's necklace stuffed inside? My fists twitch.

Brandon stares expectantly at me. "Well, I hope—"

"Hey, Alvarez!" Dave Halper's booming voice cuts me off. Something nails Brandon in the head and he blinks, stunned. "Where were you yesterday? Coach is pissed!"

Brandon glances down where a foam football bounces and rolls at our feet. He slings me a guilty look and bends to retrieve the ball. "Okay, so it's possible Coach noticed. But your sweet-talking boyfriend will be fine." He stands, right elbow poised to launch the ball.

"He's not my—" I mumble as Brandon hurtles through the crowd after Dave. But I don't finish the thought.

Because Brandon's left hand is still clutching his lock.

He and Dave disappear around a corner down the hall, and I set my books down on the floor, eyes combing the hall as I stand. Then I take a breath and fling open Brandon's locker door. Inside is an overwhelming mess of crap, the boy-sized version of a junkyard. Several food wrappers—probably from the past few weeks—litter the space. I shove one aside, smearing my hand with what I hope is melted chocolate. There are class notes from possibly years back. Folded papers and even more crumpled ones. A couple flat sheets protrude from a pile of textbooks.

My pulse pounds in my ears, but I'm already inside. No backing out now.

I look around again. No one's watching. I flip through his stack of books, searching for the small, spiral-bound notebook trimmed in silver. When I don't find it, I stare down at the notes, hoping he tore out the pages and hid them in here. I unfold them, one by one, so rapidly I end up with two paper cuts within seconds. It's all class stuff. Even a couple of tests, all with exemplary marks. But nothing mentions Melody.

Someone as smart as Brandon wouldn't stick the evidence in his locker. I reach back, dragging my fingertips behind the stack of books, and let out a growl. I'm almost finished pushing everything back, when there's a tap on my shoulder.

I jump, my hand knocking two crumpled pages and a loose pen to the tile floor. I'm caught.

But I swing around to find Gideon, eyebrows skewed. "What are you doing?"

"Nothing." I scan the hall for Brandon before grabbing the fallen items. I cram them back inside, shut his locker door, and stoop to pick up my books. "Can we talk over there?" I ask, pointing toward the less-crowded, outdoor courtyard.

Gideon walks, keeping his narrowed eyes fastened on me. "Does Brandon know you're in his locker?"

"Yeah, he said I could borrow his notes for Mr. Samuels's class," I lie calmly. "Did you go to Dave's thing last night?"

He shrugs. "Mm-hmm."

"How's your head?" He reaches out, like Brandon did. Only this time I don't flinch. I allow his fingers to brush my hair back as he inspects the bandage. It seems like my entire embarrassing display yesterday is fading to the back of his mind.

But Emily Greer rushes over, throwing an arm over my shoulder. "Did you guys hear?" She's out of breath, stray ringlets springing loose from her ponytail. "Melody Davenport never came home last night. She's missing."

"She's—" My stomach somersaults. I look at Gideon, whose dark brown eyes widen as the color drains from his face.

Emily darts off to inform the rest of the masses, and I'm left with Gideon gaping at me like he did yesterday.

The intercom crackles, startling us. "Cassidy Pratt and Gideon Hollander, please come to the principal's office, immediately. Cassidy Pratt and Gideon Hollander."

We turn down the passage to the office in silence, neither of us particularly familiar with the place. Brandon was right on one account: teachers take one look at Gideon's charming smile and magically forget his crimes. Inside, the secretary glances up from her computer and points to the principal's door.

I follow Gideon, finding the leather rolling chair behind Principal Diggs's wooden desk empty. Instead, a large man with a beer gut is seated off to the side of the room. His brown hair is gelled back, his chin is stubbly, and he's dressed in a beige law enforcement uniform with a name tag that reads SHERIFF HENDERSON.

"Hi, kids. Take a seat." He motions to the two chairs in front of the desk, which are rotated to face his own.

I move to a chair, my limbs rigid. Before I sit, my phone dings in my back pocket. I fish it out to turn it off, mumbling an apology to the sheriff. But I catch a glimpse of the text message from an unknown number and open it, my head lowered over the screen.

An icicle of fear pierces my chest, and my fingers shake around the phone.

It's a photo of a small, lined sheet of notebook paper, pink droplets smeared over the surface. It's covered in perfectly legible handwriting; I already know the words.

I wrote them.

To Brandon Alvarez.

Cold sweat breaks out over my forehead. I zero in on the photo and the caption beneath it. Just one line that makes my skin prickle and my heart lunge.

I'm so glad we're in this together.

The phone slips from my fingers, bouncing in my lap. I catch it, wrapping my fingers tightly around the screen, and look up, blinking to find Sheriff Henderson's bulbous gray eyes on me, the color of an oncoming storm.

6

"Everything okay?" Sheriff Henderson asks, a timbre of insincerity to his deep voice.

I clear my throat. "Yeah, sorry. Just my mom." But my vision is tunneling.

"Good. I've called you in to help with an investigation. Melody Davenport's family reported her missing this morning. Apparently, she never came home last night, which is unusual for her."

"Oh." The gash on my head starts pulsing again.

"Gracie Davenport said the two of you came around asking about her sister yesterday. And then my secretary received a call that we traced to your number, Cassidy. She said you sounded pretty upset, but then you changed your mind." His eyes never veer from mine.

"That's right," I say, my voice cracking. The text message spirals through my head. Brandon sent it to silence me. If I mention him or any of the details of the plan, he's going to hand that notebook over to the sheriff. "Gideon and I were in the woods yesterday, and we heard something—well, we heard Melody. And then we heard—no, *I* heard, because Gideon had to send a text—we didn't have a signal." I shake my aching head and start over. "It sounded like she was being hurt."

"How so?"

"She was with someone. At first it sounded like they were kissing. But then it sounded more like arguing, and Melody screamed."

"What time was this?"

"Maybe one or so."

Sheriff Henderson's head flinches backs, and he pulls a notepad from his jacket pocket. "Our records indicate you didn't call the station until two." His gray eyes narrow. "What took you so long?"

Your low-budget, sorry-excuse-for-a-station, that's what. I bite down growing irritation. "We tried calling right away, but no one answered."

The sheriff's face softens. "Sorry about that. We've been having trouble with the phone line. I've got someone working on it. You didn't think to stop by in person?"

Gideon looks to me, worry lines etched in his forehead. I open my mouth, but nothing comes out.

He turns back to Sheriff Henderson. "That was my fault, sir. I thought maybe Cass was confused. I should've listened to her sooner." An unspoken implication shadows his words: *I would've listened if you'd been honest with me.* "We went to Melody's house to check on her first. She wasn't home, and then Cass fell off her bike." He motions to the bandage on my head. "And then Cass—"

"Noticed Melody had posted on Instagram," I cut in before Gideon can mention the sawmill. The sheriff will want to know why I went up there, and I can't explain it without mentioning Brandon or the notebook. "So I figured I'd misheard. Gideon got me home to treat my head."

Beside me, Gideon stares with some mixture of confusion and horror.

"Hmm." Sheriff Henderson's forehead creases. "We're looking into the Instagram account." He stands up, jangling a set of keys and squinting at me. "Cassidy, how's your head now?"

It feels like someone threw a brick at my skull. "It's great."

"Good. I want you to show me where you heard this go down."

———

Sheriff Henderson parks a few houses down from mine, and we lead him to the log. I point out the spot, recounting what

I heard in full detail. Gideon shoots me a furrowed look when we get closer to the log, but I can't read it or even focus. I need another dose of ibuprofen for this raging headache.

After hearing us out, Sheriff Henderson stares down at his notepad for an uncomfortable moment. Then he motions for us to stay back as he approaches the log, clomping a perimeter around it. I wait in feverish agitation for him to spot the empty raspberry wine cooler. Brandon's prints could be pulled off of it.

But he keeps walking until he's made it full circle.

My heart swerves in my chest, and I rush closer. "Isn't there—"

But the sheriff puts up his hand. "Whoa, whoa. Easy there. I need you to stay back." It hits me with the force of a sledgehammer.

He came back. Brandon came back and cleaned up, just like he did at the sawmill. Even those marks in the dirt have been meticulously swept away.

Sheriff Henderson's eyes flick to Gideon. "So, you went straight from here to Melody's house?"

"Yes." Gideon's face falls. "I mean, no."

"Well, which is it?"

"We had to go back to the house for our bikes," I say.

"Right." He frowns. "So now," he says, scribbling more notes, "why weren't the two of you in school?"

My stomach drops to the moss-laden ground.

"We're seniors, sir," Gideon pipes up. "It's pretty common to skip a class now and then."

Sheriff Henderson doesn't look up from his notes. "Doesn't make it any less unlawful." The word *unlawful* slashes through the sounds of rushing water.

Gideon rubs at his face and I try to calm him with a look. It's my fault this has gotten so out of hand. I'm the one who asked to ditch school. The one whose secrets may have kept us from helping Melody in time. "I wasn't feeling well," I say. "Gideon offered to help me get home."

"But then you started feeling well enough to come out here." It's not a question, and the sheriff doesn't wait for an answer. He turns back to the log.

"Should we be talking to you without our parents?" I ask timidly. "Or a lawyer?" All the hours spent watching true-crime shows are failing me now that I'm the one being interrogated.

Sheriff Henderson turns to me, lowering the pen and paper to his sides. That warm smile slides onto his face again. "You two are just witnesses. You're not in my custody, and you're not in any trouble. Right now, I'm trying to find out if a girl is in danger. It's up to you, whether or not you want to help."

A guilty weight pushes on my shoulders for even asking. "We do, sir," says Gideon. "Of course, we do."

The sheriff goes back to his notepad. "Good. You said you recognized Melody's voice, but couldn't hear the other voice very well. Any guesses as to who it could've been? Does Melody have a boyfriend? Girlfriend?"

"We don't know her that well, Sheriff," I say. "She graduated last year, so we only see her at the diner now. We don't know if she's seeing someone."

"So, no idea as to who the person could've been?"

The name *Brandon Alvarez* sits on my tongue like a rotten bite of fruit. I want to spit it out. But I force myself to swallow it down. "We couldn't hear very well."

"Mm-hmm." Sheriff Henderson jots down more notes. "If you couldn't hear well, what made you assume your friend was being hurt?" He looks up, his eyes resting on me.

"She's not my—" *Idiot.* I take a slow breath, racking my brain for something. I know she was being hurt because everything happened the way I wrote it down in that notebook. Because Brandon came out here and followed my instructions, line by line. Up until the point where something went wrong. But I can't tell Sheriff Henderson that. "She screamed for help," I say, the memory resting in my throat. "And then it got quiet."

Gideon nudges a beetle-infested log with his shoe. "We saw Seth Greer and Melody arguing that morning, Sheriff. Not sure if that's helpful."

Sheriff Henderson's lips flatten as he scribbles some more. "Mm-hmm. Cassidy, where exactly were you when you heard Melody?" His gaze draws circles around us.

My heart thrashes against my ribs. I don't want to show this helmet-headed beast the hobbit house.

But it's too late. Gideon's body brushes past mine. Before I can protest, he's at the tree-lined barricade, giving up our shared secret.

Sheriff Henderson follows, sloshing straight through a puddle glowing with damselflies. He stops to squint at the pine trees. "How do you get through?"

"You kind of have to get down on the ground and push your way through," Gideon says, demonstrating.

The sheriff pulls out his phone. "Okay, I'm going to call my deputy and see if Pam's had any updates from the Davenports. Then you can show me inside there." He steps away, and I get down on my knees, scrambling after Gideon. A bundle of pine needles brushes the delicate spot on my head and I wince.

I make it through and sit in the dirt, trying to slow my breathing as Gideon paces back and forth. "You were right," he mutters, his voice low. "I wasted all that time, and Seth really took her."

"I told you she was in trouble!" I whisper-scream.

"It sounded insane, Cass," he growls.

His words knock the wind out of me. I can't catch my breath. *Insane. Pyro. Killer. Fire Girl.* Those are the names Melody and Laura call me. Never Gideon.

Now he sees what they see in me. If Melody's dead, Gideon is always going to blame me.

My eyes sting as I suck in a whistling breath. "I'm sorry."

He's right, though. And it's totally fitting. Because I'm already responsible for one death.

An hour later, Gideon and I are chauffeured back to school, Sheriff's Henderson's cards tucked into our back pockets. Gideon storms ahead of me up the front steps, and I scramble to catch up. "Giddy, wait. I'm going to fix this."

Slowly, he turns around. "Fix it?" His dark eyes narrow. "The only way this gets *fixed* is if Melody turns up, unharmed."

I want to promise that she will, but I can't lie to him again. I hate myself too much already.

"I keep getting the feeling it's too late," he says, running a hand through his messy hair. "That we gave Seth all the time he needed to hide Melody and return to the log to clean up."

"Maybe he's not the guy."

Gideon's eyes dart sideways. "Not the guy?" He lets out an exasperated puff of air. "He looked like he wanted to hurt her yesterday. You saw him yourself."

"Yeah, he seemed angry. Hours earlier. We don't know it was him in the woods. It could've been anyone." And it could've been. Between the sounds of the water, that demented raven, and the pounding of my heart, I couldn't hear the other voice clearly.

But I have more than the voice from the woods to go on.

Gideon glowers at me, and it isn't in the childish way he used to. Then he turns and paces off down the hall. I scramble to keep up until he stops at the doors to the outer courtyard. "Why did you bike up into the hills? To the abandoned mill of all places? And why did you lie to the sheriff about it?"

I twist my lips, the text message flashing in my mind. My head darts around, checking to see if Brandon is listening to my every word. The lunch bell sounds, and classroom doors fling open as students flood the hall. Gideon broods for a moment, but then he lays a hand on my arm. "Whatever you're worried about, you can tell me. You know that, right?" His dark eyes bore into mine, and I force a smile. I lean into his shoulder, trying to hold back the tears.

After the way he looked at me yesterday, I don't believe him.

"Come over tonight," I say, looking up. "I have to ride the bench at our game after school, but then I'm free. We'll figure out something. I'll help you spy on Seth."

"I'm not letting you anywhere near that guy."

I cock an eyebrow. "Just come over. Maybe by then, we'll have some news."

He nods, but his eyes tell me he's miles, maybe universes away. This time, it isn't Middle-earth.

We walk back, side by side. But an eerie hum weaves through the hall. Whispering. A hundred sets of eyes stare at us.

Kids at school often whisper about me. And they whisper about Gideon. But they especially like to whisper about the two of us together. Mostly because Melody liked to spread the thought that a guy like Gideon shouldn't be friends with a murderer like me. And when Melody graduated, her apprentice Laura carried on the tradition. We're used to it.

Which is why it stings when Gideon mumbles, "I'll see you after school," and speeds off down the hall without me.

Watching him flee reminds me of the day he left me on the log in ninth grade. It's a moment I think of often, even though the pain is still fresh.

He'd grabbed my hand in that innocent way he had a million times. Like the day we became friends on the Harris County Zoo field trip, when he stopped chasing his paper airplane long enough to take my hand and lead me away from the snickering kids and their fire jokes.

But this time, when he pulled me, it was to a seat beside him on the log.

I laughed at first. We'd overheard teenage drama unfold on the log once or twice, so I figured Gideon was staging a reenactment. At fourteen, he was about my height and stared me straight in the eyes. Eventually, his firm gaze halted my laughter. The face looking back at me was different, somehow.

Focused—on me.

"Giddy." It had to be a joke. But before I'd finished my thought, Gideon's lips pressed to mine.

I froze, dazed. When he pulled back, shy smiles tugged at our lips. He took my hand again, and a new feeling fluttered in my stomach. I had loved Gideon since the day of the zoo field trip, but in that innocent way best friends love each other.

As I looked into his dark eyes, my hand resting perfectly in his, I knew I would love Gideon Hollander in this new way for the rest of my days.

But a strange look washed over his face. Uncomfortable silence. He gave my hand a gentle squeeze. Then he let go. He jumped off the log and strode awkwardly ahead of me through the woods.

The new feeling seized and tumbled like a baby bird too young for flight. I wanted it back—I wanted *him* back. But the spot beside me on the log was empty, and it stayed that way.

There was no discussion about what happened, about why Gideon never wanted to repeat our kiss. We remained as close as ever; I refused to let my confusion push him away. But we never held hands in that careless, innocent way kids do again.

We weren't kids anymore, anyway.

I've wondered a lot over the last few years about what stopped Gideon from kissing me again. I've wondered if kissing me had been like seeing through some sort of window into my soul. If he sensed the darkness in me. The darkness that kept me from helping Melody in the woods. The darkness that had me plotting how to end her in the first place.

Now, I look up at the students still whispering. Still staring. But these aren't the typical sneers and snickers I'm used to.

Emily rushes from one clump of classmates. "Is it true?"

My heart free-falls. "Is what true?"

"That you were there when Melody was taken. Some kids saw you and Gideon talking to the sheriff."

No, they're not taunting me. They're looking at Fire Girl like she's claimed another victim.

7

After school, Gideon gets a call from his mom that he'd better turn in every assignment tomorrow or he's grounded over the weekend. Apparently, guidance counselor Haymitch informed her that Gideon is failing two classes. Next stop: academic probation, which means he can kiss football goodbye.

The two of us are seated on my bedroom floor, backpacks and books strewn about the rug. I'm trying to help Gideon get through his English homework, but he's jittery. He stops every two minutes to ask a "what if" about Seth Greer. I want to show him the threat that came minutes after I snooped in Brandon's locker. Then maybe he'd understand my need for secrecy and stop obsessing over Seth Greer.

Or maybe he'd head straight for the front door.

He can't find out about that night with Brandon. He'd believe what everyone else says about me. I'd lose him.

Even if he forgave me, he'd want to tell the cops about Brandon. And then the notebook would appear on the sheriff's desk. No, I can't show Gideon or the cops yet. Not until I find proof that Brandon is the one behind everything.

"Let's finish this." I flick my pencil against the textbook. "Besides, if anyone knows how to get justice, it's Shakespeare."

"Fine," he grumbles. "But if Desdemona's any indication, we're already too late."

We're only through one subject when my mom calls us to dinner. The kitchen smells of thyme chicken, one of Mom's staple meals. She serves it up but remains hovering over the stove. Gideon and I pick at our vegetables; our nerves have extinguished our appetites. Asher tries to make me laugh by sneaking sips of wine every time my dad buries his head in his phone. I force a giggle, but Gideon's anxious foot tapping against my chair is making me queasy.

Fortunately, Asher is eating enough for the three of us, already on his second plate when my mom sits down. She pours a glass of wine, and the bottle clanks against the table. By the time I'd gotten home from school, my mom—and half the town—already knew about my talk with Sheriff Henderson. She let me have it for not saying anything about Melody yesterday. Now she's past anger and on to whatever terror grips parents when something bad happens to someone else's kid.

"I saw Teresa Davenport hanging up flyers in town, so I stopped to help. That poor woman." She shakes her head, eyes distant as she sips her wine. Like she's envisioning hanging posters of her own child.

"Yeah," my dad says through his chewing. "Very scary. I hope that girl just went on a road trip or something and remembers to call her parents."

"Doesn't sound too likely," my mom continues, lowering her voice. "I talked to Louisa Stevens for a bit, who was helping Teresa with the posters. She says the state police already came in last night and opened an investigation."

I freeze. They'll want to talk to us.

Across the table, Asher stops chomping. "At least Cass and Gideon were able to help the cops with the details. That should point them in the right direction." Guilt ripples in my stomach. He has no idea how much time was wasted because of me. How much I've impeded this investigation.

"Louisa didn't mention any suspects?" I ask. Why is no one saying anything important?

My mom shakes her head. "I doubt that kind of thing would be publicized so soon."

I look at my brother. "Asher, you know Melody and her friends. Have you heard anything? Around the diner?"

Asher glances up from the plate, mouth askew. "Sorry, no. Haven't been over there lately." If Asher had heard something—his little sister's name at the top of the suspect list, for example—he would've told me. He's nothing if not my protector. I learned that firsthand when I was seven years old and he almost died saving my life. I can't help but glance at the scars that wrap his palm and snake up his wrist. Smoke trickles into my vision, and I blink it away.

When my eyes open again, everyone at the table is looking at me. Probably wondering why I'm asking so many questions. I lower my head. "Poor girl. I really hope she turns up. She was such a great…" I mumble, "Volleyball player."

"Is there anything we can do to help, Mrs. Pratt?" Gideon's question isn't conversation filler. He really wants to help.

"That's very sweet of you, Gideon. I'll call Louisa in the morning and ask." She smiles warmly at Gideon, whom she loves like a son. She doesn't have to deal with all of the school principal meetings over poor grades like his own mom does. My mom is left with the angelic boy who sets the table without being asked.

My dad clears his throat. "Let's talk about something lighter. Like how Asher's business is going. Any new clients?"

My brother shrugs. "Things are good. I was waiting for the right moment to tell everyone this, but I'm going to be renting an office unit in town, starting next month. It'll give me a place to meet with clients. And room for future employees."

"That's great." My dad inhales another forkful of chicken. Mid-bite, he adds, "Cassidy, maybe one day Asher will hire you."

I cringe. "Yeah, Dad. That would be great. If Asher could afford me."

Asher kicks me under the table. I yelp and try to laugh, but my stomach is in knots. "Cassidy, knock it off," my mom snaps, steadying her glass. "That's wonderful, Asher. It'll allow you some independence."

Asher turns to me. "How'd the game go, Cass?"

"We won," I say, trying to sound upbeat.

"Thanks to your hitting, I'm sure," my dad says.

Shame heats my cheeks. Luckily, my parents didn't make today's game; they don't know I only played two minutes. Volleyball has always been my thing, the court my place to shine. Every year, when Melody or Laura tried to get me to quit, it only motivated me to work harder. And it was supposed to be my ticket out of Maribel next year.

I shrug and smash a pea with my fork.

After dinner, Gideon volunteers to do the dishes. We finish drying the last dish and then close ourselves off in my room.

I press my back up against the door. "When are we going to find out something about the investigation? Shouldn't the state police have interviewed us?"

"I'm sure that's coming," he says. "I want to go to Seth's house to see if they picked him up yet."

"Giddy, I told you I didn't think it was him."

"But you didn't give me an alternative." His critical eyes pin me to the wall. "We know Seth and Melody argued yesterday. Plus, remember when we all went to Gina's last week? Seth showed up, and Melody said he was stalking her."

The last thing I want to remember is that night at the diner. The night of my colossal lapse in judgment. But Gideon's right. Seth was there, and Melody was picking on him, as usual.

"Melody didn't say he was stalking *her*. She just called him a stalker."

Gideon's head dips in irritation. "It's the best lead we have."

Actually, the best lead we have is the person who texted me at school, right after I snooped around in his locker. But Gideon needs to feel like he's doing something to help, and I'm not going to be the one to stop him.

"Okay, I'll come with you," I offer, pushing away from the door. "Maybe we can look in his car or in the backyard. See if he's hiding something."

"Stay here. I'll take Asher."

I block his path. "You're not going without me."

"Cass, this guy is dangerous."

"Then bring Asher. But I'm coming too."

Gideon sighs, and his phone buzzes. He pulls it from his pocket, mumbling, "Brandon."

Cold, sharp fear streaks through me. Brandon's threat said we were in this together. But maybe something spooked him and he's going to share the notebook. With Gideon. "Ignore him."

Gideon sends off a quick text and tilts his head. "Cass, I thought you were giving him a chance. Did something happen at the party?"

"No," I say, startled. A flush fans up my neck and guilt swells in my chest.

"Then it's still about Laura?" He passes me a knowing look. "You can be honest with me."

Gideon's wrong, of course. Honest would mean admitting what really happened a week ago at that party.

With Brandon.

I'd never wanted to go to that party, but the boys dragged me along, despite my pouting. There was a lone glimmer of promise: a party would provide an endless amount of faces for casting our favorite classic horror movies. So I stashed the notebook in my purse, planning to spend the evening with Gideon, nursing a Coke and passing the pages back and forth.

But that's not how things turned out. When we got to the house, Brandon shoved a beer in my hand and slumped back against the living room wall. Cigarette smoke and spilled booze permeated every inch of the place. I stood awkwardly, wondering how to get rid of the can and wondering how Asher and Gideon had managed to disappear.

I didn't want to be alone with him. Gideon and Asher insisted that Brandon and Laura were never getting back together, but that didn't matter to me. My resentment was rooted in principle—he'd been a willing participant in a long-term relationship with one of my two biggest tormentors.

Then the front door opened, and I cowered in a corner as Melody appeared. Apparently, she'd deigned to grace a high school party with her recently graduated presence. She strutted into the room, dress skintight, hair majestic, and several sets of eyes frolicked after her, just like old times.

But Brandon made a face. And I realized he was disgusted by the most beautiful girl in the room.

"What was that look about?" I asked, lowering onto the carpet beside him. I knew Melody's big mouth had inflicted some damage over the years. But I'd never seen anyone look at her the exact way I felt. I hadn't managed to ditch my beer, so I took a sip. Just to busy myself.

"I'm surprised she made it somewhere without her sidekick, is all." A slender, dark-haired figure passed through the door next. Brandon's head lowered. "Never mind, then."

"Wait, Laura? Don't tell me you're still hung up on the Antichrist."

"No—well, not anymore. I was for a while."

"Tell me about that," I said, my words laced with sarcasm. But truthfully, I was curious how someone could possibly be so blind to Laura's true nature.

"I just couldn't figure out why she broke up with me."

"You are quite the catch." I widened my eyes dramatically. "It's inconceivable."

Brandon laughed, and a layer of that wall I'd had up against him crumbled. "But see, I finally figured it out."

"She discovered your true identity as a demon slayer and shrank back into the fires from whence she came?"

"No." He grinned and took a swig of beer. "A different sort of devil was whispering into her ear our entire relationship, telling her to break up with me. And that devil finally got to her."

"Melody."

"You got it."

A sophomore boy reeking of body odor staggered into the wall, belting words that bore little resemblance to the ones blaring from the speakers. Brandon and I scooted away, beers in hand. "She doesn't like you?" I asked.

"That wasn't it. She's just...weirdly possessive of Laura. I wouldn't be surprised if she persuaded Laura to drop her college plans and stay in Maribel so they can work together at Gina's for the rest of their lives."

"But Laura's not just a pretty face." Something else about her that always annoyed me.

"I'm sure Melody will convince her none of that matters as long as they're together. Maybe that's why Melody has never had a boyfriend for more than two weeks. Her role as psycho best friend is all consuming."

"Maybe that's not it," I said with a devious smirk. "Maybe Melody is in love with *you*, and this was all part of her big plan to get you to fall for her instead. Actually"—I ducked my head lower—"don't look, but she's staring at you right now."

Brandon's eyes widened. His head whipped from side to side. Then he reddened, shrinking into the wall. "You got me." He bumped my shoulder with his. "What about you? Is Melody still giving you a hard time with the cousin killer stuff?"

"I wish. She's upped her game from schoolyard bullying, unfortunately."

"What'd she do now?"

My face warmed and my gaze drifted. "Let's talk about something else." I took another sip of my beer. Then another.

"Come on," he pleaded. "I told you my embarrassing tale." I attempted to stand, but he touched my arm, gently. "Hey, hey. It's fine. Keep your big secret."

"It's not a *big* secret. She has something of mine. Like…" I said, waving my beer and letting the foam slosh up through the opening, "blackmail."

"What?" Brandon's head sprung back. "Cass, that's—should we—should I—?"

"No." I grabbed his wrist. "Don't do anything. The last thing I need is for her to remember I exist."

Brandon sighed and took my mysteriously empty can. He walked over to the kitchen and came back with a full one. I grabbed it. Popped it open. Poured the lukewarm, bubbling liquid down my throat.

He settled back down. "There's got to be a way to even

the score," he said, leaning closer. "Something to keep her quiet." His now-blurry face grinned.

"What'd you have in mind? Ooh, I know! She wins a free makeover at the mall in Rosedale. But while she thinks she's getting her makeup done, she's actually getting *our* faces tattooed on *her* face."

"But how—"

"Okay, yeah, bad one." I took a few more sips. "We could send her a letter from these big Hollywood movie producers saying they want her to star in their new film. But really, *we're* the movie producers and we get some random kid with a camera to film her doing all sorts of stupid crap that we can splice together to create *Melody Davenport: Documentary of a Dimwit.*"

"Now you're thinking. Or we pay some poor sap to go out with her. If she ever threatens you again, we tell everyone she was dating a male escort the whole time."

"Are you regurgitating the plot to every movie ever watched at a thirteen-year-old's slumber party?"

"Thirteen-year-olds watch movies about male escorts?" His brows furrowed playfully.

"You might be onto something with getting her a boyfriend, though." I chugged the rest of the can. "Maybe if Melody is happily in love, she'll leave the rest of us alone for a while."

"Or, I could get *her* alone somewhere," he said, dropping

his voice. "A mountaintop with a view, like Vista de La Luna. And then, whoops. She fell."

I snorted into my sleeve. "Or you could kiss too long, and oh dear, I think she suffocated." I slapped a hand over my mouth, feigning shock.

Brandon laughed, flashing that dimple on his right cheek. "I doubt anyone could *really* get away with murder in Maribel. Everyone sees everything. When I was nine, I tried to steal a candy bar from Carver's. By noon, my mom and everyone else in town knew about it. No one kills anyone here because they'd get caught."

"You could get away with it," I said smugly. "Trust me, as a longtime viewer of the Investigation Discovery channel. You'd just have to know the perfect place. The perfect time. The perfect method. It could definitely be done."

He shook his head, an amused curve to his features. "Now I'm really curious about what she's got on you."

I turned away. "Just something on her phone."

"Something we could delete?"

"Maybe." I shrugged. "If we had her password."

He was silent for a long beat. Then he nodded once. With finality. "Whatever it is, I'm going to fix it for you."

I felt a hand on my shoulder and when I tilted my head, a fuzzy Gideon stared down at me. "Hey, everything good?" I couldn't help but notice his focus on the lack of space separating Brandon's hand and my thigh.

"Of course." I stood up, swaying a little. Gideon wrapped an arm around my hip to steady me.

"Some of us are headed to Gina's, but I'll tell Asher to take you home."

"No, I want to come. We—*we* want to come. Right, Brayden?" I giggled at the intentional fumble and motioned with a floppy hand for Brandon to follow us.

He shrugged. "Sure, *Casey*. Why not top off a few beers with a double chocolate shake? What could go wrong?"

"What could go wrong?" I slurred.

Gideon pressed his lips flat and slung Brandon a look. It sent an effervescent charge through me. Even in my muddled head, I knew what that look meant.

Ten minutes later, we squeezed into a red booth at Gina's Diner. I nestled against the wall with Gideon at my side, watching the red and white checkered tiles across the room shift and drop like a game of Tetris. Brandon sat down across from me with Asher on the end.

More kids from the party spilled into the diner until every booth and counter stool became occupied. Melody settled into the booth behind us, and I crouched low in my seat, willing myself invisible. Tina, Laura, and Dave joined her.

Our table ordered a round of milkshakes and two baskets of fries to share. Brandon asked the waitress if he could borrow a pen, and then he grabbed a napkin from the dispenser. He began scribbling, shielding the napkin with his letterman jacket–covered arms.

Behind him, Melody started blabbing about Seth, who admittedly, was leering off in the corner at an odd hour of the night. "What a stalker," she said loud enough for the entire bustling diner to hear. Seth was dressed in the Carver's standard employee uniform, a blue button-down shirt. His little name pin still clung to the front, like he'd just finished a shift. Melody spun around to face him. "You can stop staring at us now. Weirdo."

Seth reddened, his gaze lowering to his Coke.

The waitress came back to our table and started passing out milkshakes. I attempted to talk to Gideon, but Melody had used her diner employee privileges to duck behind the counter and crank up the '50s music. She and Laura began dancing and trying to tug the guys from their seats. Asher pulled out his phone, like he was regretting his decision to chaperone a bunch of children. A blushing Gideon tried to shake the girls off. Dave shrugged and got up, smiling like a dopey Prince Charming as his bulky body swayed awkwardly on the diner floor. I sat still, enjoying the show until a warm hand brushed mine. When I looked down, my palm cupped a napkin.

Brandon smiled at me from across the booth, and I was still beguiled or intoxicated enough to smile back. The napkin was folded into eighths. I unfolded as discreetly as possible.

CASS, JUST WANTED TO LET YOU KNOW YOU'RE STILL
WRONG. IT ISN'T POSSIBLE ☺

I rested my chin on my fist, a smile tugging at my mouth. Brandon was trying to keep the comradery going. The thought gave me a rush, like drinking three espressos, one after another. Joking with Brandon, sharing our darkest secrets. It was thrilling in a way nothing else was.

Out of the corner of my eye, I noticed Laura had stopped dancing to glare icily at me. She probably thought Brandon was asking me on a date.

I pressed a knuckle to my mouth to keep from laughing out loud. Let her think that. I fumbled around for the pen, knocking over a water glass. Gideon wiped it up with more napkins, but not before it had seeped through the one in my hand. I dug inside my purse and pulled out the notebook, flipping the spiral-bound pages to a clean section at the back. Then I started scribbling.

No, you're wrong. Get her to the abandoned sawmill. She won't go willingly. So take her somewhere romantic first, like the creek behind my house. There's never anyone there during school hours. Load her up on raspberry wine coolers flavored with a little something extra. Then get her to the mill and strangle her. Perfect time. Perfect place. Perfect method. Perfect murder.

Gideon's fingers unfolded, ready to receive the notebook. Instead, my hand glided across the table and Brandon's covered it. That surge of adrenaline—stronger than the ones during volleyball matches—hit me when our hands touched. I released the notebook and seconds later, he licked his lips and started scribbling again.

Gideon tensed at my side. He was looking at Brandon the way he did at the party—like he might reach across the table and grab him by his letterman jacket. Brandon finished writing and pushed the notebook into my hand again. I took a sip of my strawberry milkshake and read the response.

I HAD NO IDEA YOU WERE THIS WEIRD. TELL ME WHAT SHE DID TO YOU.

The straw slid from my lips, tiny pink droplets falling onto the pages. I rubbed my fingers over the back of my scorching hot neck and wrote.

She has a photo.

Brandon took the notebook, read, and then looked up, wiggling his eyebrows at me.

My cheeks warmed. "Not that kind of photo," I whispered, acutely aware of Gideon listening in.

Brandon gave a dramatic wink, and I giggled. He smiled

widely, deepening the dimple on his cheek. It was possible I didn't hate that dimple anymore.

Gideon leaned over the table. "What are you—" His hand shot out as he tried, unsuccessfully, to snatch the notebook. But Brandon clutched it tightly to his chest. I squealed, giggling as Brandon hurtled over the back of the booth. He did a slow-motion run, feint toss, and spin before passing it back to me. And I slipped it safely back inside my purse.

At least, I thought I did.

All I know is Brandon and I were laughing, Gideon and Laura were fuming, and everyone else in the diner was a dizzy blur.

I did a lot of reckless things that night. Drank too much. Chatted and giggled with a sworn enemy. Forgot about Gideon as the booze swam in my veins until Brandon's dark eyes became warm and that crater dimple transformed into something disarming.

The most reckless thing I did that night: falling for Brandon's act.

Now, I look up at Gideon, trying to bury my thoughts about Brandon. As long as he has that notebook, I can't say a word about him. To anyone. Gideon leans against my desk, studying me. I reach out and touch his shoulder reassuringly. "I am being honest with you."

8

A few minutes later, we're all piled onto my bed. Gideon is convincing Asher to drive us, since hiking into sketchy neighborhoods in the dark isn't the safest. Asher's forehead wrinkles. "So then, where are we going?"

"Remember Seth Greer?" I ask. "He was in your grade."

"You mean creepy Seth from behind the bleachers?"

"That's the one. Do you know anything about him?"

Asher pauses thoughtfully before nodding. "He was creepy. And he lived behind the bleachers."

I sigh. "We saw him and Melody arguing yesterday morning outside the diner. And now Gideon thinks he was the person in the woods. So we're going to spy on him."

Asher shrugs and heads off to tell my parents we're going

for ice cream. Then the three of us cram into Asher's Prius, me in the passenger's seat and Gideon in the back.

Seth's house is two streets from Melody's, in a neighborhood where rusted chain-link fences barely squeeze between the houses. We park at the end of the block and turn off the engine. It's dark, but the streetlamps cast a faint glow.

Asher digs through the glove compartment for his flashlight. "What's the plan?"

"We could knock on the door and try to get Emily to invite us in," I suggest.

"So this is like *The Lost Boys*." Asher turns to grin at me. "We're vampires."

"It isn't funny," Gideon mutters.

"I meant we don't have to sneak around," I say. "Gideon and I are friends with—well, we *know* Emily. I can ask for help with the physics homework. You could just be along for the ride," I say, motioning to Gideon.

"What about me?" Asher asks. "You need two people with you to ask for physics help?"

"Maybe you should stay in the car." I smirk. "You can be the getaway driver."

Gideon sits up in his seat. "Or we're just the distraction. We provide Asher the opportunity to sneak around outside and dig up stuff on Seth."

"I might even be able to get inside," Asher offers.

"No." Gideon shakes his head. "Too risky. Seth might be

home. Cass and I can manage in there. I just want to know more about Seth. If he was seeing Melody, or if he got called in for questioning. I'm hoping Emily will give me something."

"Try taking your shirt off," Asher suggests.

Gideon rolls his eyes and unbuckles his seat belt. "Okay, so that's the plan. One small problem though. How's Cass going to convince Emily she needs help on an assignment?"

I hadn't thought that far ahead. My grades are the one thing I have in common with Asher. The difference is my brother flew through school barely reading more than the titles of his textbooks, whereas I spend all my free time studying.

"Doesn't matter," Asher says. "Emily won't be listening to Cass. Not with Gideon in her bedroom." He has a point. I unbuckle my seat belt and ease the door open. Asher whispers, "Wait. What am I looking for?"

"Something of Melody's," Gideon answers. "See if Seth's car is unlocked. If not, dig through the trash."

"You two are buying me ice cream for real after this."

Gideon and I click the doors shut quietly, leaving Asher in the driver's seat as we tiptoe down the dark street. There's a chill in the night air, and I zip my hoodie up higher. When we reach the sidewalk, I whisper, "What are we going to do if Seth answers the door?"

"Ask for Emily, I guess."

"Or we could just ask him if he took Melody," I say wryly.

"Trust me, I would. But if he knows we're on to him, he'll be less likely to make a mistake."

The porch lights are off as we approach the house, but there's a black or gray Honda parked in the driveway. Gideon rings the doorbell, and my heart thumps. I feel like a criminal, skulking in the shadows, waiting for someone to open the door. *Keep breathing.* We're just here for homework help.

There's no answer, so he rings it again. My gaze darts from one dark window to the next. "I don't think anyone's home," I whisper. Gideon rings the doorbell one last time before we shuffle back down the steps.

I motion for Asher to come out of hiding. His door clanks shut, and he emerges from the darkness, flashlight in hand. "No one home?"

"Nope," Gideon answers. "Let's see if the car's unlocked." He tries the handle, but it doesn't open. "No luck."

"I guess whoever has the flashlight should probably take trash duty." I nudge Asher.

"We'd better hurry," he says. "The neighbors are going to see us digging through the trash and call the cops."

"It's fine. The cans are on the side of the house," Gideon says, pointing. Headlights emerge in the distance, and he gestures for us to get down. My heart pounds as I duck behind the Honda. If it's Seth or Emily, we're caught.

The blinding lights near us, and my heartbeat quickens.

Cold, rough cement digs into my palms. My eyes shut. But the lights dim behind my lids as they pass by the Greer home. We release a collective breath.

I stand up. "I'm done." Despite the cold air, my hands are clammy. "This is stupid." We're not even focusing on the right suspect. "The cops can do this."

"Cass, the cops aren't doing anything," Gideon snaps. "If they were, you and I would've been called in by now. We have to do something." Soft rays from Asher's flashlight trickle over him as he stands up, pained eyes fixed on the front door. His hands lift and fall at his sides. If Melody never turns up, he'll always feel this way. I want to tell him exactly how he can help. I want to fix this for him.

I sniff, biting my lip to hold back the tears, and place a hand on his shoulder. But his body stiffens. Asher's light flits from Gideon to me, like a question.

Maybe I can tell the truth. Yes, Brandon will turn in the notebook. But if I get the cops looking in the right direction, they might find the proof to nail him. They might even find Melody alive.

Gideon and I stare at the asphalt. It blends into the night, encasing us in a giant, black sphere as my mind wrestles with itself.

We clamber into the car in silence, and Asher starts the engine. As we trail away, light winks at one of Seth's windows. Someone's watching us.

Asher parks in the driveway, but we don't make it to the door before it opens. My mom emerges, hand on hip. She points from me to Gideon. "Two detectives came by here looking for you."

Gideon and I exchange a look. A sob racks my body. My mom gathers me into her arms as I burst into tears.

"It's going to be okay, Cassidy." She helps me inside and onto the sofa, taking a seat beside me. Asher slouches into the recliner across from us. "They just want to go over what you told Sheriff Henderson."

Gideon remains standing, shifting nervously. "Mrs. Pratt, did they say anything else?"

My mom digs a card from her pocket. "They said for you to call this number." She shakes her head. "They wanted you both to come in tonight, but I said it was a school night and they'd have to wait until tomorrow."

Gideon straightens. "Mrs. Pratt, I really think we should call now. It's not that late, considering it could make all the difference in the world for Melody Davenport."

My mom inhales deeply. "That's up to your mother, Gideon. I already left her a message, so she should be calling soon. I'm not sure if Cassidy's in any shape to be interviewed tonight. But Cass," she says, turning to me, "if you decide to go, I'm coming with you. You kids are too young to be handling all of this without an adult."

She ambles to the kitchen, and Gideon takes her place on the sofa, wrapping an arm around me. "Well? Think you can handle talking to those detectives?"

His dark eyes soothe me until I feel myself nod. I'll show the cops the threat, explain what's written in the notebook. Maybe they'll believe my version of events; maybe they won't. But I have to try. "Just let me wash up."

In the bathroom, I splash some water over my face and look up at my reflection, hoping the cops won't read the guilt oozing from my red, puffy eyes.

As I take the towel down from the rack to dry off, my phone buzzes in my back pocket. I slide it out and unlock the screen. Another message from Unknown pops up, and my vision zooms in and out of focus, so I can barely read the words.

Hope the cops don't find Melody's phone.

Keep playing with fire and you're going to burn.

Or burn the ones you love.

The lines chill me through, but they aren't the only reason I'm paralyzed minutes later as Gideon calls empty words through the bathroom door. His light knocking turns to pounding, the doorknob rattles, and his voice grows louder and more desperate.

There's a photo of me attached to the message.

I'm wearing a white T-shirt and spandex shorts, but I'm not in the gym; I'm crouched somewhere I never should've been in the first place. My saucer eyes gape at the camera and smoke fills the background.

I know the photo well. Because Melody showed it to me after she took it.

Two weeks ago. On Election Day.

9

"Cass, hello? What's going on?" Asher's voice now. More hammering. "Open the door!"

There are no windows in the bathroom; still, my gaze ricochets in all directions, searching the walls. I fumble the phone over the sink and then clasp it tightly between both hands. I stuff it in my pocket. *Breathe*. With trembling fingers, I turn the doorknob.

As soon as the door cracks, Asher shoves his way in. "Why didn't you answer us? What's wrong?"

"Nothing."

Brandon is watching me.

Or has it been Seth this whole time? Is it really a coincidence that this threat was sent minutes after I snooped around his house?

Whoever he is, he doesn't just have the notebook. A shiver wracks my body. Somehow, he got into Melody's phone.

Asher hovers over me for a few beats. Then he shakes his head and wanders back down the hall.

I try to shoulder past Gideon, but he blocks the doorway, forcing me to meet his eyes. "Hey, are you okay?"

I let my head dip. "I'd rather wait until tomorrow to talk to the cops."

Gideon jerks back. "Cass, I know this is rough, but think of Melody. We're the only witnesses."

It's impossible to think of anything *but* Melody. I'm thinking about how that gold necklace was wrenched from her neck. I'm hearing those bone-chilling sounds she made before going silent. "I know, but I'm not feeling well." This is true. All my resolve to face the detectives and tell them the truth has crumbled into tiny fragments. They're churning now in my stomach. Whoever's doing this knows I had a motive.

Gideon guides me back to the living room. He sits beside me, placing a hand on mine. The phone presses into the underside of my thigh. I dig it out, rubbing my fingers over it, desperate to show him the message.

Asher wanders in holding a glass of water. I take it, my phone sliding to one hand. "Thanks," I mumble as he moves to the recliner.

If I share what's on my phone, the two people I love the most will try to intervene. And this maniac will do whatever it takes to protect himself. He'll make sure I'm locked up, and this town will think Melody was right about me all along.

If that's not enough, he'll find other ways to silence Asher and Gideon.

Until I figure out who's doing this and find proof, I can't say anything. To anyone. I sip the water, letting the possibilities tumble through my brain.

Brandon hated Melody. The most obvious answer is that the notebook never made it into my purse. It fell and he found it. Or he reached under the diner table and snatched it when I wobbled off to the restroom. I'd had so much to drink that I simply believed he could be trusted.

Still, someone was watching us at Seth's house. Maybe Melody wasn't exaggerating when she said he was stalking her. It would explain the scene outside the diner and his presence the night of the party. He could've noticed the notebook fall from my purse. It gave him a plan and someone to frame for it. And a smart guy like Seth could've figured out her phone password.

"Cass." Gideon removes his hand, twisting to look at me. "Your mom can drive us to the station. We'd probably be back in an hour."

"I'll go first thing in the morning."

Gideon opens his mouth to protest, but Asher straightens. "Let her sleep, Gideon. You can call and talk to the detectives now. They don't need both of you right this second." He rests his head on his palm. "You're just going to repeat the same story."

Gideon scoots to the edge of the sofa. "I never know what story Cass is going to tell these days." He stands and trudges down the hall. Moments later, he returns with his backpack, continuing past us to the front door.

"Gideon." The phone is heavy in my fingers. No matter what I do, I'm going to lose him.

"Tell your mom thanks for dinner." He opens the door and strides out. I have the urge to run after him. To show him the text messages. To tell him what Brandon said at the party. Mostly, though, I want him to stay.

And he wants to get as far away from me as possible.

The door clicks shut and Asher raises a brow. "What was that about?"

My phone is starting to slip from my sweaty fingers. "He thinks I'm keeping things from him."

"Are you?"

If I lie one more time tonight, my soul is going to melt into a black puddle on the floor. I bite my bottom lip to keep the words and the tears back.

"It'll be fine," Asher says. "I'll talk to him." He runs a hand over his dark hair. I notice the smooth, shiny pink skin that runs along his left palm, puckering into a ridge that disappears beneath his sweatshirt sleeve. The scars continue up his arm. There are more on his right forearm. He shouldn't have those marks, those permanent reminders of what a disappointment he has for a sister.

When I was seven years old, I was playing out back with a neighbor, Sara Leeds—Melody's younger cousin and the reason Melody has made my life in Maribel a living hell.

My dad had built us an enormous wooden playhouse with white scalloped trim, functioning windows, and slatted shutters. There was a little plastic table inside, and my mom let Sara and I decorate it with an old tablecloth and some tiny porcelain teacups. Sara and I brought our dolls for a tea party. Mine looked like me, blue eyes and brown hair, and Sara's had blue eyes and blond hair like she did.

We were being kids, feeding our dolls cakes made of grass and pebbles on the fancy tea set. But I had an idea to make it even fancier. My mom kept some old candles in the garage, and I'd seen where they kept the fire starter in the kitchen drawer. Sara agreed that a candlelit table would take our tea party to the next level.

I dug up the candles and lit them after several fumbled attempts, the scent of apple pumpkin spice swirling around us.

I turned around to bake up some more of those lovely cakes, knocking one of my mom's china teacups onto the floor. It shattered, and Sara threatened to tell on me.

I moved toward her, begging her to keep quiet. But I bumped the candle. It toppled over, and the whole place went up in flames. Smoke soon filled the space, and before anyone heard our screams, I passed out.

That's what I think happened. The last thing I really remember is yelling at Sara to shut her mouth about that stupid teacup.

I woke up in the hospital. All I cared about was my doll. I kept asking about it until my mom finally told me it was gone. Burnt up. Later, I learned that Asher pulled Sara and me out, but only I survived.

And I haven't stopped hearing about it since.

I was closer to the playhouse door when Asher got to us. I bear faint scars on my legs, where some burning boards fell on me. Asher's scars are from when he went back in for Sara and the rest of the place crashed into a flaming heap. The scars—both of our scars—aren't just a reminder to Asher; they're a reminder to me of how I killed my first friend and almost killed my brother.

Now, I tear my gaze from the marks and shake my head. "No, Asher. I can handle Gideon myself."

His shoulders sag. "Okay. Forget it." He stands up and walks off down the hall. Regret pinches my insides.

I follow suit, shutting myself in my room. I try to finish my homework, but my mind continues to wander. The closest thing I have to a homework-related thought is about Gideon. *Poor Gideon. He'll never finish his English homework without me.* Mostly though, I think about Melody and about the threats on my phone. And if there's any way to get this guy without losing everything.

The next morning, two detectives are on my porch. The one who greets me is a tall man with dark curls. "Good morning. Cassidy Pratt?"

I nod.

"I'm Detective Reyes from the Oregon State Missing Persons Division. This is Detective Sawyer." He motions to a stout woman whose brassy hair is pulled back into a bun.

"Hi."

"Is it okay if we ask you a few questions?"

I scan the houses around us. Whoever's doing this could be watching me right now, waiting for an excuse to make good on his threats. "You should come in. My mom will want to know you're here."

"Not a problem. Thank you." Detective Reyes allows his partner to scoot past him inside the house.

I shut the door and gesture toward the living room. "Please have a seat. I'll get my mom."

"Thanks," says Detective Sawyer, continuing through the foyer, toward the sofa. I scurry down the hall to my parents' room, my heart thumping.

When I return, following in my mom's wake, the detectives introduce themselves again. My mom nods nervously, and I cower two steps behind her. Detective Reyes stands. "This shouldn't take too long, ma'am. We just need to go over your daughter's statement from the day Melody disappeared."

My mom turns to me with an uncertain look. "Maybe I should call my husband."

He smiles warmly. "It's just a routine follow-up. Cassidy is a witness, nothing more." He points to a photo on the mantel. "Is this the rest of the family?" My mom perks up and follows him to the other side of the room, no doubt eager to blab about Asher.

That leaves me with Detective Sawyer. She looks nice enough. Her head flicks to the empty space beside her on the sofa, and I sit. "So Cassidy, Sheriff Henderson gave us your statement. We're just here to follow up on a few things. We spoke to your friend"—she flips through a notepad like she can't remember—"Gideon Hollander. Why was it you didn't want to talk last night?"

Someone is pinning this on me. "I wasn't feeling well. I think all the stress from everything with Melody got to me."

Detective Sawyer stares at me, unblinking for a long beat. "Sorry to hear that," she says, flipping back through her notepad. "Now, there's one thing I'm still a little unclear on." Her lips twist. "Why did you and Mr. Hollander go to Melody's house instead of the sheriff's station?"

"Like I told Sheriff Henderson, I couldn't be positive about what I'd heard. The forest was noisy, with the birds and the creek. And I didn't see anything. I didn't want to alarm everyone until I was sure."

"If you weren't sure what you'd heard, how did you know the voice belonged to Melody Davenport?"

I pick at my fingernails. "She and I were in varsity volleyball together last year. She was—*is*—very loud, and she has this high-pitched laugh. It's...unusual. One girl at school called it a kookaburra bird call, so we looked it up on YouTube and it sounded exactly like Melody's laugh." My foot refuses to stop tapping against the wood. "Anyway, Gideon and I heard that sound in the woods. Melody made it, but then, she got quieter. They sounded like they were"—my eyes divert to the wall—"doing other things after that."

"What kinds of other things?" Detective Sawyer's face is stoic.

Seriously? "Like kissing, I don't know. That's what kids sometimes do in that spot."

"And do you sometimes listen?"

If I touched my face right now, my hand would scorch. "No! No." I lower my voice. "Gideon and I usually go out there because it's quiet. We weren't expecting people."

My mom stirs from her conversation with Detective Reyes. "Cassidy, is everything all right?"

"Yes, Mrs. Pratt," Detective Sawyer answers. "Everything's fine." She smiles and turns back to me. "Just a couple more questions for now." Her chin rests on the end of her pen. "Did you recognize the voice of the other individual?"

My teeth clamp together so hard my jaw hurts. Detective Sawyer's eyes are fastened on mine. My tongue itches to push out the name Brandon Alvarez. But then I remember the wink of light in Seth's window. The truth is I don't know who's doing this. Giving the cops false information will only make things worse. "I couldn't hear it well enough, ma'am."

"So, no idea?"

If the guy with the notebook gets arrested, he'll hand it over. I tug harder on my fingernail. "No, sorry."

Detective Sawyer frowns. "Mr. Hollander wasn't with you the entire time. Is that correct?"

Terror locks my spine into a stiff, upright position.

"For example, he wasn't in the"—she pauses—"*clubhouse* when you heard the cry for help. Or when you heard the other voice."

This lunatic already got to the detective. He handed over the notebook. She knows I have no alibi.

"So it's possible," she continues, angling her head in thought, "that the second voice could've belonged to Mr. Hollander." Her lips curl smugly.

A crack resounds in my head. Black. Tiny flickers of light. I can't breathe. I can't speak. Was this what the threat meant the whole time? *Or burn the ones you love.* Is he going to pin it all on Gideon? "No!" I finally say with too much force. "Gideon was sending a text. We both heard Melody talking to someone before he left. She wasn't talking to herself!"

Detective Sawyer flinches and leans back toward her side of the sofa. Like she's afraid of me.

This is exactly what Melody always wanted. For everyone to believe I'm dangerous. Now that she's missing, she's finally getting her way.

But *is* she missing?

Am I being threatened because I was there the day she was taken? Or am I simply the target of Melody's most brilliant scheme yet? The photo was on *her* phone, after all.

I've ripped this fingernail tip off too low. Stinging pain shoots up to my elbow. My mom rushes over. "I think Cassidy's had enough, Detectives."

"Yes," Detective Sawyer says, her eyes shining with fascination. Or satisfaction. She turns to my mom. "Thank you, Mrs. Pratt. We'll be in touch."

My mom walks the detectives out, and I retreat to my room. I shut the door behind me and call Gideon, but he doesn't answer.

10

When I arrive at school, Gideon's bike is chained to the rack in front of the school steps. He has a truck, but he only uses it when the weather's bad. Normally, he'd be waiting for me by the fountain, but he's obviously still mad at me. I need this argument between us to end so I can have my best friend back.

As I enter the double doors, an array of red curls accosts me. "Hey, Cassidy!" Emily glances quizzically from one side of me to the other. "Where's your other half?"

"I was actually just looking for him. You didn't see him?"

"No. I'll help you look, though. I was putting up these posters, but I'm finished." She points to the walls adorned with her handiwork.

I glance up at the colorful butcher paper advertising the

Sadie Hawkins dance in three weeks. "Nice. Are you heading the dance committee again?"

"No, but I'm one of the core members. You gonna ask Gideon?"

"I doubt I'll go."

"Don't say that." Emily frowns. "I won't complain about you freeing up Gideon for someone else, though. Not like I'd have a chance with him anyway."

She glances at me wistfully, probably wanting some word of encouragement. Too bad I'm in the worst mood ever. "I wouldn't know."

"Oh." Emily's babbling stops for a moment. Then she smiles and continues talking like I'm the first person she's seen all year. We wander the halls, pausing for me to peek through the tutoring center door, where Peter is helping someone who isn't Gideon. As we approach the doors to the outer courtyard, a couple of juniors—Henry Belton and Jordan Lee—enter. When Henry sees us, he tilts his head and whispers to Jordan, who sneers and makes *Psycho* stabbing gestures. The two trot off, snickering.

My fists curl, but I notice Emily has gone quiet. Her eyes glaze the tile floors. "That wasn't about me?" I ask.

Emily shrugs and keeps walking. "Doubt it. The Seth stuff took on renewed life when Melody went missing."

I'm not the brunt of a joke for once. It doesn't feel the way I thought it would.

Her eyes glisten. I never realized how much Seth's sister was affected by all of the creepy stalker talk. We make it outside, past the open courtyard and along a path to where the grassy fields border the campus. Several boys are tossing a football and I spot a shirtless Gideon. My cheeks warm. A group of freshmen girls gathered on the outskirts of the field seem to feel the same way. He nears them to run down a misfired ball, and the girls race one another to get to it first, squealing as a small brunette with milkmaid braids hands it off to him.

From far away, his eyes snag mine, and he hesitates. But he turns back to continue passing the ball. My heart twists. He's never ignored me like that before.

"Do you want to call him over?" asks Emily, twirling a blazing red spiral around her finger.

"Nah. He must've mentioned something about playing ball this morning and I just forgot. Let's go."

Her hopeful expression sinks. We plod back inside to wait for the bell.

At morning break, I glimpse Gideon hiding within the masses of students by the lockers. The dark circles under his eyes are visible from a distance. But he disappears, and I'm left standing alone by my locker.

My eyes sting as I exchange books. I don't know what else to do, so I trudge over to the group gathered in the courtyard, hoping I can finally confront Brandon.

Laura slinks through the crowd to stand beside me. "You okay?"

No, I am not okay. I can't confide in my only friend without putting his life in danger. I can't be honest with the police, or they'll think I had something to do with Melody's disappearance. I have no viable options, and I feel like I'm suffocating.

But there's no way I'm telling Laura Gellman any of that.

"I'm fine, thanks."

"Well, I'm always here for you, if you need anything." I'd like to knock the saccharine smile off her mouth, but her delicate face would probably crack. "Ever since Melody disappeared, I just—I could use a friend too."

Ah, yes. The real reason Laura's talking to me. To garner sympathy now that her BFF is missing. "I'm really sorry about Melody. You must be a nervous wreck." To be honest, she does look especially high-strung today. Her always-haughty voice sounds a bit squeaky.

"I'm wondering if the cops are working all the angles," she adds.

"Angles?"

"Yeah, you know. Taking into consideration all the people in town who have a propensity for that kind of thing."

Is that a dig at me? My eyes narrow. "Actually, Laura, I was in the middle of looking for your ex. Have you seen him?"

Laura's concerned expression melts away like ice on hot

asphalt. "Why would I know anything about him?" She spins around and heads down the hall.

I duck outside to the back courtyard. A group of guys sit along the low brick wall at the back of the fenced-in area, laughing over someone's phone. On one of the picnic tables, a girl sips from a canteen while reading a paperback. I stop at the vending machines, digging through my wallet for quarters for a soda, when a hand falls on my shoulder.

I jump, turning straight into Brandon. "Hey, Cass." His voice is low, eyes prodding. "Can we talk real quick?"

I freeze before spitting out, "Sure." Then I follow him to a spot in front of the wall, away from the huddle of boys.

"Hey," he whispers, leaning in close like he did at the party. This time, his breath smells sweet, like he's been sipping cherry cola rather than beer. "So you were there in the woods when someone took Melody?"

"Yeah." I try to gauge his expression.

"It's totally creepy, right?"

Almost as creepy you acting surprised. "Mm-hmm." He's visibly shaken, but I can't read his eyes. I know I'm tired, but it's almost like *he's* leery of *me*. The way people are always leery of Fire Girl. The thought rattles me, and I take a step back.

"Cass." He lays a hand on my wrist. Gently. But alarm bells blare in my head. I want to shake myself free. "I know you didn't have anything to do with this."

I blink. How did he manage to twist everything around? *Keep cool.* If he has the notebook, the last thing I want to do is spook him. His hand lowers.

"And you know I had nothing to do with this, right?"

I nod. "Of course." Because we know each other so well. "We weren't the only people in Maribel that Melody pissed off."

"No." He shakes his head. "Still, it's such a coincidence. I mean, after everything we said."

"Yeah, I know. But we were just messing around," I say, hoping to provoke him.

"Right," he says, but I hear the doubt blaring through that meek, one-syllable word. "I don't know the details, but I can't get over the similarities to what you wrote."

Is he taunting me? I stick my fists into my kangaroo pocket. "You know what's even weirder? I can't find that notebook anywhere."

He pulls back, mouth open. "It's gone?" But that sparkle lights his eyes. He's definitely testing me.

"Almost like someone took it and carried out the plan."

His brows cinch together. "I hope not. That would almost make it...*our fault*. Right?" He frowns, spinning around before I can answer. An uneasy feeling pins my sneakers to the cement. I never expected Brandon to fall to his knees and confess to whatever I heard in the woods that day.

But I didn't expect him to be so convincing. He looked genuinely concerned that *I'd* done something to Melody.

In third period math, there's a warm-up equation on the board, so I tug out a sheet of lined paper and copy it down. Thoughts about Brandon swim around in my head, preventing me from solving it. Mrs. Larson is chatting with a girl up at her desk, allowing the classroom chatter to swell to a dull roar. I try to tune it out, to block out the memory of Brandon's face as he examined me in the hall. But behind me, Stephanie Reed giggles loudly. "Laura's going to kill you!"

Tina Robbins shushes her. My ears perk up.

I turn in my seat, quirking my lips slyly. Despite being one of Laura's unfortunate minions, Tina has never been anything but sweet to me and everyone else in this school. "What'd you do now, Tina?"

Her round cheeks bloom pink and she glares at Stephanie. "I told you to keep your voice down, Steph." Her eyes flick my way. "Nothing. It's nothing."

Stephanie twists a strand of raven-black hair and grins. "It didn't look like nothing when you got into Brandon's car." Stephanie, on the other hand, is the opposite of sweet.

Tina's eyes widen with panic. "He just gave me a ride to town after you guys ditched me. You can't say anything. I'm not the only one who could get in trouble. Brandon told Coach Vargas he was sick. He could get benched."

My brain thrums in my skull. *No.* "Wait? Are you talking about Tuesday?"

Stephanie nods. "Coach ended practice after you got hit

with the ball. Something about zero tolerance for bullying. Which was kind of ridiculous because Laura was the only one laughing—"

"We would never do that to you, Cass," Tina cuts in, but Stephanie's eyes trail off in disinterest.

My jaw clenches. Of course Laura started mocking me as soon as I was out of earshot.

"But it was kind of the best punishment ever," Stephanie adds, "because she ended practice before we had to run lines."

"Did you and Brandon *drive around* all afternoon?" I use air quotes and Stephanie laughs into her palm. I focus on my warm-up paper, doodling meaningless lines like I'm half-invested in the conversation. But my heart is thumping.

Tina huffs. "Can you two please stop? It was *one* time. I'll probably never see him again, so there's no point in talking about it."

Tina and Stephanie continue quietly bickering, but I don't hear any of it. I slump down in my seat, trying to piece my shredded mind back together.

Brandon was in town with Tina the afternoon Melody was attacked.

He couldn't have been the voice in the woods.

11

I head to volleyball practice seventh period, hoping it will take my mind off things. Instead, the topic of Melody's disappearance springs up before we finish warm-ups.

"I heard she was kidnapped by that weird guy, Sam or Steve," Kate Lowe calls from the back of the court. "Remember? The super-creepy guy who used to stare at us in the cafeteria?"

"Seth," Tina corrects.

"Yeah, Seth. That's what I heard."

Two years ago, Seth was completely normal, other than the fact that he spent a lot of time in the library. But then he started becoming more and more of a loner, hanging out under the outside bleachers where the cheerleaders practice.

He started wearing eyeliner and rumors began floating around that he stalked girls.

In a larger town with a larger school, a kid like Seth would probably go unnoticed. But at Maribel High, Seth became the token weirdo. And after high school, he became the strange, silent local drugstore clerk whose eyes follow you throughout your trip to pick up deodorant or shampoo. His gaze can burrow through your clothes, until you become so uncomfortable that sometimes you just walk out without purchasing anything on your list.

Emily was right about the boys in the hall today. It didn't take long for our tiny school to circulate its own version of what happened to Melody. But...could their version be the right one? If Seth found out what I did to him two years ago, he would have another mammoth reason to want to pin all of this on me.

Laura pipes up now from behind me. "No, I heard she ran away from home because her parents got mad after they caught her with so many guys. She was always kind of, you know."

She dashes past me and I glare at the back of her head. It's just like her to speak ill of the recently disappeared. She never had the guts to say anything like that back when her BFF was running this place.

Kate passes up the ball, but it's a misfire. I see the flash of white and dive for it, realizing too late that our middle blocker, Lillian Jeffries, has called me off.

We collide, tumbling into a massive heap. The ball rolls pathetically away, back under the net.

"Watch what you're doing, Cassidy!" yells Lillian, rubbing her forehead. The sentiment is echoed by the rest of the team. Kate whispers under her breath, "Shh. Don't piss off Fire Girl. What if Melody was right about her?"

What if she was? I'll never know if Melody was right about me, since I can't remember what happened after I fought with Sara Leeds in the playhouse the day she died. Melody has always seemed so certain I started the fire on purpose. The last time she gave me hell for it was two weeks ago.

On Election Day.

It was the day we were to elect the new captain of the varsity squad. Coach wanted us to decide for ourselves. She must not have fully trusted us, though, because she asked Melody—last year's captain—to stop by practice for the occasion. She took over like she'd never left.

Kate and Lillian had already talked me into putting my name in. I knew I'd be up against Laura, but they promised I'd have the votes. Melody held the basket with the slips of papers containing the names, pausing before reading them. There were a few qualifications she had to go over, just to ensure that all of the candidates were worthy of the title of senior captain. I wasn't nervous about that part; the qualifications are the same every year. I have a perfect GPA, I've been playing volleyball since freshman year, and I've never had any disciplinary issues. Lillian gave me a subtle thumbs-up. I was already envisioning typing the title out on a college application: Senior Captain of Varsity Volleyball.

Melody began reading the list. "Number one. Candidate must have a GPA over 3.5." *Check.*

"Number two. Candidate can have no suspensions during the previous three school years." *Check.*

"Number three. Candidate has been a member of either varsity or junior varsity volleyball for three years." *Check.*

My cheeks started to swell. I could feel it coming. But Laura turned to wink at me, and my stomach dove straight into the gym floor.

"Number four." *There is no number four. There's never a number four.* "Candidate must have a clear criminal record. This includes arsonist-type activity that resulted in the death of any other individual." My face burned as she looked up from her list. "Our leaders should be able to protect us, not endanger us, after all."

All heads pivoted in my direction. My ears grew hotter and my throat constricted. Melody proceeded to pull out the tiny slips of paper and read the names. Once every name had been read, she placed a perfectly manicured hand on the pile of papers and said, "Well, that's thirteen votes for Laura, and one vote for Cassidy." Then she brought the hand up to her mouth. "Oh, Cass, you didn't vote for yourself, did you? That's so tacky. Plus, you didn't even qualify." A shrill kookaburra cackle echoed off the gymnasium walls.

Most of the girls stared at their feet. Tina looked at Laura in horror. Lillian mouthed, "Sorry, Cass," like someone had put a gun to her head.

I ran from the gym. I had no plan. I just had to get outside before I cried or tore someone in half. Portable classrooms lined the back of the campus, their doors facing the dirt road behind the school. I headed toward them, prepared to duck and hide until the tears passed.

But someone shouted my name. *Melody.* What the hell did she want now? I picked up speed, skirting the wall and stealing to the front of the portable wing. I tried one door after another until I found an open one and slipped inside. It was the chemistry room.

I shut the door behind me, ready to face a confused Mr. Ladd, the teacher. But the room was empty. Mr. Ladd must've been making copies or getting coffee.

I lowered onto the paper-thin carpet, the laughter from the gym still ringing in my ears. Then the tears came.

My attempts to calm down only made my nose drip harder. I was mid-sniffle when the door clicked open. I jumped to my feet, ready for Mr. Ladd to yell at me for being in his room without permission.

But in walked Melody. She paused in the doorway, hair windblown. Pink lipstick still intact. Brown leather bag slung over her shoulder like she'd stepped into a department store. "Cassidy, what are you doing in here?"

I stood beside a filing cabinet, wiping at my nose.

"Is this still Mr. Ladd's room? He doesn't know you're in here, does he?"

I sniffed. "Why are you following me?"

She batted her blue eyes innocently. "Coach sent me to check on you."

"I was just leaving."

"Cassidy, are you"—one more blink as her body shifted to block the doorway—"crying?" Cue long, dramatic sigh. "Here." She dug into her bag like I was a two-year-old and she was trying to find a piece of candy to shut me up. Instead, she pulled out a cigarette and a lighter. "Take it," she said impatiently.

"I don't smoke."

Melody rolled her eyes and slid the cigarette between her glossy lips. She lit it, took a long drag, and her mouth curled around the sizzling paper. "That's right," she said, removing it with two slender fingers. She blew a puff of smoke in my direction. "You pyro people have other ways of coping with stress." Her eyes skipped over the room. "I think I can accommodate."

"I appreciate your effort." I moved toward the door, trying to brush past her. "But I'm good."

She lifted the lighter then, clicking on the flame and pointing it at me until I backed up. "Just wait a minute. You'll feel better if you light something on fire." She still smiled, but her gaze sharpened. Enough to cut glass. "You know, like you lit my little cousin on fire."

A tingle ran from my scalp to my lower spine. I had to play it cool. Everything I did—every tear I shed, every nervous twitch—would be the talk of Maribel High by the next morning. "You're going to set off the smoke detector." I played with the ends of my ponytail, which started sticking to my sweaty palms.

Melody flicked her chin at the ceiling. "These portables don't have smoke detectors. No alarms. No air-conditioning either, for that matter." Then she grabbed a rag off the whiteboard sill and lowered the lighter. She examined the ink-smudged fabric quizzically as it ignited. Its once-crisp edges twisted and blackened, and wispy fumes spiraled into the air.

"Knock it off, Melody." Louder this time.

"Come on, Cass. Don't act like you're not enjoying this." She lifted the burning rag like a flag. Up and down. The smoke fanned, filling the room, and my mind darkened.

I shut my eyes, but the flames still flashed in my head. Only this time, I wasn't standing in a portable classroom. I was seated in a small playhouse. The faintest scent of apple pumpkin spice still lingered under the scent of burnt wood. Beneath the crumbling table, my doll peeked out, its big blue eyes staring up at me.

Sara was sprawled unconscious on the floor.

I blinked to find Melody staring at me with enormous doll eyes. My heart jolted. I was back in the portable, but I was still seeing things. "Wow." Her voice came out small. Squeaky. The voice of a child. "This is really working, isn't it? Like some twisted therapy for psychos."

It *was* working. I was remembering. I only wished I could go further back. To just before the playhouse ignited. "I said knock it off." Again I tried to push past her, but she blocked me with the burning cloth.

"I'm only—ouch!" Melody dropped the shriveling remains of the rag onto the shabby carpet and her finger flew into her mouth. By her feet, the smoking edge of the fabric brushed a cardboard box of papers—probably homework Mr. Ladd had set by the door to grade—and the whole thing caught fire.

"What is wrong with you?" I screamed, frantically searching for something to put it out. The box erupted, smoke gushing. Flames crackled and leapt in every direction. I finally spotted the fire extinguisher clear across the room. Melody stood in a daze, like she couldn't fathom how this had happened. Beside her, fiery tentacles crawled from the box to the bookshelf lining the back wall. They climbed up the spines of the books like a red, hot phantom, igniting the wooden frame and reaching the ceiling.

But I didn't want to let the fire go. Not yet. First, I wanted to remember. I shut my eyes again.

This time, I didn't find myself in the playhouse. There was no hint of apple pumpkin spice. Instead, I saw Melody inside the portable classroom. I saw myself charge past her.

Slamming the door with her still inside.

Holding it shut as her screams rang through the melting walls and the flames ate her alive.

My eyelids flung open.

A cloud of smoke shifted over the ceiling, followed closely by flames. Like a bright orange tsunami, they covered the ceiling. *Flashover.* I'd heard the term after my playhouse burnt down. Molten droplets poured overhead and smoke cascaded around us. Melody was still standing there, useless. So I dashed toward her, shoving her out of the classroom before the fire consumed her.

I turned back to try for the fire extinguisher again. But the smoke swirled thick around me. The room swayed. I swayed. Then I collapsed onto my knees, searching deep inside for an ounce of strength to pull myself to my feet. I looked up to find Melody watching me from the door frame, her eyes still far too big. Far too blue.

She had her phone. It barely flashed through the raging flames, but I caught a glimpse of silver-white amid the plumes of smoke.

Melody was snapping a photo of me while I was trying to put out the fire. "What are you doing?" I screamed. "I just saved your life and you're taking pictures?"

"Just some insurance," Melody sputtered through a cough. "Let's go! It's out of control!"

I covered my face with the bottom of my practice shirt and sprinted after Melody. Once we'd made it far enough from the portable, I pulled out my phone.

"What are you doing?" she shrieked, snatching it.

I wheezed and tried to grab the phone back. "Calling nine-one-one before every building on campus catches fire."

"If you call them, they'll know you started the fire."

"But I didn't," I protested, glancing back at the billows of smoke and gasping for breath.

"Really?" Melody sneered. "Because that's what it looks like." She held up her own phone, exhibiting the photo of me crouched before the growing flames.

"But you—"

"No one will believe it was me. Not with the photo. Not with your history. You'd better let someone else spot the smoke and call."

"It might be too late." Behind us, the bungalow ceiling creaked and moaned.

"I'm going back to practice," she said, slapping my phone back into my palm. "You should get out of here." She started moving alongside the wing of portables, out of view from the football field and the practicing cheerleaders.

"Melody, wait! You can't show anyone that photo."

She paused, mouth twitching like she was working not to

smile. "You want me to keep quiet about the fact that Fire Girl is back at it again?"

Despite the heat from the flames, a chill wracked my body. "Please. I saved you."

Melody's mouth softened, but her eyes sparkled. "I might be able to keep it to myself. For a price."

I clenched my fists so hard my nails drew blood. "What's that?"

She licked her lips and spun around. "I'll let you know." Then she sprinted off toward the side door to the gymnasium.

Shouts of "fire" erupted from the football field. The cheerleaders in the common area began to squeal. I climbed the fence behind the last classroom and never looked back.

That night the local news reported that a classroom at Maribel High had nearly burned to the ground. No one had been hurt, but everything in the building was lost, and there was minor damage to the surrounding classrooms. The fire chief believed it to be a result of arson. No arrests had been made.

No one had seen me enter the portable—no one except Melody, who seemed hell-bent on proving to everyone in Maribel that I was a bad seed. And the proof was on her phone. All I could do was wait.

I never told Gideon about Election Day. Or Asher. I was too worried they'd try to fix it and authorities would believe Melody over me. I want to tell Gideon now, to enlist his help against Seth or whoever's doing this. But this person threatened the ones I love; the cops already think Gideon's involved. I can't put him in any more danger.

All I know is the cops came up empty. I'll have to dig without involving Gideon or anyone close to me. And I might not have to do it alone.

12

The next day, I snatch up Emily Greer as my partner for our U.S. History decade assignment and invite her over after school. It's easy; Emily follows around us volleyball players—even the lowest on the totem pole—like we're celebrities.

That afternoon my mom is surprised but pleased when I introduce her to Emily. My mom loves Gideon but constantly encourages me to make more friends. Sweet Emily exceeds her expectations.

The two of us settle into my room, using my laptop to research our assigned decade: the 1930s. My room door is wide open, and, five minutes in, Asher strolls by. He pauses when he notices my usual companion has been replaced.

"Hi, Emily," he says, and her freckles vanish in a wave

of red. Asher pretends not to notice. "How's your brother? Haven't seen him around much." He smiles like he has no clue he's nearly killed her. Asher and Seth were never friends; this is formality and Asher being Asher. Last week, he stopped to ask my mom's friend Louisa Stevens about her sick dog. I threw up a little in my mouth.

Emily continues to stare, so Asher turns to me. "What are you two working on?"

"Just a project for U.S. History."

"Ah, yes. The good old decade assignment. Well, I'm off to finish some work. Happy studies, ladies." He tips an imaginary hat and heads down the hall.

Once Emily recovers, it's clear her mind is not in the 1930s. "I can't believe Asher Pratt knows my name," she breathes. "Does he have a girlfriend?"

Sighing, I set my laptop aside. "No, he's pretty busy with his company."

Emily rests her chin on her palm dreamily. "Yeah, I remember he was super smart."

"Right...so, what's *your* brother up to these days?" I pick at my fingernails and try much too hard to act casual.

"Seth? He's still working at the drugstore. Not much ambition. Not like Asher."

"What's he like, anyway?"

Emily's eyes sink to the wood floor warily.

"I'm not making fun of your brother, I promise. I wouldn't

do that." Emily's lips purse, but she stays quiet. "I just mean, do you guys hang out much? I hang out with Asher all the time, so I was curious."

Emily looks back up with a grin. "It's not because you have some mammoth crush on my brother?"

I manage a chuckle. "You got me. I just wanted a date with an older guy."

"Well, I'm sorry to inform you, he's taken."

My eyes widen before I can stop them. I nod, trying to mask my shock. "Oh, that's great. Who's the lucky girl?"

"You tell me. He's been so secretive about it. I've never even met her." Emily rolls her eyes. "But I know she's real. At least, I'm pretty sure she's real."

My heart flaps in my chest. "How do you know she's real?"

"Well, he goes out to meet her all the time and brings her stuff. I guess he could eat the chocolates himself, but why buy the flowers?"

My foot jitters and my palms slip over the back of the laptop. Gideon and I assumed the argument in front of the diner was Melody telling off her stalker. Was it actually a lovers' spat? Between Melody and the guy she didn't want anyone to know about? It would explain why they were in the woods together. I run a clammy hand through my hair and shrug. "Maybe he became a vegetarian."

Emily giggles. "Can we please go back to talking about *your* brother?"

I let out a long breath. "Because why would we actually talk about the 1930s?"

One way or another, I'm going to have to get into the Greer house.

After Emily leaves, I find Asher in the kitchen, eating ice cream. It's my favorite—peanut butter chocolate crunch from Daisy's Ice Cream Parlor in town—so I help myself to a bowl. "Hey, Asher, I wanted to ask you something about Seth."

Asher squints. "Are you and Gideon still looking into that guy?"

"Sort of. Except I'm doing it alone because Gideon is MIA."

"What? Cass, that doesn't sound safe." His spoon clanks in the bowl as his fingers move to the scars on his left hand.

I pretend not to notice, the way I always pretend when Asher goes into security guard mode. "Just tell me what you know about him. All the kids think he took Melody. They're even giving Emily hell about it."

Asher's eyebrows lift, but he shrugs. "Well, you can't blame them, I guess. You walked by those bleachers. I'm sure you remember how uncomfortable he made everyone feel."

I set my spoon down and lean in. "Yeah, but is that it? Did he ever actually *do* anything to anyone? The cops don't seem to be looking at him."

"There were rumors about him figuring out girls' locker combinations and taking stuff," he says with a head tilt, "but I'm not sure he was ever caught. Girls would say he was following them around."

I busy my mouth with a bite of ice cream as guilt swishes in my stomach. But I can't stop myself from blurting, "Emily said he has a secret girlfriend!"

Asher's shoulders straighten. "Okay." He draws out the word.

"Well, what if...what if it was Melody?"

"Melody and Seth?" He shakes his head and chuckles. "I know you're trying to help, Cass, but let the cops do their jobs." He rests a hand on my shoulder. "It was one thing when Gideon and I were with you. But if Seth's the guy, he's more dangerous than everyone thought." Asher gets up and ambles toward the kitchen door, bowl in hand. "Just stay away from him, okay?" He waits for me to nod and then motions past the door. "I'm taking mine to my room. I've got a little more work to do."

"See you." I spin back around, my head nearly sinking into my bowl. I'll never find the proof I need by keeping far away from Seth.

I stay, swirling the ice cream around with my spoon in the quiet of the empty kitchen. After a minute, I check my phone again, a habit I picked up the moment Gideon began to distance himself from me.

Minutes drag by. I stare at the tiny screen on my phone for most of them, willing the glowing beacon of a new text message to replace my reflection. I'm too antsy to sit here. I grab my phone, shrug on my backpack, and head out the door.

I hop on my bike, headed toward Gina's Diner. Maybe I'll have some coffee and get a little homework done. Maybe, since Melody worked at the diner, I'll catch some town gossip.

And, just maybe, I'll run into Seth Greer. He was there the last time I went to Gina's.

When I hit the main drag, I spot a familiar car parked in the small lot across from the diner. It's a blue Honda Civic with a peeled and puckering Maribel High Football bumper sticker.

Brandon Alvarez's car.

Brandon's in the front seat, so I duck behind the wall. He had an alibi: Tina Robbins. No wonder it seemed like he was interrogating me yesterday. He thinks I followed my own plan and got rid of Melody.

But maybe Brandon can help me. He already knows about the notebook, and he isn't a "loved one." Maybe he'll be able to help with my investigation. I remember that furrowed look of concern at the party. The finality of his words. *Whatever it is, I'm going to fix it for you.*

Would he help me now?

If he's headed to the diner, I can accidentally bump into

him. I wait a few minutes, but he doesn't budge. His head is tilted toward his lap, like he's texting someone.

I can't wait like a creep forever; I'll have to flag him down.

I speed across the street to the lot. Brandon's head remains low, his engine off. Must be one interesting conversation. My last few steps are cautious; I don't want to startle him.

I approach the car and peer through the front window. The object in Brandon's hands isn't a phone at all. It's a small, white box. The kind you'd get from a department store to put jewelry in.

Something else in his hand gleams in the refracted window light. He palms the shiny object into the box. It goes into his jacket pocket, and his hand reemerges with car keys.

I duck down behind the car next to his, my legs quivering beneath me. My hands grip the warm asphalt as I take in a shallow breath.

The gleaming thing in the box.

It looks like Melody Davenport's necklace.

13

Brandon's engine rumbles to a start, filling the air with toxic fumes. After he drives off, I let out a long breath. Then I whip out my phone, type a quick text, and send it before I can talk myself out of it.

Can you meet me at HH?

This is our secret code for the hobbit house. In ninth grade, Gideon and I discovered the acronym doubles for Hathaway Hall at school. We figured this might become useful if anyone tried to torture the location out of us.

My legs are shaky when I stand. I have to talk to Tina again. Somehow, there must be a crack in Brandon's alibi. Brandon *was* the voice from the woods.

My phone buzzes with Gideon's response.

When?

My heart lifts. *Now*

OK. OMW

See you

I can't do this on my own. The past two days, I've given him space, but I'm done with that now. Mad at me or not, Gideon's the only person I can trust. And I need him on my side so we can come up with a plan. Together.

I just have to convince him to keep quiet about everything, so he can stay safe.

I arrive at our hideout. It's as magical as ever, but draped in yellow tape and veiled in a darkness that can never be lifted, no matter how much sunlight streams through the crowded evergreens.

Still, I hope once we're together in our special place, he'll have to forgive me. He'll have to listen to me.

I do a quick scan for cops and duck under the tape. When I get through the trees, I kick aside the vines and grass. I pull aside the tarp and step down, using the wooden crate. It had been such a pain to haul that big block of wood out here. We ended up having to rent a shiny red wagon from a neighbor kid in exchange for a pack of Twizzlers. The crate had a dual purpose though, acting as a tiny table whenever we needed to write prank letters or share a hobbit-sized snack.

Once inside, I sit against the splintered boards and wait for Gideon. Leaves crunch, and whatever's gripping my insides loosens. I didn't really think he would stand me up, but I'm relieved to see his face lowering into the hideout before me.

"Hey." I take in the familiar scent of his shampoo mixed with playing football in the grass, the sight of his truant's smirk and those deep, dark eyes. I've missed him, even if we haven't been apart long. Our fight created a chasm between us.

And in the fading light of dusk, I notice that Gideon's winsome smile lines have vanished and instead, harsh creases gather on his forehead and between his brows. He won't meet my eyes, like he's afraid to.

"Thanks for coming."

He nods tersely. "What do you need, Cass?" It's absurd to need a *reason* to meet Gideon, and the question hits me like a volleyball to the gut.

"I don't want things to be like this anymore. I *miss* you."

Gideon shakes his head slowly. "It doesn't work like that."

"Why?" I shrug, pleading. "I know you're mad that I've kept things from you, but I didn't have a choice. I tried to help Melody. I went with you to spy on Seth."

"And bailed before we got anywhere! And then, what, you felt sick when the detectives wanted to talk?"

"No, Giddy. I—someone sent me something. A threat."

Gideon's eyes widen and he inches closer. Overhead, an eerie wind sings through the trees. "What are you talking about?"

"I got a text after Seth's house, threatening to pin the

whole thing on me. That's why I couldn't go with you to talk to the detectives."

His head slumps forward and he passes a hand through his dark, disheveled hair. I try to touch his arm, but he recoils. Like I'm some sort of diseased creature.

Maybe I am.

"It was kids from school messing with you, Cass."

"No, Giddy."

But his eyes are lost. "I should've helped her," he says into his hands. "I should've listened to you. At least she would've had a chance. Now she's probably dead"—his voice breaks—"and I let it happen."

A rogue tear drips down his face until he swats it away. Despite all the times he's comforted me through a cry, I can't remember Gideon tearing up since his dog died in third grade. Sorrow writhes in my chest. I want to reach for him, but I keep my distance, worried he'll bat me away like that solitary tear.

"Please, just listen. I know who did it."

His head lifts slowly. "Who?"

"You have to promise you won't go to the cops or confront this person. Not until we have proof."

"Tell me."

I take in a tremulous breath, the scent of damp wood doing little to aid my voice. "Brandon."

Gideon draws back. "What?"

"He's hiding Melody's necklace in a box in his jacket pocket."

"He's your brother's best friend."

"And I don't trust him! Have you seen the missing-person posters?" They're plastered all over town; they're hard to miss.

He hesitates, but half nods.

"The gold necklace with the musical note. I think Brandon has it."

"You think?" Gideon lifts a hand impatiently and releases a pathetic laugh. "Oh, good. As long as you *think*, then we might as well go to Brandon's house and tie him up ourselves. Is this about the diner? Something did happen between you two, didn't it?" For a second, his eyes soften and he reaches for me. "Did he hurt you?"

Tears sting behind my eyes. "No, Giddy, nothing happened."

"Then what is it?" His voice is raised and hoarse. "What is your goal here, Cass? The fire hasn't made your life easy, I get that. And Brandon's ex is the worst of your tormentors. But do you really think this story about him is going to make things better for you?"

His words strike and stab like nails. *This story.* Daylight has dwindled. Gideon's dark eyes recede into the wooden walls around us, leaving me nothing to grab on to. I wipe away tears and peer into the dark. I can't see my best friend's eyes, but I know they're glowering at me.

I could fix this. I could tell him about Brandon and the party, about the notebook. I could make him see it's not just a story. But Gideon doesn't trust me anymore.

Which means I can't trust him. I don't know what he'd do with my secrets.

Gideon's foot creaks on the crate. Light barely trickles in through the treetops. I forgot my flashlight. We'll become stranded out here once those few rays are extinguished.

Nothing has gone as planned. There is no forgiveness. No hug. No *see you tomorrow*. Not even a supportive hand offered as we pick ourselves up out of the hole in the ground. Instead, shrouded in twilight, we trudge and stumble our way back through the pines, the sound of twigs snapping like brittle bones beneath our feet.

14

In the morning, my mom tells me the whole town is helping to search for Melody. My heart drops—I watch enough true crime shows to know this means that the cops have already given up on finding her alive. Every day that goes by decreases our chances of finding her, and Melody disappeared on Tuesday. Four days ago.

But if the whole town is participating, Brandon might be there, which means I can pump him for information.

Asher and I walk toward the woods behind my neighborhood, Sheriff Henderson's instructions fresh in our ears. My parents paired off to search the forested area behind the diner. Asher studies the small area circled in red on our map. I peek at the map, trying to calm my nerves. I've managed to keep some amount of hope alive—that Melody simply ran away from this tiny town in search of bigger things. That she was abducted but will connive her way into getting released, the way she conspired to get me left behind last year for our away game against Millington. Even hope that this is all some sick joke she's playing to torment me.

But today we could find her body in these woods.

I peek up from the map, wanting to share all of this with Gideon. But he's standing over by the tent, pretending not to see me.

I notice Tina and Laura up ahead, squinting at their own map.

"Asher," I say, nudging his arm. "I've got to talk to Tina real quick."

"Mm-hmm," he mumbles without looking up.

I dash over to Tina and tap her lightly on the shoulder. No need to call Laura's attention. Tina turns around, smiling when he sees me. "Hey, Cass. Need a partner?"

"I'm actually partnered with Asher. But I wanted to ask you something."

"Sure, what's up?"

One look at her smiling face and my nerves falter. *Just say it.* "Look, I know nothing happened between you and Brandon last Tuesday."

Tina's smile freezes, then slowly deflates. "Excuse me?"

"You weren't driving around or doing anything with

Brandon all afternoon." It's a gamble. But deep down, everyone—Tina included—already wonders if I'm crazy. What's the worst that could happen? "My question is *why did you lie?*"

Tina blinks. "I don't know what you're talking about."

"Why would you spread a rumor that you were with Laura's ex," I say, leaning in close, "when you weren't?" I straighten again, taking a step in Laura's direction. "I mean, she's right over there. Maybe you want to explain it to her."

Tina pulls on my sleeve. "Wait." She gnaws her bottom lip, her eyes zipping over to Laura and then back to me. "Fine. I lied. But I'm not telling you why."

I exhale slowly, so she can't see my relief. "Really? Maybe we should see what Brandon thinks about your little rumor."

"It wasn't my rumor," Tina snaps. "Stephanie saw me get into the car and started blabbing about it. I didn't tell anyone on purpose."

Guilt tumbles in my stomach. "I'm not going to say anything. I just need to know. Did Brandon put you up to this? Did he tell you to say you were with him all afternoon?"

"No." She shakes her head. "He just gave me a ride. Cass, please. I can't have people asking me about why I was in town or why Brandon drove me. You have to let this go."

"Tell me exactly what happened, and I give you my word it will stay between us."

Tina's head slumps. "I was one test away from academic

suspension." A few yards away, Laura stirs, so we move a few steps farther from the tent. "Coach was going to call my parents," she whispers. "No more volleyball. I promised I'd get my grades up, but there weren't enough hours in the day. I remembered Dave talking about this guy behind Carver's who can sell you something to help you stay awake." She glances anxiously behind her to make sure no one is listening. "When Coach ended practice early, Brandon was already getting into his car. I needed a ride from someone who wouldn't ask questions." Her face flushes. "Please don't tell anyone. If Coach or my parents ever found out—"

"Tina, it's okay. I won't tell anyone." I regret this whole conversation, for making Tina—one of the few nice people on our team—admit something so shameful. But I have to push it, or it was all for nothing. "I need to know one more thing. Where did Brandon go after he dropped you off?"

She frowns. "I don't know. He let me out and drove off."

"He didn't say anything about where he was headed?"

"Why is this so important? Is this about the diner the other night? I saw Brandon flirting with you, but I didn't think you'd actually fall for"—she peeks behind her again, where Laura's chatting with some guys from school—"someone like him."

"What does that mean, *someone like him*?" Does Tina know about Brandon? The real Brandon?

"Nothing." She gives me an unreadable look. "Just be careful, Cass." Then she turns back to the search tent, and joins Laura and the guys. I speed-walk back to Asher.

So there is a crack in Brandon's alibi. He was unaccounted for long enough to lure Melody Davenport into the woods.

Asher is still engrossed in his map, oblivious I ever left. I kick a pebble as someone behind us shouts, "Hey, Pratts! Wait up!"

Brandon.

He stops beside me and my heart whirrs like a wind-up toy.

He's wearing the jacket from yesterday. It's one of those green parkas with all the pockets. A couple bulge, but I can't tell if any of them hold the box.

"Hey, Brandon." I wave and take a step closer. Then, holding my breath, I force myself to lean in for a hug.

Brandon's body stiffens beneath my arms, but I brush a hand over the bulgiest of the pockets anyway. My fingertip knocks something, making a faint, hollow tap. It could be the tiny box, the one holding Melody's necklace. I let out the breath and pull back, smiling awkwardly.

Asher and Brandon exchange goofy expressions as we pick up our pace. When we reach our circled area of the forest, Asher points. "The sheriff said to look here carefully. If we see any disturbed patches or anything that might belong to Melody, we have to find an officer. We aren't supposed to touch anything."

"We'd better get started," Brandon says with a shrug. "There's a lot of ground to cover. Should we split up?"

"Definitely," Asher says. "Shout if you see anything, Cass."

"I will." The boys wander off in opposite directions, and I move in a straight line. I examine the forest floor, pushing aside twigs and leaves with my shoes. It's a perfect, sunny fall day. The kind that sends the slightest breeze through the woods, kicking up the scent of orange honeysuckle. The kind Gideon and I might spend skipping rocks over the glassy surface of the reservoir. Or doing any outdoor activity—other than this.

Half an hour later, footsteps break my focus. I look up, expecting Asher. But it's Brandon.

"So, where's Gideon?" he asks, stepping closer. My eyes comb the trees for my brother, but there's no sign of him. Panic flutters in my chest.

"He's around," I say. "Searching with his mom."

"Right." Brandon bites his lower lip. "Here, let's go this way." He points toward a large patch of shrubbery, tugging on my wrist with his other hand. I flinch and wrench my arm away.

His forehead wrinkles. "What's wrong, Cass? You're acting weird."

"No, I just have to finish up to that white rock. That's where the red circle on the map reaches."

"I already searched that. Besides, these plants up here

need checking." When he points again, I notice dirt embedded under his fingernails.

"We weren't supposed to touch anything." I stare at Brandon's dirty fingers.

He wipes his hands on his jeans, pink blossoming over his cheeks. "I thought something was buried over there." He glances over his shoulder. "So I dug around a little. Turns out it was an old granola bar wrapper. Nothing important."

I nod, but my eyes veer to the once-stuffed jacket pocket, now flat against his chest. Then my gaze travels back to the path I never checked. I don't think Brandon's digging had anything to do with a buried granola bar wrapper. He's trying to keep me from that patch of soil I would've crossed in a matter of moments. I want to call out for Asher, but force myself to follow Brandon.

We check a shrub, quickly discovering the only thing it hides is a deadly armor of thorns. I'm still picking them from my clothes when we meet back up with Asher.

"Nothing?" he asks. Brandon and I shake our heads in silence. "Me neither. I guess we should head back to the tent and ask what's next."

I scurry after him, Brandon close at my side. As we duck out of the forest, I peek over my shoulder one last time. I scan for a marker, some detail to help me remember how to get back to that area Brandon kept me from searching.

It just may be where he buried the box.

In the morning, I almost oversleep due to the complete absence of sunlight. There's only a drab, gray sky. Fog covers the family car as we clamber inside to go to church. We park in front of the quaint white building, its spire top lost up in the haze. As we exit the car, the leaden sky opens up and leaks over our heads.

When the four of us pass through the open doors of the church, hair wet and drooping, we're swept up immediately by a tide of whispers and cries.

Louisa Stevens approaches and whispers in my mom's ear—surely an attempt to protect Asher and me. But she has to raise her voice to make it distinguishable above her own sobbing. "*They found—Melody's—body.*"

I run into the bathroom and throw up in the first empty stall.

Afterward, as I wash up, I consider hiding out in the bathroom. I can't face those crying people and their mourning faces. But it's harder to look at the face staring back at me in the mirror—the one responsible for the girl now lying cold and lifeless.

Melody's really gone. She was horrible to me, and I often wished her out of my life. But I never truly wished for *this*.

I rinse my mouth, checking in the mirror for a fraction of a second. Then I trudge back out to my parents to endure the nauseating whispers and wails.

I don't hear a word from the pulpit, other than the prayer said for the Davenports.

Athletic practices are canceled on Tuesday for the funeral, but I don't attend. Instead, I get completely ready in a sleeveless black shift dress, tediously apply eye makeup, and style my hair into loose, bouncing curls. Then I wait until my family is halfway out the front door to inform them I'm not feeling well.

I'd like to spend the funeral destructive crying—that thing that happens when you sob over your freshly painted face. But I have a mission. While everyone else is at the funeral, I'm going back to the woods to dig up the necklace. Once I'm sure it's there, I'll leave an anonymous tip with the sheriff. Hopefully, Brandon left his fingerprints behind.

As soon as my family's car engine trails off down the street, the doorbell rings. I squint through the peephole to find Gideon standing there.

I fling the door open and throw my arms around him, resting my cheek against his chest. His rhythmic heartbeat is soothing, but his arms stay bridled at his sides. Slowly, his body loosens and his arms enfold me. I never want to move, but the moment ends. Gideon steps back and eyes me.

His face turns a deep red, and his eyes divert to the floors. "Sorry, were you headed to the funeral?"

"No. My family's there, though."

Gideon's eyebrows angle in confusion. "You're not going? Because of the threat?"

I wrap a curl around my finger. "Not exactly. Why aren't you at the funeral?"

"I figured it might be a good time to investigate, while everyone's there. Those detectives aren't doing everything they can. Seth was barely questioned before they sent him on his way." His voice drops. "They're saying whoever did it tossed her body into the reservoir like garbage."

My stomach spins and careens like a wrecked carousel. I picture Melody lying on the muddy bank, blond hair tangled in the slimy rocks and broken bottles. Blue eyes open and empty. "What else are they saying?" I whisper, blinking away the image.

"They're doing an autopsy to make sure she didn't just fall into the water—you and I know that didn't happen. They're also saying the necklace wasn't on her. That the killer kept it as some sort of trophy."

Kept it in a small white box. I fold my hands together, but I can't contain my mouth. "Giddy," I say, struggling to catch his eyes, "I told you I saw the necklace. Brandon stuffed it into his jacket pocket."

"No, you said you thought you saw something that *could've* been the necklace."

My shoulders sag. "Well, I'm going to look for it. Good luck finding anything at Seth's place, since I saw where Brandon buried the necklace in the woods."

Gideon's hand moves to his temple and up through his hair, rumpling it. "You really think he did this?"

"Yes."

"Cass." He reaches out to touch my arm, but thinks better of it. Instead he fidgets with the pocket of his jeans. "Seth has that necklace."

I grit my teeth. "I explained to you guys three years ago how I felt about Brandon."

"He's not a killer because he dated Laura Gellman."

"He's a killer because he killed someone!"

Gideon sighs. "You've got to give me more than that."

I want to tell him. I do. To lay out the reasons Brandon's the guy. But I know Gideon. Once he hears about the fire and the notebook, he'll trust the cops to take me at my word. And they won't. They'll see that photo. The notebook where I described in detail how to kill Melody. My history. They'll start investigating me, and Brandon will get away with everything. He'll be free to do this to the next girl who crosses his path.

Gideon squints at me hard before his shoulders fall. "You look really pretty, Cass." And he might as well have said, *You're dead on the inside, Cass*. He swivels around and heads for the steps.

My heart slithers down to my feet. He can't leave this way. "Where are you going?" I shout, scampering after him in my bare feet.

He stops in the driveway. "To Seth's place. Are you coming?"

I stand before him, my eyes drifting to the half-open door, then back to his pleading expression. If I tell him, maybe I'll end up in prison. Maybe Gideon will hate me even more. Maybe he'll find some way to forgive me and help prove my innocence. The list of *maybes* is infinite.

But if I don't tell him, there's only one outcome: he'll walk down that driveway and never show up on my doorstep again.

And I guess that's the thing I fear more than any of it. I blow out a long breath, rustling my perfectly curled hair. "Look, I'll tell you how I know. But you're coming with me."

Gideon's brow furrows and then softens. "Fine," he says, motioning to the door. "Lead the way."

I peer down at my funeral attire. "I need to change first."

15

Two minutes later, jeans and a ratty T-shirt replace my dress. I shrug on a hoodie, tie my hair back, and dash out the door.

Gideon is waiting in the driveway. "Okay, talk. Where are we going?"

"First, to get shovels." I hurry around to the side door, and Gideon follows me inside the dark, musty garage.

"Why do we need shovels?" he asks as I push one into his hands. I grab the second shovel, and the moment seems so insane that a chuckle escapes my lips. Here we are in the most grievous situation of our lives, yet we're both holding shovels, like nothing has changed since we were ten years old.

He flashes an incredulous expression and darts out the door, shovel in hand.

I follow. "Because I know where Brandon's hiding spot is." I tug out the crinkled map with the red circle and point. "That's where we're headed. He was acting strange during the search on Saturday. He actually pulled me away from my designated area."

Gideon stops to raise his brows at me. Then he marches, pushing and hitting at branches as he crosses them. "I still don't understand why you're so certain he killed Melody."

"Giddy." I pull at his arm and this time, he doesn't wrench away. "I should've told you this before. But this person is dangerous."

Gideon spins around, wariness crinkling the corners of his eyes. Sighing, he lets the metal end of the shovel sink into the dirt. "Cass, I know I haven't been there for you with whatever you're going through. But I'm here now. If I'm going to help you, I need to know what you're hiding."

I shake my head. "You'll think I'm horrible." A squirrel chitters nearby, and it sounds like laughter, mocking me.

Gideon drops the shovel and places both hands on my shoulders. "I'd never think that. Go on, tell me."

I twist my lips and toss my shovel to the ground. "In September, I put my name in for varsity captain."

His head tips back. "I didn't know that."

I tuck my hands inside the kangaroo pocket of my sweatshirt, curling my fists. "It didn't end favorably for me. But that's not the only reason I didn't tell you."

My hands fidget inside the pocket, and Gideon digs his fingers inside to hold them. The warmth of his hands settles me, and words begin tumbling from my mouth. Everything. The vote. Melody. The fire.

Gideon listens intently, his eyes fixed on mine. His fingers run over my palms as I get to the part about leaving the portable classroom a pillar of smoke.

His expression turns grave and his hands fall still. "You just let it burn?"

"She had a photo that"—I swallow—"*looked* like I'd started a fire in a room I wasn't even supposed to be in. She said if I called or if I told anyone, she'd say she walked in on me starting the fire." My eyes flood. "No one would've believed me over her. Not after what happened to Sara."

Gideon's gaze absorbs mine. "Why didn't you tell me this?"

"Because you would've done the right thing!" Shame rushes into my cheeks. "You think everyone is like you, Giddy," I say quieter. "You would've told the cops it was Melody. You would've trusted them. And they would've taken one look at that Fire Girl photo and trusted Melody."

"But I could've been there for you. You've been all alone."

"I know. I just—" I let Melody frighten me into keeping my mouth shut. Because I believed her. I believed everyone in town would trust her word over mine. Just like sometimes I believe she's right about what happened to her cousin. Seeing the flames on Election Day, feeling the heat, brought some of it back.

And I think, deep down, I wanted to let Melody burn the way her cousin did.

Gideon's head tilts. "I still don't understand what all this has to do with Brandon."

"It was that party a couple weeks back. When you guys thought Brandon and I were getting along so well."

Gideon's shoulders stiffen. A guarded look crosses his face.

"Look, nothing happened. We just talked. But it was what we talked about that has me positive he's guilty."

"Go on."

"We talked about killing Melody Davenport."

He doesn't respond, which is the worst response.

I shake my head. "I know how it sounds. But I was angry at her and waiting on pins and needles for her to start passing that photo around. I didn't mean anything I said to Brandon."

"What did *he* have against Melody?" Gideon's head drifts slowly away from mine, and his hands slip from my sweatshirt pockets.

"Apparently, she was responsible for breaking him and Laura up. I thought he was bitter-babbling, like I was. At the diner, that notebook we were passing back and forth— it's sick, I know. But it was a joke. At least, I thought it was. What happened in the woods, though, was exactly like what I wrote down in the notebook." I pull out my phone and hand it to him, letting him scroll through the anonymous messages.

"And Brandon took the notebook. He's using that and the photo to silence me."

Gideon hands back the phone, his eyes glazed over. "I guess this explains why you biked up to the abandoned mill."

"I'm so sorry. I...didn't want to get you involved."

Gideon's hand moves to my back and he pulls me in. His breath is warm against my neck, and, for a while, we don't talk or move.

Finally, he whispers into my hair, "I'm glad you told me."

"And now you're dying to say, 'They're coming to get you, Cass' in a spooky voice."

"No." His chin brushes my ear. "At least, I wasn't going to reference *that* exact movie."

I growl.

"I just can't believe Brandon would do all that." It stings. He pulls back, looking straight into my eyes. "I didn't mean—I believe you. But I wish I'd known all of that about Melody. You should've confided in me instead of Brandon."

"I see that *now*." But again, Gideon's wrong. He was the only person who never looked at me like I was Fire Girl. Now that I've told him the truth, I don't know what he sees. "So... you're still going to help me?"

"Of course." His hand closes around my wrist. "Let's find that necklace. But Cass, we're going to have to show the detectives the threats. The only thing we can do is get ahead of this creep."

"No, no, no, no. It'll look like a premeditated thing. And I was there, at the murder scene. They'll never believe me."

"It's the only move we've got. I'll admit the whole notebook situation doesn't look good. But we've cooperated with the detectives so far. They may be able to trace the texts to the killer. We might be able to get this guy. Trust me, please. I'm not going to let anything happen to you."

I want to believe him. I look in his calming eyes, my body warming and melting beneath them like chocolate under a blazing sun. His face lowers. It's so close to mine. His lips begin to purse, and for a split second, I wish for something harder than I've wished for anything.

But Gideon's lips part, and he says, "I'd give anything to go back in time one week."

My cheeks catch fire. It was a stupid wish. "Me too."

"She's really gone, Cass. And it's our fault."

"We didn't kill Melody. But Brandon wants to make it look like we did. That's why we can only trust each other from here on out."

Gideon's eyes fall. "Unless there's more you're hiding."

My hands clench. "This is why I didn't tell you." I tear myself away and bend over to retrieve my shovel. "Are you going to help me look for the box, or not?"

He exhales and leads the way. A chill in the air whips through me, and I miss the warmth of his chest even more.

Gideon's walk is determined, but he pauses to hold the

larger branches aside for me as we travel deeper into the forest. The pine scent, the bickering, the shovels—everything seems just as it was when we were kids.

But now Melody's ghost is hovering in the air between us.

"I feel like we should've been there by now," I say. The shovel bounces off my shoulder repeatedly, bruising it. I want to snatch the map from him. Is he even going the right way?

"We're close. Let me take that," he says, reaching for my shovel. He heaves it over his shoulder, and it clanks against the one resting there. After several yards, he stops to survey the area. "It should be right around here." He checks the map again. "Does this look familiar?"

"Yeah. That's the thorny shrub of death over there," I say, flicking my chin at it. "So up ahead. That's the spot Brandon didn't want me to search." Sure enough, there's the large white rock tucked within a cluster of trees. "Somewhere around here." I point to a large patch of bare dirt and Gideon hands me a shovel. "This area's a lot bigger up close. I hope we can dig it up before the funeral ends."

"We don't have to dig it all up." He hefts his shovel higher onto his shoulder. "First we have to check for signs of disturbance. It's rained some, which won't help things. But we should be able to tell if he buried something here in the last couple of days."

"Okay." I examine the area, tiptoeing over the rocks and weeds.

Gideon sighs and points. "This part looks like it's been touched."

I push my shovel into the soil, and it sinks. "Yeah, this could be it."

An hour later, the forest floor is strewn with mountains of earth. Craters are woven amid the peaks, making the area look like a foreign planet. My nostrils and lungs are coated in a fine layer of dirt. But there is no box.

Gideon taps me on the shoulder. "Cass, we have to get back. Your family thinks you're in bed. They'll worry, especially after what happened…"

"To Melody." I scan the piles one last time before nodding. "You know what, you go. I'll handle my family."

"No, I'm walking you back. It'll be dark soon, and you couldn't even find your way out here in broad daylight."

I slap a dirt-coated palm against my thigh. "Fine." We grab our shovels and speed-walk out the way we came. "I guess I was wrong." My head hangs as I walk. Gideon puts his free hand on my back, but my muscles tense.

"It's okay, Cass. We can check Seth's place."

I wiggle out from under his hand. "I don't mean wrong about Brandon! I mean I was wrong about where he hid the box." We breach the edge of the forest and follow the back fence around to the side of my house. "We probably have a few minutes until they get back. Let's sneak over to his house and try to get into his room. With both of us looking—"

But I don't finish my sentence. Something snags our eyes as we round the corner of my house: my family's gray sedan is parked in the driveway.

Reclining against hood of the car is Asher, and he doesn't look pleased.

16

"What are you two doing?" Asher hisses, moving toward us. The freshly dry-cleaned scent of his black suit mingles with the breeze.

"I asked her to come with me," Gideon says. "She was helping me bury my neighbor's dog. She was old, the dog. And my neighbor. That's why she needed help."

My heart thunders in my chest. Still, my lips threaten to curl. Gideon loves to spin stories, but they're usually grounded in truth. Listening to this outright lie is bizarrely comical coming from him. Especially since he's trying it on Asher. I pick at my dirty fingernails.

"Right." Asher's tone is dubious. "But I thought Cass was sick."

"I started feeling better, and I wanted to help. That poor lady." Now I'm practically prying my nails from their beds.

Asher's face falls. He knows we're lying, and he's hurt. Guilt sloshes in my stomach.

"Well, I hope you two had fun doing whatever it was you were really doing," says Asher dryly. My cheeks warm. "Because they buried Melody today, and you missed her service."

I'm dizzy. All that digging and walking and lying. "We're just going to put these shovels away." I motion to the garage.

Asher reaches for Gideon's shovel. "I'll help with that. You can go home, Gideon," he says, yanking the handle from his grip.

"Asher," Gideon says, "hold on a second."

"Go home, Gideon."

"Wait a minute."

Asher ignores him, turning to me. His brows furrow and he points at the front door. "You know Mom and Dad are in there, right? They may have already walked into your room to check on you. If you come with me right now, I can help you sneak back in there. But if it's too late, you're on your own, Cass. I can't explain to Mom and Dad why you missed Melody's funeral to be with your *boyfriend*."

I shake my head, hoping I shut my bedroom door after changing clothes. "Keep your voice down." I can't leave things with my brother this way. I lob Gideon a helpless look.

Before he can stop me, I blurt, "Asher, there's something you should know."

Asher's impatient expression doesn't wilt.

I glance behind me at the street and drop my voice. "The real reason we weren't at the funeral is because we were trying to find Melody's necklace. Brandon has it." Asher frowns, but I keep talking. "He told me he hated her. And then a couple days ago, I saw him with her necklace."

"Is this about Laura Gellman? Cass, I told you—"

"I'm not making this up! Gideon believes me, don't you?" I turn to see Gideon's gaze lower to the pavement, his teeth clamped onto his bottom lip. He renders a curt nod.

"I see," Asher says, lugging the shovels to the garage. He walks off, leaving Gideon standing with his dirt-encrusted hands in his pockets, and me with my fists balled.

This ends today. Right now, I'm going to sneak back into bed and finish pretending to be sick. But the first chance I get, I'm confronting Brandon. I'm done with everyone believing that guy over me. "I'd better go inside," I mumble to Gideon. "See you later."

"Cass," Gideon says, but he doesn't attempt to follow me.

Once I've settled under the covers, a book I have no attention span to read in hand, there's a knock on my door. "Come in," I call, expecting my mom.

But it's Asher. "How are you feeling?"

I roll my eyes and pull the covers up higher. "You don't need to come in here and tell me not to blab about Brandon. I promise I won't say a word"—I cough and mutter—"until after I find that necklace."

"I wasn't going to mention Brandon. Maybe it was too soon to stick the two of you together." He shrugs. "You did seem to be getting along well. There were sparks and everything."

"Gross."

"So it's back to Gideon, then."

My teeth clamp. "Did you tell Gideon he shouldn't date me?" A startled expression crosses Asher's face. "Don't deny it. I saw how you made him feel terrible just now. You must've said something to him."

Asher steps closer to the bed. "Cass, it's not like that. I was just upset that you two ditched the funeral."

"You made him promise not to date me."

"Not exactly," he says, cheeks flushing.

My head tips forward.

"I was worried. Your freshman year, after Brandon…"

"Went to the dark side," I offer.

"Yeah. I started hanging out with you and Gideon, and everything was great. Then he told me how he felt about you, and"—he shrugs—"I just told him to be careful."

"You *what*?" Heat courses through me, half rage at Asher, half a warm thrill hearing Gideon's feelings confirmed.

"You'd been through so much with the fire, and things were good between you two. Between all of us. I didn't want it to fall apart. You could've gotten your heart broken and lost your best friend at the same time. It would've been too much."

"I hate you, Asher." And I hate Gideon for telling Asher about us. But then my brother's fingers graze the scars on his left wrist, and my anger fizzles.

"Because you know I'm right."

I press my lips flat. Asher may have wrecked my chances with Gideon before, but a sliver of hope grows now, pushing my spirits skyward. Maybe Gideon still feels this way.

Asher starts wandering the room. He twists the crank on the little music box he gave me for Christmas one year. "You Are My Sunshine" plays while he flips open a book from the shelf and returns it. I wonder, as he fingers the edge of one rugged, white hardcover, if he remembers the hours spent on this floor, reading *Fox in Socks*. I lean back against the headboard, listening to the music swirl around the room, until a chanting breaks out over the notes: "When beetles battle beetles in a puddle paddle battle and the beetle battle puddle is a puddle in a bottle…"

I crack a smile. "'They call this a tweetle beetle bottle puddle paddle battle muddle.' That was my favorite part."

"It is the most enthralling scene, no one can argue that.

Though I'm pretty sure I can quote the entire book, thanks to you." He moves on down the line, giving the rocking horse a nudge. When he gets to the porcelain doll, he stops and turns to me. "Edna's chipped," he says with a note of hurt. He picks up the doll and examines the tiny hand that cracked during an earthquake. "Do you want me to fix it?"

"No, Asher, it's fine."

"It would be a simple fix."

It gnaws at me that I didn't take better care of Edna. The doll was a gift from Asher to replace the one the playhouse fire consumed. Asher named her after the neighbor down the street who used to complain about her sciatica on a daily basis. As much as I wanted to love that doll, she only reminded me of Sara and the mistake I'll never outlive. She's been sitting here beside all the presents I've outgrown on the shelf, right next to a framed photo of Sara and me. The photo rubs at a raw spot in my heart, but I won't take it down. Forcing myself to look at it is the least I can do for her. "Sure, Asher, that'd be nice." I never remember to stay mad at him for long.

Clutching the doll at his side, Asher peruses my collection of volleyball trophies. This doesn't take long, as it's one-fourth the size of his own collection. He looks up suddenly. "I'm sorry about Gideon, okay? I know how you feel about me talking to him on your behalf, but if you want—"

"I'll let you know."

He shrugs, smiling softly. The creases on his forehead are now smooth. "Fine. Feel better." He winks before ducking out.

The rest of the evening, Gideon barrages me with coded texts about telling the "doctor" what I told him. But I know the desperate detectives will jump at the first opportunity they get to arrest someone.

Maybe tomorrow. Parents couldn't get me an appointment today.

??

See you at school tomorrow

I wake up from a nightmare about the fire so vivid that my eyes are wet and swollen. Asher and I were in the playhouse, where we spent every summer moment before the fire. Where my mind has spent so many nights attempting to replay how the whole place went up in flames. But in the dream, instead of finding myself stuck and crying for Asher to help me, his screams rang out over the crackling and crashing.

The playhouse in the dream expanded so it was longer and larger than any real house. I tried to push through the smoke to find where the screams were coming from. Every time I found my way through a door, the house extended farther so that I stumbled into another cloudy room. My lungs were bursting when I finally caught a glimpse of Asher, pinned underneath a fallen beam. He wasn't screaming anymore, and his eyes were empty, like glass. I called out to him. I shouted I was coming. When I finally made it through the last door, I was outside on the too-green grass, watching the entire playhouse crumble, engulfed in dancing flashes of red.

I rip off the covers, the overwhelming need to see my brother and hear his voice pulling me from the bed. Quickly, I dress for school, then knock on his door.

"Come in."

I open the door to find Asher wearing the bizarre combination of house slippers and a suit. "What happened to you?"

He looks puzzled until I indicate his choice of footwear. "Oh." He grins. "I've got a meeting in town later."

I can't see any natural connection to what I want to say, so I blurt, "I'm sorry I missed Melody's funeral. Nothing excuses me. I didn't sleep much last night thinking about it." Asher sits down on the bed. "Was it a nice service?"

He nods and fiddles with his tie. But his eyes flood.

"Sorry," he murmurs, blinking a few times. "I just realized *Zombie Bride* was on last night and I forgot to set the DVR." He struggles to smile. "It obviously made me emotional."

Guilt prickles in my chest. This is all my fault. Not just because I didn't help Melody. Because everything I said to Brandon that night at the party—everything I wrote in that notebook—encouraged him. "I'm not sure there's any real way to get over something like that, Asher."

He laughs weakly. The front door chimes, and he wipes at his eyes.

"I'll get it." I scurry down the hall and through the foyer. I pull open the door to find a familiar parka framed in the doorway. But I can't find my voice to say hello.

Brandon squints at me. "Hey, Cass. Asher's expecting me." He stretches his neck to peer over my shoulder. "He's home, right?"

I clear my throat. "Yeah, sorry. He's in his room." I spin around. "Come on in and have a seat in the kitchen. I'll get him."

"Thanks." Brandon steps through the doorway and my limbs shake as I follow him. "Asher!" I yell. I'm not letting this guy out of my sight. "There's coffee in the pot if you want some," I say to Brandon.

"Sure. Thanks."

"Cream or sugar?"

"Black."

Right. Like his murdering soul.

I grip the carafe with trembling fingers and pour Brandon a nice, hot cup. "Asher!" I call again, lifting the mug. But my quivering fingers lose their grasp, and it tumbles to the floor, shattering.

Ceramic shards leap across the tiles and brown liquid pools, branching off through the grout.

I dash to the counter to grab a towel. "Here," Brandon says, leaning over in his chair. He grabs at the biggest chunk of ceramic, and a small object tumbles from his jacket pocket.

The box.

17

Brandon nearly topples from his chair. The ceramic shard falls from his hand as he snatches the little white box.

I drop the towel to the floor. "What's in the box?"

"Nothing. It's just—"

"Show me what's in there, Brandon," I demand, taking two quick steps toward him. He lowers the box to his lap, fingers covering it protectively.

"Cass." Brandon's eyes plead with me.

"Why don't you want me to see?" The force and volume of my voice climb.

His chin sinks. "Because you wouldn't understand."

"Of course, I wouldn't understand! You're still going to show me what's in there!" I shout, crossing the slippery tiles and lunging at him. I grab his arm and try to wrestle the lid away as he clamps it back over the box.

But I catch a glint.

"Cass, calm down!" Brandon yells.

"I won't calm down until you show me! You've got Melody's necklace in there!" I'm on him now, scratching and yanking, but his hands tighten on the box.

Footsteps pound in the hallway. "Cassidy!" Asher stomps toward me. "Get off him!" He pulls me back, and I grunt, trying to wrench myself from his grasp. "What are you doing?"

"Brandon has Melody's necklace! He killed her!"

"Cass." Asher tries to lay a calming hand on my shoulder, but I twist away.

"I heard him that day in the woods! Brandon did it. The proof is in that box."

Asher's eyes are wide. His head swivels to Brandon, whose body hunches over the box. Hope flickers.

Then my brother says, "I'm so sorry about this." He turns back to me. "Cassidy, get out of here."

I halt, my espadrille landing on broken ceramic with a crunch. "You're really not going to make him show us what's inside?"

Asher's face is stoic, his tone razor sharp. "Get out."

"This is unbelievable."

Asher pushes me toward the door, and I have no choice but to obey. But Brandon's voice rises over my protests. "Here.

You want to see what's in the box? Go ahead and look." He tosses the lid to the ground, holding the open container on his lap. I wiggle out of Asher's grip and dart toward it.

A metallic flash curls my stomach. Inside is the same gleaming thing Brandon held between his fingers outside the diner on Friday. When I see a small, silver bracelet nestled into the bottom corner, my breath catches.

There's a charm, but it isn't a musical note; it's a heart, engraved with *Love Brandon*.

I was so certain it would be the gold necklace—the one from the posters and the news—that I simply stare at the bracelet, blinking to make sure it's not some trick of the mind.

"I brought it here to show your brother. It's for Laura."

A present for Laura. A present he didn't want me to see because he knew I'd judge him for trying to win her back. My mind continues reeling, trying to work out how it could be anything but Melody's necklace. I don't dare touch it. And I don't dare look either boy in the eye.

"I-I'm sorry." My gaze falls to my feet.

No one responds. Brandon looks at me, his body slumped in exhaustion, eyes wide with fear. Asher stares at the wall. I stand helpless, a familiar desire seeping into my veins.

That desire to watch something burn.

It's an uncharacteristically cold October in Maribel. Even our sturdy Douglas fir trees seem unprepared as wind knocks their needles to the ground and that frosted layer lingers into late morning.

As kids, Gideon and I despised the colder months because it meant our hideout would be buried beneath the pillows of white. As we've grown older and our ventures to the hideout have grown fewer, our hatred has withered into a dull resentment. The cold steals the one place we can escape together.

This year, I barely notice the cold move in. There's nothing to share, no one to share it with.

It's been a week since Melody's body was discovered. The Oregon State Police investigation into the alleged homicide is well underway, but no one feels comforted. No arrests have been made, and regardless of the outcome, it's too late for Melody. Investigators determined she died before entering the water, putting rumors that she slipped and fell into the reservoir to rest. As long as the investigation is open, the police won't release information regarding the manner of her death, so the town has been inventing its own versions as to how she was killed. One story claims she was bludgeoned. Another claims her throat was cut. With every version, I remember the chilling sounds from that day. They flood my mind and haunt my sleep.

If there is any evidence, the police haven't found it. The days plod by, and no leads spring up.

Apart from school and practice, I haven't ventured from my house much. I spend any spare time with my books. Fictional worlds help take my mind off of everything from the safety of my bedroom. I can't set foot in town and risk running into Mrs. Davenport, or Gracie. I don't want to think about how they have to walk past Melody's empty bedroom, knowing she'll never sit at her desk or sleep in her bed again.

Asher's been avoiding me ever since my charming display in the kitchen with Brandon. He decided to expedite his move to town, probably to escape me. During work hours, he hides out in his tiny office kitty-corner to Gina's Diner. After work, he comes home and pretends I don't exist.

Gideon refuses to speak to me. He's upset that Seth is still free and that I've kept the threats from the detectives. Plus, Asher told him about the necklace fiasco. Since Gideon aided my Brandon investigation, he was humiliated by association.

I keep texting Gideon that I'll help him look into Seth. And I push aside my nagging worries about crossing Seth's path again. If Seth has the notebook and the Election Day photo, I'm in a world of trouble. And if he found out what I did the last time we crossed paths, two years ago, this is personal.

Monday morning, I drag myself through the double doors of the school, letting its familiar stale scent overtake me.

Before I can peel off my coat, Emily, Laura, and a few others surround me.

"Isn't it freezing out there?" asks Emily.

Laura nods. "Yeah. What is going on with this weather? No Gideon today?"

Such a natural segue. My pulse quickens as I walk, hoping for some wormhole out of here.

"Yeah, you two used to be Siamese twins," Tina says, smacking her gum. "Is something wrong?"

When I don't respond, Laura fills the void in the conversation in her own, special way. "He came on to you, didn't he?" Her feigned concern floats through the air like a foul odor.

"We're fine," I lie. The truth is that my birthday came and went over the weekend—the big eighteen—and Gideon sent a freaking birthday card. I read the distance between us in his messily scrawled writing.

Hey Cass, hope you have a great birthday.
Love, Gideon

It was my first birthday without him in twelve years. "We just... We don't have to be together *all* the time."

The bell rings, startling me. But I soon recognize its rescuing power and rush off to first period.

At morning break, I spot Gideon on my way past the

open auditorium door. His words from the day of the funeral reverberate in my head: *You look really pretty, Cass.* But I remember his eyes glistening with disappointment. I can't meet those eyes again, so I watch from a distance, my head partially hidden behind the door.

Gideon sits alone on the auditorium steps, handsome as usual, though thinner. Shadows fill new hollows in his cheeks and jaw. I watch a bit too long—knowing Laura and the others will probably catch me—and Gideon does nothing notable.

I'm about to tiptoe away when his head veers suddenly to one side. I follow his gaze until my eyes settle on the reason he seems so still and unoccupied.

Gideon is watching someone too.

He's watching Gracie Davenport.

Something I can't identify pricks up in me. Gideon stands, taking the steps down and exiting out the other set of doors, and I follow. He remains focused on Gracie's blond head, which bobs down locker-lined Hathaway Hall. She continues toward the courtyard doors and Gideon follows behind her.

I stop at my locker and spin the combination, watching from behind its door as Gracie exits, her head downcast and her normally styled waves drooping limply in front of her face. She seems to be operating in a dream state, pushing the door open by memory. I don't want to risk following the two of them outside on my own, but I have to know what Gideon is up to.

Emily walks by, unaware of my half-concealed presence behind my locker door. "Hey, Emily! Wait up!" Hastily, I swap out my books and slam the door. Then I scurry over to her. "Are you headed outside?" She was clearly walking toward the auditorium, but I take my chances. "Because some fresh air sounds great." I flash her a big, fake smile.

Sure enough, she alters her path toward the courtyard, returning the grin until we approach the back doors. "Looks freezing out there," she says, hesitating. "I don't have my coat with me."

"We won't stay for long. I just need a little breather before third period."

Outside, the air is biting and blustery. Emily shoots me an impatient look. She has a point. What is Gracie doing out here? I scan the courtyard, keeping my head facing Emily. I have to appear engaged in conversation.

Gideon's seated on a bench, no sign of being affected in the slightest by the frigid air, staring at Gracie. She's sitting on the low red brick wall bordering the courtyard, wiping her face. Her violent shivers are noticeable from a distance. As I watch, guilt and sorrow swell in my chest.

Gideon has been pulled out into the freezing cold by a familiar tug. It's the tug that made him stay behind for theme park day in fourth grade, when Johnny Larson's parents refused to sign the permission slip. That same tug made Gideon the only sophomore at the senior prom when he found Katie Shaw crying by the drinking fountain and asked if she would be his date. It's the tug that made us friends in the first place, when he rescued me from the second graders and their Fire Girl jokes.

It tears him up to see someone this way—anyone really, but I bet he feels responsible for Gracie. And I know his mind is spinning, turning over and over, wondering if and how he can fix her.

The thought reaches into me like an invasive woodland vine. It coils around my brain, around my limbs. Filling. Squeezing. Immobilizing. I stand frozen as Emily's pleas to go inside bounce off my ears on the back of the harsh, whistling wind.

18

Eventually I hear Emily's pleading and follow her inside. I've watched long enough. Watched my best friend slip away.

I've got to get him back. Even if that means diving headfirst into whatever game Seth Greer is playing.

Emily said he still lives at home. It shouldn't be too difficult to get inside his house and look for Melody's necklace or phone or some proof he's the guy. Maybe if I'm lucky, I'll find that crumpled notebook while I'm at it. And I can burn those pages. This plan means breaking my promise to Asher about staying out of the Greer home. But I ignore the twinge of guilt and ask Emily if we can meet there for our project. She seems reluctant at first—which I attribute to her interest in Asher—but she agrees.

In the daytime, the Greer house is a faded tan, the paint peeling off in patches. One of the rotting porch posts buckles, causing the overhang to tilt. The lawn is an overgrown field of yellow weeds. Emily walks in front of me, ducking her head inside the front door before allowing me to pass.

"My room's this way." She squeezes by me in the tight hallway, knocking the poster board I carry. The poster was my excuse to ensure that—one way or another—I ran into Seth today. Since he wasn't at the drugstore, I'm hopeful he'll make an appearance here. Emily opens the first door and goes inside. I hang back, peering down the dark hall, which contains two more closed doors, before making a sharp turn.

"Is anyone else home?" I ask, attempting nonchalance as I follow her.

Once inside, I have to blink away the blinding pinkness of the place. Emily's room looks like the venue of a four-year-old girl's birthday party. There aren't any actual balloons, but the number of heart-shaped pillows, Disney princess posters, and bubble gum–colored beads strung from wall to wall could fool anyone. "My parents are at work. Seth might be here. He hasn't been sneaking off with"—her voice drops—"*you know who* much lately."

Because that would mean hanging out with a corpse.

"Yeah," continues Emily, "I don't want to know what's going on there." She manages to wince without losing her smile.

"Why not?"

Emily balks. "Why don't I want to know about my brother's love life? Do you talk to Asher about that kind of stuff?"

I pause thoughtfully. "He doesn't have a girlfriend. But I think he'd talk to me about it, if he did. We talk about everything." Well, we used to, before I accused his best friend of murder.

"That must be so great." Her face softens wistfully.

"I take it you and Seth aren't very close."

"I mean, I love him, but he hasn't exactly made my life easy. Every time I go anywhere, it's the same thing. Oh, you're *Seth's* sister. And then there's the look." She lets out a loud breath. "I know there's never been an ounce of truth to the rumors about my brother, but still. It's like...I resent him anyway. I know that sounds terrible."

"No, I get what you mean. It can't be easy getting teased for something that has nothing to do with you." It's not even easy getting teased for something that has everything to do with you.

"Yeah." The curve of her lips finally wavers. The ripple of guilt comes back.

We hunker down on the carpet, poster and books sprawled out on our laps. I rest my back against the ruffled pink tulle bed skirt bordering Emily's bed. I'm anxious to get this over with. I keep straining my ears for footsteps or some sound to give away Seth's presence in the house.

I sit up, pushing my textbook off me. "Hey, can I use your restroom?"

"Sure." Emily points toward the open door. "It's the one on the right."

"Thanks." I creep down the hall to the bathroom, pausing by the door on the left side—probably Seth's room. The wraparound part of the hall likely leads to the master. It's quiet on the other side of Seth's door, so I press my ear up against it. Heart pounding, I reach out to place a sweaty hand on the knob. I inhale and twist.

The door opens easily and I lean in, expecting to find the space where all the princesses from one room over come to be executed. Instead, I step inside to find something resembling Asher's room. The walls are lined with classic rock posters, and a shelf is stocked with books I've never heard of. I get a quick flash of the first time I spoke to Seth, my sophomore year, in the school library. He wasn't into wearing all black and stalking girls yet. He was reading a hardcover— something about ants—and I paused by his table to ask if it was good.

He smiled and lowered the book. "I'd say you were welcome to check it out after me, but it's my own personal copy."

I raised a brow. "You already read everything in here?"

He laughed, light and easy. "High school libraries don't typically carry books of this nature."

I brought a hand to my mouth and looked over my shoulder. "You're not saying our school has something against insects, are you?"

"Something like that." His lips curled. "But you can take a stand for the six-legged creatures and borrow it from me."

I pointed to my volleyball jersey. "I don't have much time for extracurricular reading at the moment. But maybe later."

Now, the books strewn over his desk show that his love of obscure reading material didn't go out the window along with his old wardrobe. I turn to face the opposite wall, where the bed resides. It's pretty bare, surprisingly absent of the heavy metal posters and graphic novels with creatures devouring body parts that I'd expected.

Also absent: Seth.

I do a quick scan of the room. The closet is open, revealing a dark, monochrome wardrobe. When I spoke to Seth for the first time in the library, he was wearing green. It turned his hazel eyes into emeralds.

The second time we spoke, his jeans and Converse sneakers were just like everyone else's, and his eyes looked amber above his yellow shirt. That second time we were in the library again. Seth seemed to like the library, back in the days before he swapped it for the bleachers.

I approached the table where he was seated, just like the first time. "So, I see you finished your encyclopedia," I said. "Or did you give up?"

His lips quirked at one side. "Finished it. And *Volleyball for Dummies* in between, just in case you came back in here.

So I'd have something to talk to you about." His eyes met mine, and my cheeks ignited.

Some people might have found this behavior creepy, borderline stalker, but truthfully, I didn't. I thought it was kind of sweet. After feeling rejected by Gideon for so long, having a guy put real effort into getting me to notice him was flattering. "Really? And what did you learn?"

"Okay, I made that up. That book might not even exist, but I did a little research. Did you know that volleyball dates back to 1895?"

"They didn't give us a history lesson. Just a uniform."

We kept chatting until the librarian shushed us, and I headed off to my locker, beaming the whole way.

I lean inside the closet now, rifling through black shirts and jackets. There's a wink of metal, and I halt. But it's only a zipper. I grab the molding to catch my breath. What am I doing in here? Am I really going to find Melody's necklace hung up next to tomorrow's outfit? I back out of the closet, tripping over a black boot that toppled from the shoe rack. I recover, hoping Emily's house has thick walls.

I dash over to the desk, pulling open each drawer in turn. All I need is that necklace, her phone, a love note she sent him. Anything that proves he was seeing her.

The drawers are just as orderly as the rest of the room. There are stacks of paper, envelopes, half-filled-out job applications, and a little tray of pens neatly arranged in

compartments. Someone as intelligent as Seth shouldn't be
stuck working in the dinky town drugstore—especially not
when it means being harassed on a daily basis. He must've
stayed for Melody. I flip through the papers, stopping when
something colorful catches my eye. Hidden beneath the forms
is a collection of photographs. They're quite good; it seems
Seth is somewhat of an amateur photographer. There's a blue
jay perched on the branch of a tree, its lilac-colored blossoms
bordering the scene. Beneath it is a photo of a sunset taken
from a nearby hiking spot. I dig further, uncovering an image
that makes every nerve in my body coil.

In it, a girl bends over to retrieve something from the
floor. I recognize the medicine-filled aisles on either side of
her. The photo looks like it was snapped from behind the
drugstore counter. I also recognize the blond hair and slim
figure of the unsuspecting shopper.

It's Melody Davenport.

I slide the photo into my back pocket and rummage
through the remaining drawers, checking over my shoulder
every few seconds. But there's nothing.

I turn to face the bookshelf, my last hope for finding
something to prove Seth's connection to Melody. A thump
resounds from the next room. Emily has shifted from her
position on the floor. I don't have much time before she comes
to check on me. I kneel down, my fingers skimming each spine
until they brush a familiar cover. Last year's Maribel High

yearbook; Asher and I share a copy. But I stop because a slip of paper pokes out from between the pages, like a bookmark. I ease the book from the shelf, my hands shaking beneath its weight. As I let it fall open to the bookmarked page, my stomach springs into my throat.

It's the volleyball page of the activities section. My photo is at the bottom, alongside the faces of Laura Gellman, Stephanie Reed, and the rest of last year's varsity squad. But my eyes are immediately drawn to the middle row. There in the center of the pristinely posed group, Melody Davenport's smile shines brighter than anyone else's. Her long blond hair is curled to perfection, making Lillian Jeffries's and Kate Lowe's photos on either side pale in comparison. But there's another reason Melody's photograph stands out among the others.

Her eyes have been removed.

Dark, jagged holes stare back at me as my trembling hands try to keep the book from plummeting to the floor.

I snap a quick photo with my phone and close the yearbook. Thoughts screech in my head, but I have to return the book to the right spot. I thrust it back in, then turn around to find a dark shape in the doorway.

19

Seth Greer glares at me from across the room, blocking my path out the door. I try to catch my breath but manage only shallow intakes of air.

"S-sorry," I stammer. "I was looking for the restroom." This lie takes up whatever air supply I had, so Seth's clothing isn't the only black in the room. My vision tunnels, his menacing hazel eyes at the focus.

He doesn't reply, but takes a step toward me. Should I call out to Emily? No. I need to get him talking. I'm already in deep; I have to make sure he was the one in the woods with Melody.

"Um, is it"—I point out the hall—"the one across the way?" No answer. Just another step closer. Okay, one more try. Then I'll resort to screaming and bulldozing past him. "I'm Cass. We've met before, in the library?"

"I remember." His voice is eerily calm. "Did you come by to borrow that book?"

I slap my head like I'm remembering. "Oh, yeah, about the ants."

"Termites."

"Right. I'd love to borrow it. I've been wanting to learn more about termites." I cringe at the squeakiness of my voice.

"Oh, it's not about termites," he says with a smirk. "Not really." Another step. "It's about a teenage serial killer."

I take a ragged breath. "I can see you're still into reading." My hand shakes as I motion to the piles of books.

One step closer. "And you? You're a writer now. At least, you sure can weave a story."

He knows. He's talking about that day, two years ago.

It was the day Seth and I spoke for the third time. Our conversation started in the library again, but this time it continued into Hathaway Hall. His eyes were a hazy green, like a lake you could just float off into. He wore jeans and a plaid shirt, and a cowboy joke danced on the tip of my tongue.

But Melody Davenport called me over, and I had to say bye to Seth before she could embarrass me in front of him.

"I've noticed you've been getting pretty friendly with that nerdy guy." Her coy smile made my teeth hurt. "What would Gideon think?"

I had always made a point not to answer the girls' questions about whether Gideon and I were a couple. If I answered in the affirmative, it would've been an outright lie. If I answered in the negative, it would've meant that Gideon was single. So I just left it ambiguous, which it sort of was. Still, Melody's threat hit a nerve.

"That guy?" I asked, tossing a thumb over my shoulder to where Seth stood at his locker. "No way. That guy's stalking me. He told me he read an entire volleyball guide just so he could learn more about me."

"Uck. Perv." Even while fake gagging, Melody was gorgeous. "He probably just wanted to look at pictures of girls in spandex."

I shrugged. "Probably."

Melody gasped and nudged me. "He's totally staring at you."

I turned around, and Seth's eyes met mine. He waved and gave a shy grin.

I smiled and then twirled right back around to face Melody. "So scary, right?"

"We should go warn the others." Melody skipped over to where more volleyball players huddled around a cement planter. That kookaburra cackle reverberated off the lockers in her wake.

It was a lie that got away from me. Then it rolled like a tumbleweed, picking up bits and pieces as each student added to the rumor. If Seth was spotted near the bleachers, it was because he was stalking cheerleaders. If Seth ate in the cafeteria, it was because he was spying on girls.

I don't know what made Seth decide to give in to the rumors. To be the dark, solitary creeper we said he was. Maybe it was because he couldn't even pass through the library anymore without hearing the teasing, the whispers.

I know what that's like.

And I know what it's like to want to give in.

I felt bad about Seth. I almost apologized, but he didn't know it was me. Melody was the loudmouth, so he likely credited her for his newfound infamy. I managed to get Maribel High talking about someone else for a change, and no one was the wiser.

But right now, Seth's bladed glare is unmistakable: he figured it out.

He knows that every problem he's had in the last two years, every problem his sister has faced, is thanks to me. And I never could've done it without Maribel's sweetheart, Melody Davenport.

I throw one more desperate glance at the bookshelf before turning back to Seth. "Give it to me."

His eyes narrow. "What are you talking about?"

"My notebook. You have it, and I want it."

He lifts one dark brow.

"Look, you psycho, I know what you did, and what you're trying to do to me. You'll never get away with it."

"You and Melody always had a knack for name-calling. But I'm confused. You're in my room, digging through my stuff, and I'm the psycho?"

You and Melody. He sees us as a team. Together, we ruined his life. And now he's taking the two of us down as a team. The second I leave this place, Seth is going to hand that notebook over to the Oregon State Police.

The only way around this is to give them Seth, to totally slash his credibility before he gets the chance. I didn't find Melody's necklace or phone, and I'm not sure how helpful my snapshot of Seth's yearbook is going to be.

But the creepy photograph he took of Melody is tucked safely inside my back pocket.

The closer he gets, the more I see how his eyes match his clothing again. This time, he's cloaked in darkness and his eyes, lined by his dark lashes, are piercing, onyx black. The kind of eyes that seek revenge. Time to get out of here.

"Emily is waiting for me," I say forcefully. "We're working on a project."

He steps aside, allowing me to pass. But not without shooting me one last look: a warning. As I exit the room, his soft baritone meets my ears, slicing into my memory with the

ease of a steak knife, taking me back to the woods. "Hope
you find what you're looking for."

The door closes behind me, and then the loud music
starts.

20

The next day, Emily is chatting away at my side on the way to fourth period, but I'm too anxious to listen. I have to show the cops what I found in her brother's room. And I need Gideon to come to the station and vouch for me, but he won't even answer my texts.

We pass a boisterous group of sophomore boys congregating behind the lockers. Words like *psycho* and *stalker* bounce around, and I peek at them; they're looking right at Emily. She continues fiddling with something in her locker, like she doesn't notice. But her ears are crimson. I spin around, and Emily's hand clasps my arm. She shakes her head, eyes pleading. "Ignore them."

This isn't fair. Despite how unstable or evil Emily's brother is—more than these boys even know—she has nothing to do with it. I never meant to hurt her by spreading those rumors. I just liked having the attention off me for once.

I growl under my breath and go back to stuffing books into my backpack. The high-pitched laugh of one boy whose voice hasn't changed yet makes my scalp itch. Emily's arm trembles as she reaches for a folder.

I don't think I can keep it together.

One of the boys, a scrawny thing with braces, calls out, "Hey, Greer! How's your brother?"

That's it. I slam my locker door, dropping my backpack to the ground in the middle of the hall. Two steps in, a tall blond boy impedes my path.

Peter McCallum. I shuffle back as he tells the sophomores in a firm, composed voice to get to class. As their eyes roll and they trudge off, that obnoxious laugh still echoing off the metal lockers, he says something else. Too low to catch.

Peter turns around and walks over to us. He stoops to lift my backpack from the ground, handing it to me. I stand, dazed, as Emily speaks for both of us: "Thanks for that."

"No problem." His flashes a crooked smile.

I find my voice as he steps in the direction of the gymnasium. "Wait. What did you say to those guys?"

"I told them they'd be late for class."

"Yeah, but after that. You whispered something."

He shrugs, grimacing in a silly way. "I can't tell you."

"Come on."

Peter sighs. "I said they shouldn't make fun of Emily's brother because he's probably looking for his next victim." He shrinks back, his eyes lowering. "Sorry, Emily."

Emily doubles over next to me, her body shaking, and I freeze. But after a moment, giggles break through the strained silence. Emily is shaking with laughter.

"That was a good one," she says, grabbing her backpack. "I've gotta use that one. You ready, Cass?"

"Yeah, okay." I force a smile.

"Thanks again," Emily calls to Peter. She's still chuckling as we walk to class.

I spend all of fourth period debating my next move. When the bell rings for lunch, I speed to my locker to escape Emily. I have to turn her brother in. I have to tear her family apart. If the teasing was bad before, she's going to get eaten alive after this.

Gideon's locker is ten locker doors down from mine. I know he has to retrieve his lunch and exchange books. He's been avoiding me, and I've let him. But that's over. He has to come with me to the cops.

I finish at my locker. Still no sign of him. I grab the two textbooks I need and slam my locker door. Lunch can wait; I have to find him.

When I pass the auditorium, the doors are ajar. Faint sounds of laughter trickle into the hall.

The school must be holding auditions of some sort. I

nudge one of the doors and peer through the crack. The large space is lit by a single spotlight, but it isn't the voices of the drama club or the choir filling it.

It's Gideon and Gracie. And they have a football. Gideon runs up and down the aisles of the auditorium. He tosses it to Gracie, who dashes up an alternate, stair-filled aisle, catching the ball with ease. Then Gideon catapults himself up onto the stage, shouting, "I'm open!"

Gracie laughs, launching the ball up to him. It's a decent throw.

The way they're acting together—have they been spending time with each other? The thought steals my breath. How did I let it all slip past me? A friendship between Gideon and Gracie is impossible. He has to see that. He can't nurse every wound; this is one he has to leave to someone else. I have to make him understand.

This football game in the auditorium must be Gideon's idea, as it is both athletic and prohibited in nature. I watch as they continue passing, their giggles echoing off the walls. Gracie's smile spreads as Gideon trips over a step, falling onto the squeaky floor with a crash. She looks beautiful and happy. It seems Gideon's project has been a miraculous success.

I hate her. My empty stomach finally catches up to me as I pull my head back from the gap between the doors. I flee down the hallway, sore and dizzy—like I've been knocked off the auditorium stage by a linebacker.

In the indoor courtyard, Emily is eating lunch with Peter on a cement planter. They're laughing in conversation until Emily spots me and waves me over. The last thing I want to do is talk. But I manage a hello and sit down, pulling out my sack lunch to busy my hands.

Emily turns from Peter to offer me a potato chip. "I lost you after class. Where'd you go?"

I take a chip and nibble on it, trying to invent an answer. But when I look up, Laura Gellman is flitting down Hathaway Hall toward us.

She stops in front of me, eyes shining devilishly. "I'm so sorry about Gideon. You must be devastated."

I stare blankly. It's only been a few minutes since I saw him—what happened? Did the police arrest him? Detective Sawyer knew he had no alibi. This is how Seth is finally going to make good on his threats. Not by going after me.

By going after the one I love. My heart lurches.

"What are you talking about, Laura?" asks Emily. I'm trembling, despite Emily's skeptical tone.

"Oh," purrs Laura, clearly enjoying this. "Maybe you don't know." Her hands press together in front of her thin V-neck sweater.

I've had enough. I stand, moving toward her so quickly that she shuffles backward. "Laura, I swear if you don't spit it out, I will walk to the cafeteria and buy a coffee just so I can throw it into your smug face."

A deep chuckle resounds behind me, and a tiny trill of hope that it's Gideon works its way into my head. But I turn, remembering Peter.

"Well, if you're going to be so hostile, never mind." Laura huffs and swings herself around.

"Laura," Peter says, "just tell her. You've got the poor girl all worried now, probably for nothing—no offense." I want to hug Peter, our savior twice in one day.

Emily echoes his sentiments. "Yeah, Laura, just tell her."

Laura backs up like we're a pack of vicious carnivores. "Fine. But I think it should just be Cassidy who hears this. She may need her privacy."

Peter rolls his eyes. "Fine. Go have your private meeting."

I follow Laura to a cutout in the hallway where the drinking fountains are tucked away. She pauses before speaking, like she has to prepare herself. "I saw Gideon"—she cups a hand over her mouth and it's outrageously annoying—"with Gracie Davenport."

"Okay," I say, unsure where this is going. "Gideon's allowed to have other friends, Laura. Is this your big secret?"

"No, Cass. They were *very friendly* together." Laura flinches, retracting her shoulder like I might explode.

Walk away. But the question slips from my mouth. "What do you mean, *friendly*?"

"You know, touchy-feely. Grabbing her hand. Her nudging his arm. That type of thing. Way more flirtatious than the two of you ever were. And I heard she asked him to Sadie Hawkins. Anyway, I thought you might want to know before you saw the two of them together." She reaches out to touch my arm in a comforting gesture.

I yank my arm back. "Why would I care about that? He can be *friendly* with whoever he wants! This is the news you thought would be *devastating*?" My breathing is labored now. The people in the hallway stop mid-conversation and mid-bite to gawk at the shouting person.

Fire Girl is coming unhinged.

Laura smirks. She only has to see my glistening eyes and hear my strained voice to know that I *am* devastated. Gideon and I were never together, not in a romantic way. But the way he cut me out of his life and went and got a girlfriend—or whatever Gracie is—just like that, makes it look like a breakup.

Tears well in my eyes, one blink from splashing all over my face. I want to knock that smirk off Laura's face. But it's gone, replaced by something else. "Cass, I'm—"

"Yeah, I know. You win."

"I didn't—"

"Leave me alone." I brush past her, hurrying out the back doors. The outside air is frigid, but I don't care. Its effect is numbing, and right now I want to be numb. I stand at the far end of the courtyard, shins scraping against the low brick wall, screaming into my hands through bared teeth. The tears fall, creating salty pools in my open palms.

"Cass? Are you okay?"

Emily. Can't she see I need to be alone? But her hand comes to rest on my back, and I just keep crying.

The bell rings to end lunch, and her hand remains there. I've become used to being alone the past two weeks. But Emily cares that I'm hurting more than she cares about being on time for class. Like Gideon used to.

Once I've composed myself, Emily helps me to the bathroom. Our history decade project is scheduled for this period, so I have to clean up. I close myself inside a stall, taking slow, deep breaths. "How are you doing, Cass?" she calls through the stall door.

The tardy bell has long since rung, and if we don't hurry, we'll get a zero. I clear the lump from my throat and reply, "I'm okay. Just a sec."

I come out, staring straight down at the sink while I wash my hands.

"I'm guessing she told you something about Gideon," Emily says. My gaping eyes dart to each stall in alarm, and she reassures me, "It's empty." Her gaze falls from the scratched opaque mirror. "It's okay. You don't have to tell me if you don't want to. I thought you might like to get it out. But you don't have to."

"Thanks." I rub at my red, makeup-smudged eyes. "I want to tell you. But let's get this presentation over with first. How do I look?" I turn to face her with a warped, doubtful smile.

"Cass. You always look amazing. No wonder Peter's in love with you. But if we're going to get there before class ends, we'll have to run."

I join her in sprinting through the hall to U.S. History, not sparing a moment to blush over the Peter comment. Emily holds the large poster board of the 1930s. It flaps against her side as she scuttles along, huffing every couple of yards. I force a laugh to match Emily's as we invent our excuse seconds before diving into the room.

I settle into my seat, tired and achy. Not from the hallway sprint—from knowing I can't ever open up to Emily. Not really. She's been so kind to me, but the only way to stop all of this and get Gideon back in my life is to smash her heart. Her brother is a murderer, and I have to be the one to break it to the world.

Today.

21

The photograph of Melody is stowed in the pocket of my backpack, and I still have that yearbook photo on my phone. Since Gideon can't seem to go two steps without Gracie Davenport pasted to his side, I'll have to take my chances talking to the detectives without him.

After history, I grab my things from my locker and whirl around, crashing right into someone. My books plummet to the floor, and everyone in hearing distance turns to stare at me for the second time today. Enormous blue doll eyes zip toward me from every angle and I shut mine to blot them out. I take an uneven breath and mutter, "Sorry." Then I stoop to help whoever's picking up my books.

"It's fine. Here." The voice sets my skin aflame. The

bustling hall comes to a blurring stop as I look up at Gideon's dark eyes and scruffy jaw. I accept the book, and our fingers brush. Gideon's cheeks blush pink against his olive skin.

"Giddy," I say breathily, wanting to take in everything about him. But he won't make eye contact. He rubs his hands together, like he can't wait to wash off the filth.

"Hey. How are you?" He mumbles the words like a kid forced to talk to an ancient relative. Bags still line his eyes, and his jeans sag. The old Cass would've told the old Giddy to go eat his lunch. But I don't. The nickname doesn't even fit him anymore. This person lacks every trace of Giddy's playful nature.

"I have to talk to you." I lower my voice. "It's about Seth."

"Not here, Cass." He attempts to sweep past me, but I sidestep in front of him. When I don't budge, he relents, turning into a nearby corner of the hallway.

I follow close behind. "Where would we talk about it? You avoid me all the time. You never return my texts anymore. Gideon"—his full name sounds wrong when I say it aloud—"I'm sorry about everything. I have to live with my mistakes every day."

He stays silent, tugging on the strings hanging from the neck of his green hoodie.

I huff through my teeth. "I have proof Seth was stalking Melody."

Gideon's eyes widen. "What do you have?"

"Photos. I'll show you in the truck. Come on."

He pauses, clearly still unsure I can be trusted. My stomach pinches. I never imagined *he*, of all people, could ever feel this way about me too. Then he exhales loudly and hurries beside me toward the front doors of the school. "How did you get them?"

"I went in his room and took them."

"Aren't you afraid of what he'll do when he realizes they're gone?" He pushes a door open with one arm, letting me pass.

"Of course, but I refuse to mess up again. I've got to make sure this guy can't hurt anyone else." The icy-cold air hits us, and I wrap my arms around myself.

"So then, you'll show the detectives the threats?"

I bite my lip. "I can't. When they read the notebook, I'll look even guiltier than Seth. And the cops forgot all about the fire in the portable. If they see the photo—with my history..."

Gideon's glance is sharp. "Seth is going to turn over that stuff anyway. As a last-ditch effort to save himself."

I shake my head. I've thought about this. "The notebook, yes, but not the photo. That would be as good as admitting he had Melody's phone."

"So your grand plan is to give them half the truth." Gideon sighs. I can feel him drawing further away. We get into his truck and he calls the detectives.

As he speaks to Detective Reyes, my head swirls. Maybe

he's right. Maybe I should just hand over my phone and trust the detectives.

Or maybe that's the worst thing I could do.

Gideon hangs up, tossing his phone onto the center console. "They want us to meet them at the diner." He starts the engine. We turn onto the road leading from the school and the truck lurches over a pothole, messing with my nervous stomach. I force myself to breathe slowly and steadily, but Gideon slaps one hand down firmly on the steering wheel. "Cass, if you withhold evidence, you're not letting the cops do their jobs."

"Giddy, everyone already knows I killed a girl! You think they're going to care about Seth's photos when they have it in writing that I wanted Melody dead and planned out how to do it?"

He exhales loudly. The cab is still bitingly cold, and my entire body shakes. "Show me the photos," he says.

I pull out my phone and Gideon glances away from the road to view the eyeless yearbook photo of Melody. Then I dig out the print of Melody in the drugstore. "Well, do you think it's enough?"

His shoulders roll. "It's something. If they could trace those text messages he sent you, it would be solid."

"He used a burner." The texts won't do anything but give Seth an edge. The next few minutes crawl by in silence. I should keep my mouth shut. "Why are you hanging out with Gracie Davenport?"

"Leave her out of this."

The command is curt and final, and it stings. The cab has started to warm, but the space between us is like ice. I'm not sure it will ever melt away. "Fine," I say, opening the chain of anonymous threats. I read. Reread. "I'll show them everything."

Gideon removes a hand from the wheel and squeezes my shoulder. "It'll be fine, Cass. You're doing the right thing."

The right thing. If I do what Gideon wants, I'll be walking out of that diner with my hands cuffed behind my back. I grip the phone tighter between my clammy hands. The trees in my periphery blur and zigzag until I shut my eyes and take a deep breath.

I exhale, open my eyes, and delete the entire chain.

An hour later, I walk out of the diner unsteadily, like I can't remember where we parked. Gideon is waiting on the curb, where he promised he'd be if I needed him, and I sit down beside him. Inside, Detective Sawyer listened to me and looked at the photos. She asked to keep the print. Then she thanked me and said I could go.

I keep waiting to expel that big sigh of relief—especially after seeing the grateful look on the detective's face—but it never comes. It just hangs in my chest, suffocating me.

It isn't just that breath stuck in there. It's also my secrets.

My guilt. I thought they'd be purged along with any statement to the cops, but the sickening feeling refuses to budge. "I couldn't do it," I say, staring at the gum-encrusted sidewalk. "I'm sorry. I panicked."

Gideon doesn't speak. I wait for him to get up and drive off without me, but he just sits there. I don't know what else to say. I failed him. I failed this town. Most of all, I failed Melody. It doesn't matter what I discovered. It doesn't matter that I single-handedly found her killer and worked up the guts to turn him in.

Melody is not coming back. She's gone. My fears, my selfishness, kept everyone from helping her, and nothing I ever do will change that.

Gideon stands up, offering me a hand. I take it, and he pulls me to my feet. But he doesn't look at me as we walk to his truck.

I made a choice. And I lost him.

Now I have to go home and wait. Wait to see if Seth talks his way out of this, using me as the scapegoat. And I have to do it without Gideon, which is fine because I don't deserve him.

I guess I never did.

22

After practice the following afternoon, Asher and I turn on the TV for the first time in weeks. We're watching a reality special about the world's most brilliant jigsaw puzzle–solving teens, when a local news story breaks. An update on the Melody Davenport case.

My heart thumps in time with the blue lights flashing on the screen.

The news reporter finishes going over the basics of the case—not that I need a recap—and a photograph of a young man appears on the screen. Seth Greer. The reporter goes on to explain that this young man has been arrested concerning Melody's alleged homicide.

"Wow, Cass." Asher's eyes are fixed on the screen.

"I know," I breathe. After Gideon dropped me off yesterday, I apologized to Asher about the Brandon stuff and the way I've been acting lately. I needed someone on my side. He said all was forgiven, but he still seemed wary of me. His eyes were vacant. I broke something between us, and my attempt to fix it felt like slabbing on cheap glue.

At least we're on speaking terms now. He wasn't happy about my investigative work, but he eased up when I told him about Seth's collection and the threats.

Now, my hands shake as I look at Seth's photo on the screen and listen to the story of how my efforts actually ended in someone's arrest.

The reporter continues, explaining that Melody's DNA was found in the trunk of Greer's car. Anyone with information concerning the case is encouraged to call the Oregon State Police Department. A telephone number flashes in yellow at the bottom of the screen.

A little cry of relief escapes my lips. I clear my throat as Asher's eyes drift to me. My chest relaxes, but not all the way. An unsettling thought needles its way into my mind and takes up residence there: I wish the reporter had mentioned the necklace. Just to eliminate all questions forever and put me in the clear.

Still, the police found Melody's DNA. The fact the detectives haven't come for me means that DNA evidence prevailed over the notebook.

"You did good, Cass." Asher scoots closer to me on the sofa, wrapping an arm around my shoulder. "That creep is getting what he deserves."

I'm setting out forks and plates for dinner when my phone buzzes.

I grab it. Gideon.

It's over.

I heard. They got him. Giddy, I'm really sorry.

I go back to the table, letting the utensils clink against the plates. Then I push my pride aside and send another text.

Do you want to come over? Asher's here. We can watch a movie.

Sorry, I can't.

Of course not. You're busy with Gracie Davenport. I growl, slamming a knife down so hard it pierces through the tablecloth.

Over by the stove, my mom startles. "Cass, what's wrong?" She checks and stirs her dish one more time before setting the spoon down. Then she steps closer, straightening her apron and peering at me.

"Nothing. I'm sorry. It's just Gideon."

My mom hasn't asked about Gideon. She probably figured I was fine with my replacement friend. I expect her to ask now, but she doesn't.

"Also, I just... Did you hear about what happened with Seth?"

Mom winces. "Yes, sweetie, I did. I know you're close with Emily. Is that what this is about?"

I nod. "People already teased her relentlessly because of Seth. And that was when it was all just rumors. Now..." My eyes wander to the sizzling meat on the stove.

"What if you invite her over? She probably needs a little time to process things with her family, but in the meantime, you could reach out to her. Let her know you're still her friend and you're here for her."

"You don't mind?"

"Of course she doesn't mind," comes Asher's voice from the doorway. "Why would she mind?"

"Well, things are probably going to be chaotic for Emily and her family. And if she comes over here—"

"We'll handle it."

He pats me on the back as my dad wanders into the room, headed straight for his chair. He mutters, "Terrible," clears his throat, and takes a sip of wine.

My mom returns to the stove, motioning for Asher to help her.

"What's terrible, Dad?" I plop down into my seat.

"This whole ordeal with the Greer boy."

"I can't say I'm surprised." Asher gathers up the pan with a potholder. "He was very strange. Disturbed, I guess."

"The Greers have been my patients for years," continues my dad. "It's unreal."

Asher and I nod. His knife punctures a steak still steaming in the pan. As he drops the meat onto my dad's plate, I watch the bloody liquid seep to the edges. A few drips leak onto the cream-colored tablecloth.

Seth wasn't always strange and disturbed. I made him that way with the rumor I spread. A little of this destructive part of me leaked out and dripped into his life. And then into Melody's.

Gideon was right to drop me. I've already left my mark on him; he'll never be the same after all this. Maybe I shouldn't invite Emily over; maybe I should tell her to get away from me while she still can.

Emily, understandably, does not attend school the next two days. Over the weekend, she texts me that reporters are camped outside her house. Her devastated parents contacted a lawyer and then hid under their bedcovers. Emily has been doing her best to comfort them and assure them it will all be cleared up soon.

The following week, when the reporters finally fall away like the last leaves of an autumn oak, she agrees to come over for dinner.

I open the front door to find her bouncy red curls hidden beneath a navy-blue beanie. She wears large sunglasses, though clouds block out every last ray. She peeks behind her before ducking inside. I shut the door and pull her into a hug, letting her cry on my shoulder for a change.

But every tear tugs on my conscience. I did this to her. And though I'm certain her brother killed Melody, it doesn't make it any easier.

At dinner, Asher is charming as usual. Emily nearly starves herself—maybe due to her traumatized state, maybe out of some self-conscious delusion that her eating will ruin her chances with him. Asher makes getting a smile out of Emily his personal mission.

"How did the big decade project turn out?" He flashes his crystal eyes from her to me. Emily practically swoons straight into her full plate of spaghetti.

"I think it went well," I answer for both of us. "Mr. Samuels seemed to like our old movie clips."

"I still think you should've presented in costume," Asher says with a devious grin. "You know, bowler hats, gabardine suits." He winks at Emily and her face suddenly resembles a giant strawberry, bright red with freckles dabbled about.

I laugh. "So we blew it because we didn't dress like 1930s businessmen."

"I'm sure you two did fine," my mom says. "You've been hard at work on that thing for weeks." *Fine*, not *great*, the word she would have used to describe any project of Asher's. Still, my mom is doing her best to make Emily comfortable. She doesn't think I'm capable of making a friend stick.

She's right.

"Thanks, Mrs. Pratt," says Emily, recovering from her spell as a mute strawberry.

My dad, on the other hand, seems confused by everyone's treatment of the elephant in the room. He's quiet, refusing to join in the conversation. He keeps squinting across the table at Emily, like she might try to use her knife on someone. I'm not sure if she notices, but my stomach clenches. I can't wait to flee the dinner table.

"Don't you two have a big dance this weekend?" my mom asks suddenly. "Sadie Hawkins, right?"

"Mom," I whine. "We don't want to talk about that." I sip my water and look to Asher for help. He sees my pleading eyes and his mouth twitches. I sigh. That twitch only means one thing.

"Oh, but Cass, you must tell us who you're asking to the dance," says Asher, a chuckle escaping halfway through his words.

I glare at him. "You know I don't go to dances." Especially one where I'd have to watch Gracie throw herself at Gideon all night.

Emily perks up in her seat a little, like she's enjoying the show. "Why not, Cass?"

I take a bite of spaghetti, just to buy time. How can I explain to someone like Emily, who lives and breathes school spirit—who is on the dance committee—that the idea of a school dance triggers the same physiological response in me as imagining a thousand needles stabbing me in the face?

My noodle has disintegrated to nothing by the time I swallow. "Um, I don't know. It's just not my thing."

My dad sighs loudly and takes a long gulp of wine.

Point taken. "Well, I'm finished. Want to go to my room, Emily?" I look at my mom hopefully, and she smiles her approval.

"Sure," Emily says, picking up her plate.

"Not necessary." Asher reaches a hand across to stop her. "You two go. I'll clean up."

Asher's finger must have skimmed Emily's, because she freezes and stammers, "O-o-k-kay. Th-thanks."

Once Emily and I settle onto my bed, the topic can no longer be avoided. I hand her one of the sugar cookies my mom baked earlier today and lean back against the bed frame. "So, what's been happening?"

Emily shakes her head. "Just"—she shrugs—"a lot. And my parents don't know how to deal with it. I don't even think they would have gotten Seth a lawyer if I hadn't mentioned it."

"Didn't he ask for one?"

"Well yeah, but just the state-appointed guy. He needs somebody good. This is murder we're talking about."

I nod. It's strange staying silent, pretending to agree while everything in me screams that Seth needs to remain in prison for the rest of his life. Still, that tiny, nagging thought is fighting to surface again. Despite my efforts to smother it, I have to know for certain. "This is ridiculous," I huff, shaking my head. "What was this supposed DNA evidence they found?" It's a natural enough segue; the media hasn't revealed this detail yet.

Emily's face turns ashen, and I regret asking. "I don't know."

"Did anyone mention the necklace?" I nibble on a cookie, trying not to seem too interested in her answer. "You know, Melody's necklace that went missing? Was it part of the evidence?"

"I don't think so. But no one's telling me anything—that's part of this nightmare."

"Have you talked to Seth yet?"

"No, I..." Her words catch as she blinks away tears.

"It's okay. You can tell me."

"It's all my fault," she whispers.

"What? No, Emily. None of this is your fault."

"You don't understand," she says, rubbing her eyes. "I didn't go talk to my brother because I *never* talk to my brother. I haven't in the last two years."

"Well, you're very...different."

"He wasn't always this way. He changed. He was always smart and reserved, but he wasn't this loner guy."

Guilt curdles in my stomach. "Really?"

"I think it's because of me. I see you and Asher, and you're so close. If I'd had that kind of relationship with Seth, maybe he wouldn't be the way he is now. Or maybe I would've seen it. Maybe I could've stopped it." Her eyes widen and she claps a hand over her mouth. "Not that I think he killed Melody. I—oh no." Her head falls onto her knees.

"Emily, I know you don't." I reach out to touch her shoulder. "I know you don't. You can trust me. I promise I won't say anything." There it is again. That sick feeling, like my spaghetti sauce is climbing back up my throat. Because if it comes down to me and Seth again, I know I won't keep that promise.

The truth is, as Emily's true thoughts spill from her mouth, the knot I've had in my gut since that day in the woods eases. Even Seth's own sister believes, deep down, that he killed Melody.

"Okay," Emily says, that cheery look working its way back onto her face, "let's talk about something else. I've had nothing but Seth's problems on my mind for the past week."

"Sure. Name it."

"Let's talk about why you're so against going to the dance. Even Asher thinks you should go."

"No, see, he was purposefully trying to embarrass me."

"Cass, I'm supposed to go to that dance. And we both know I can't, not after everything that's happened." She sniffles. "And right now, you're my only friend."

I take a deep breath.

"Would you consider going in my place? You wouldn't have to do much. Just hang some posters before the dance and then report to the rest of the committee if any issues come up during the event." She leans in, hopefully.

"Oh, Emily, you know I would... Isn't there, like, any other way I can help?"

"Why don't you want to go? Really? I know it might not be your favorite thing, but you look terrified at the thought. I trusted you. Trust me now."

I lick my lips. "Okay. This is going to sound ridiculous in comparison to everything you're going through"—Emily nods for me to go on—"but it's about what Laura said in the hall a couple days ago."

"About Gideon."

"Right." I proceed to tell Emily about Gracie Davenport asking Gideon to the dance. "I don't think I'm jealous of him going to the dance with Gracie," I say, finding it difficult to explain my feelings while leaving out a million details. "I just..."

"It's like he's moved on," Emily graciously cuts in. "I get it. You guys were best friends and now he spends all of his time with her. Totally makes sense."

"Yeah, I guess that's it." And that *is* it, mostly.

"I think getting your own date to the dance will make you feel so much better." She grins exuberantly. "And I know just who."

"I'm not sure." But suddenly, her plan strikes me as brilliant. By going to the dance, I can keep an eye on Gideon— just to make sure his mission to help Gracie Davenport doesn't include disclosing my part in Melody's death. And if my being there with a date happens to make him a little jealous in the process, it would only be a bonus. "Who'd you have in mind?"

"Peter, of course. It's obvious he has a thing for you. And he's totally hot."

Peter McCallum, with his blond hair and narrow green eyes, is the polar opposite of Gideon in the looks department. But it's funny I never noticed it before, because Emily is right. He is attractive, which always made his single status a bit of a mystery. I've seen his glances and heard Gideon's jabs, but I've never given him much thought. "You think he likes me?"

"Everyone knows it. And I have insider knowledge." Her eyebrows lift playfully. "The other day when Peter sat with me at lunch, he spent the whole time asking about you." She pauses like I need a moment to let the meaning sink in. "Seriously, Cass. He'll say yes."

I smile nervously, disbelievingly, at what I'm about to say. "I guess I could ask him."

Emily squeals and claps her hands. "Yay! Oooh, you guys are going to be the cutest couple ever."

"Are you sure I can't convince you to come? You're kind of my only friend right now too. I want you there. I promise to be your bodyguard."

"No one would go with me. Unless it was in a *Carrie* sort of way."

"Let me handle that." I begin rattling off the names of the

worst guys at school in an attempt to cheer her up. Dougie Melborn, the only junior in high school who is perpetually dirty, is first on the list. He isn't dirty in a simply hygienic manner. He is actually, physically filthy—like he was rolling around in the mud before school.

"Just imagine the red-haired, dirty babies the two of you would make one day if everything goes well." I laugh, clutching my sugar cookie–filled stomach. "But I wouldn't spend too much money on a dress for the dance, because one slow dance with him will have you covered in mud and probably whatever bugs live inside the dirt clods on that guy."

Emily struggles to breathe between giggles. "Fantastic. So you get Pretty Peter and I get Dirty Dougie."

"Oh, let me think a bit more. I'm sure I can come up with someone—maybe not quite as good of a catch as Dougie though."

"Please don't trouble yourself," she says. But her enormous grin and red, tear-streaked face only make me laugh harder.

23

I wait until after school to approach Peter. There were plenty of opportunities earlier in the day, as Emily made clear by repeatedly tugging on my sleeve. But I'd rather do it when I'm free to run home and hide under my covers if he turns me down. Emily assures me he won't, but the dance is only three days away; he must've been asked by now.

I spot him by the fountain in front of the school, which is only a fountain in name. Water never flows from it—it was shut down years ago after one too many giant bubble bath pranks gone wrong. So it's just a gray stone statue of our mascot, Maribel the Mermaid, surrounded by a circular concrete wall. Students usually sit here, waiting for the morning bell or for their rides after school.

Peter waves in the brisk but affable way people do when they expect the other person to return the salutation and continue walking. But I stop in front of him, so he's caught off guard. His intensely focused eyes broaden the slightest amount.

"Hey, Peter."

"Hey, Cassidy." The end of my name drifts upward, like a question. He scoots over on the wall, making room for me. Sitting down is clearly not an option in case this conversation ends abruptly and unfavorably for me; however, standing before him at the entrance of our school makes me feel like an enormous attraction.

My gaze sinks to his sneakers. *Stop it.* I bring it back up to focus on his green eyes instead. But his eyes make my head swirl. "I just wanted to ask really fast if you had a date for Sadie Hawkins."

His eyes widen and narrow again. Just when I'm sure I've made him uncomfortable, he answers, "Nope, nobody asked me." He shakes his head, slowly. "That's why I'm sitting here, waiting for one of your kind to come to her senses. I figured if I did a little posing, modeling out here by the stunning Maribel"—he gestures to the statue behind him—"some pretty girl would have to stop and think, *I need to be the mermaid who gets to go to the dance with that model guy.* So far, no girls have experienced such a revelation."

I try to restrain the smile stealing across my lips. "Oh,

okay, well, I was just wondering. Hope it works out for you. See you later." I wave and stride toward the steps leading to the parking lot.

"Seriously?" comes the deep voice behind me.

I laugh, whirling back around to see Peter wipe fake tears from his eyes. I take a couple steps in his direction. "You know, when I woke up this morning, I had no intention whatsoever of going to the dance, but when I saw you next to the mermaid..." I shrug, wielding a look of incredulity. "I just... I want to know. Can I be that mermaid, Peter?"

He tilts his head, resting it on an index finger. "I think that might be okay." His grin is subtle and crooked, and my heart quickens. "Pick you up at six?"

"Yeah, sounds perfect. You'll have to do some searching for a corsage to match a long green flipper, though." I practically skip down the steps as he calls after me.

"I'll start looking today!" I have the most ridiculous smile plastered across my face as I fly to my bike. Maybe Emily is right. Maybe this is exactly what I need.

Poor Emily was right about one thing: her Sadie Hawkins's prospects. I never did find her a date. I asked two guys, but one laughed in my face and one heard the name Emily Greer and just looked at me like I was lost. Then he practically ran away. Emily said it was fine and would free her up to help me get ready for the dance. After all, there's a lot to do in just two days.

We work after school on Friday, getting the last bits of my ensemble together on Saturday morning. I skip lunch to hang Emily's posters before the rest of the committee shows up to finish the decorations. I sneak in and out of the gym, heaving the enormous ladder all around the room, without running into a single babbling committee idiot.

In the afternoon, Emily curls my hair into loose, polished waves and does my makeup, painting smoky gray eyes and glossy pink lips to create a version of me that looks out of place above my jeans and T-shirt.

I slip into the short, blush-colored dress we found at a little boutique in Rosedale, its color like an extension of my own pale skin. Emily says Peter won't believe his eyes when he sees me in the dress, with its spaghetti straps and form-fitted bodice that flows into a bouquet of tulle. The hem kicks slightly outward, forming a splash about my thighs. I secretly hope it will make that impression on another guy at the dance.

When Peter rings the doorbell, Emily sends me on my way with a smile.

Before the dance, we go to dinner at a small but fancy Italian restaurant thirty minutes from Maribel in the middle of nowhere. Inside, candles illuminate a dimly lit room. This amplifies the whole "date" aspect of the experience, it being just the two of us sharing a cozy meal with a single red rose displayed on the table between us. In the spirit of Sadie Hawkins, I inform Peter I will be paying. To this, he simply laughs and responds, "We'll see." The challenging edge to his tone reminds me of Gideon, momentarily coating our outing in a gloomy film.

We settle in and place our orders, and Peter's upbeat nature eventually puts me at ease. "So, you and Laura seem like you're on really good terms." He smiles slyly behind his water glass.

"Is it that obvious?" I make an embarrassed grimace. "Have you ever seen *The Omen*? Not the remake—the original?"

"No," he says, letting the word trail. He stares at me, the corner of his mouth inching upward. "Isn't that movie, like, a hundred years old?"

"Well, yeah," I say, "but Gid—my brother and I have something of an affinity for classic horror." I make a twirling gesture with my hand, knowing how nerdy I sound. "Anyway, there's this old hag lady who's actually a demon sent from hell. And, I swear, Laura reminds me of her pretty much on a daily basis."

Peter's mouth drops open for a moment. Then he bursts into laughter. "Wow. So you like her a lot then."

"Yeah, I really hope she comes tonight. I'm sure she'll find a way to make my first school dance more memorable. You know, by introducing the Antichrist to the masses of dancing students. Or by letting us all take part in whatever evil plot she's working on to destroy the universe."

Peter tries to compose himself, shaking his head like he can't believe me capable of such remarks.

"Sorry, I should shut up now. You probably think I'm horrible."

"You don't know what I'm thinking." That little corner of his mouth is still raised. Heat fans out across my face, like wildfire. "I hope her *news*," he says, adding air quotes, "wasn't anything too terrible."

The waiter comes with our plates, and I see it as my window of escape from answering his question in any manner of detail. "Oh, of course not. Laura just gets her kicks out of trying to make everyone else believe their problems are worse than hers. This looks great." I motion to the plate before me.

I've ordered this fettuccine here before with my family, so I know exactly what it will taste like.

"Yeah, it does," Peter says, blowing on a forkful of noodles. "So, tell me. What else should I know about you, other than your unique taste in movies?"

I used to have a starting spot on the volleyball team. I used to have a best friend. I'm responsible for one death, maybe two. I take a sip of water, eyes planted on my plate. "I'm pretty boring. You know I play volleyball?"

He cocks a brow. "Small school, remember?"

"Sorry. You go first. What should I know about you, Peter?"

"Easy. I order a double chocolate milkshake from Gina's twice a week, even when it's snowing outside."

I frown dramatically. "That's very disappointing."

"Well, it hasn't won me any awards or anything, but is it really that bad?"

"I'm afraid it is." My eyes travel up to his, a grin inching over my lips. "To a Daisy's Ice Cream fanatic. Gina's milkshakes have got nothing on Daisy's."

Peter laughs and I take a bite of my fettuccini, trying not to choke as I chew through giggles.

"Battle of the milkshakes might make for a decent second date," he says, halting my laughter. "I'm glad you asked me to this thing tonight."

I go back to staring at my food. As if twisting the noodles onto my fork is the highest form of science, requiring my full concentration. "Well, I was kind of forced into it, remember? Maribel the Mermaid made me do it."

"That's right. Well, I take it back then. I'll just thank her on Monday."

I don't want to look up because my face is probably as red as it feels, but I venture a glance. Peter has stopped chewing. His emerald eyes peer at me through those slits, a smile cracking beneath.

The flutter I felt at the fountain returns. I nod. "I'm sure she'd appreciate a thank-you."

We make our way back to Peter's car after dinner, and I

realize things are going quite well. Maybe because Peter never explicitly asked me about Gideon, and also because Peter's personality is a lot like mine. And it's easy to get along with yourself at first, having so much in common and everything— that is, until the dark things nestled deep within emerge, and you find that you might not like yourself as much as you thought.

On the car ride to the dance, our bodies seem to be drawn together despite the armrests between us. The game of sideways glances back and forth out of the corners of our eyes is exhilarating. By the time we make it to the school parking lot, one of Peter's hands has drifted from the steering wheel to rest dangerously close to mine.

Part of me wants to know what will happen if we stay in the car together another minute. But the other part bolts from the passenger seat the second he hits the breaks.

"Hey! I was supposed to open the door for you," he scolds, coming around to meet me. "Mermaids," he mutters, eliciting a laugh from me. As nervous as I was leading up to the dance, being with Peter is fun. Thrilling, even.

I might not even have to pretend to like him.

24

We step into the school gymnasium lined with the Sadie Hawkins posters Emily slaved over. Inside, the large open room is decorated like a night sky. Long black fabric drapes the walls and thousands of twinkling lights float across the ceiling. Cardboard cutout trees in the fashion of Van Gogh's *Starry Night* are displayed around the room, and swirling clouds adorn the walls. A yellow moon painted with a gallon of gold glitter is suspended from above, accompanied by a smattering of gold stars. Spotlights shine from the ceiling, making the girls' dresses sparkle.

But the corners of the room remain out of the spotlights, with only the delicate glow of the twinkling lights to illuminate them. In one such corner, swathed in shadows, I spot Gideon.

At first I don't recognize him because a girl's arms are looped around the back of his neck—an accessory I've never seen on him before. But we near them, and the two dark figures emerge: Gracie's head on Gideon's shoulder, and his hands on the small of her back, his chin tucked into the crown of her head.

A horrible sensation grabs me. It's like parts of my body have plummeted to the floor, leaving room for my heart or soul to tumble straight through. I stand in the doorway staring while Peter makes his greetings. I can't pry my eyes off them. Part of me wants to tell Gracie myself that I let her sister down. To get it out in the open, once and for all. I heard her sister's pleas and did nothing about it.

And part of me wants to tell her to stay far away from Gideon Hollander.

When Peter returns, I have no choice but to lift my silver kitten-heeled pumps from where they seem fastened to the floor, one at a time. I take his hand as he escorts me out to the dance floor.

The first song is slow and easy, and I worry I'll never perk up enough if something more upbeat pulses through the speakers. I ask Peter if we can get punch.

"You're not tired already, are you?" That lopsided smile lights his face. "I was worried about you, because of the mermaid stuff. I can't imagine you're very accustomed to dancing."

"I'm fine," I say, rolling my eyes. "Just thirsty. Even mermaids need to drink." He follows me to the punch table, where I scoop myself some of the red drink, gulping it down as Peter chats with a boy in our grade whose name I don't know. He nudges Peter and whispers in his ear. Peter nods before leaning toward me.

"You might want to slow down a little with the punch. Someone already got to it."

I stare blankly at him, and he raises his eyebrows a few times, nodding toward the plastic cup. And then it hits me: someone spiked the punch. I glance bemusedly at my empty cup and toss it into the trash. I guess the punch tasted a bit off. Still, I don't hate the tingly sensation coursing through my body when Peter leads me back onto the dance floor.

Maybe it's the alcohol, but I've somehow acquired the boldness to direct Peter to a better spot. One with a clear line of sight to Gideon and Gracie. Where maybe they'll have a clear line of sight to me. With Peter.

It's another slow song. Gideon and Gracie are dancing closely and effortlessly, like they've been dating for months. It pressures me to make the same sort of display, and the punch is rallying me on.

My hands begin on Peter's shoulders, and his rest loosely on my back. He's making light conversation, joking about how we should've had the dance outside if we wanted a night sky theme—which would've been ludicrous due to the outdoor temperature. I laugh and slowly inch my fingers behind his neck, drawing myself closer to him in the process. I don't look around for Gideon, but simply will him to see us as I gaze into Peter's eyes. My face hovers inches from his, with a demure look I hope will encourage his fingers to move somewhere a little less safe.

As though controlled by a puppeteer, Peter's hands wander to the small of my back, and then just a tad lower. My spine tingles. Then he does something surprising: he breaches the miniscule gap holding our faces apart, bringing his lips firmly to mine. I startle, but allow myself to lean into him, returning the kiss as warmth radiates through every inch of my body.

We part, smiling shyly back and forth. And I feel an undeniable tug—a need as real as breathing itself—to find out if Gideon saw. I excuse myself with a squeeze of Peter's hand, mumbling that I need to say hi to someone. Really, though, I'm hoping to catch Gideon's eyes trailing after me. I tiptoe on sore feet toward the punch table, worried I won't find anyone to talk to.

With relief, I notice Lena from my English class over by the punch. Might as well sneak a few more sips of red stuff in the process.

Lena's short, with a severe black bob. Her hot pink gown is too big, making her look like a child playing dress-up. I focus on the punch, serving myself a bit. Then I step back from the table to face her. "Oh, hi, Lena!"

She squints a little, struggling to recognize me beneath the extra makeup, before smiling. "Hi, Cassidy!"

"Who are you here with?"

She giggles, pointing to a gathering of boys that now includes Peter. I turn my back to them, hiding my punch in front of me. "David Townsend," she says in a squeaky voice, still giggling. Her face is redder than the punch, which she's clearly been consuming. "I didn't want to ask him. But he kept following me around school, so finally I just figured... why not? You know?"

I nod, though I definitely don't know. She seems to have invited her stalker to the school dance. Still, I laugh and add dramatic gestures while we speak. It has to look like I'm enjoying myself. "And how is everything going so far?" I ask with an inquisitive raised brow.

"Not as well as it seems to be going for you," she says approvingly. "Peter McCallum is like...the most gorgeous guy at school. And you two were getting *very close* out there." Suddenly uncomfortable, I take a giant swig of my punch, downing it in one flick of the wrist. "I guess that means you and Gideon Hollander broke up. He looks pretty cozy out there too."

"Oh no, we were just friends." But the mention of Gideon is just the excuse I need to steal a glance. They're still out there, dancing now to an upbeat song, smiles wide. Gideon spins Gracie, whose blond hair seemingly flutters about her in slow motion. His hand is on hers—the hand that led me to so many adventures when we were kids. The hand that led me to the log when we were fourteen.

A wild thought crosses my mind: I should just march over there and take that hand back.

I reach in front of Lena to scoop up some more punch, gulping it down until the tightness in my stomach is eased by fiery warmth. "Well, I'd better get back to my date." I toss my cup into a nearby trash can along the wall and veer toward the dance floor.

I'm soon met by the unforeseen obstacle of a spinning, hazy room. It was difficult to navigate before, when it was simply dark and flickering. Now, as I stagger dizzily through the maze of people, I repeat a command to myself: *Do not fall and look like a drunken idiot.*

Fortunately, Peter intervenes. He takes my hand and brushes a stray hair out of my face with a gentle stroke. "You okay?"

"Yeah, let's just dance." I lead him toward the throngs of swaying, jumping, and convulsing students. The toasty, fuzzy sensations are accompanied by a feeling of invincibility that makes me want to move until I can't recognize myself.

So I do, and Peter dances with me, surprise blooming across his face. He laughs and watches me with fascination.

"I didn't think smart girls could dance like that." He pulls me close as the tempo of the next song slows.

"Well, you're a pretty good dancer for a smart guy

yourself." The world spins faster by the second, so I rest my head on Peter's shoulder. I don't dare close my eyes; this causes the nausea to roll in like the tide. Instead, I hold on to him with my eyes slightly open, watching the room rotate with Gideon at its center—a distant, beautiful figure, twirling and floating to the vibrations pounding in my brain.

A twinge of guilt about Peter has been growing steadily as the night goes on. He's a nice guy who deserves my attention. If things with Gideon weren't caving in on me, I may have found myself falling for Peter and his intellectual charm.

Instead, I'm selling this fake smile and this fake fun girl who dances, and I can tell by his face he's buying every second of it. And he's probably thinking that this is his moment—dancing to this cover of "Can't Help Falling in Love" and me holding on so tightly—when he finally gets the girl and the rest will be history.

With this thought, the nausea finally courses its way high enough in my throat that I panic. I tear myself away from Peter and attempt to locate the nearest exit. My kitten heel turns sideways and I stumble, nearly falling onto the squeaky wooden floor.

"Cass, are you okay?" Peter calls, trying to catch up.

"Yes, I just need a minute. Be right back!" I shove my foot back into the silver pump and do my best to dash through the whirling dresses and arms that fly about, despite the rocking of the room.

Bursting into the crisp night air, I'm blinded by the street-lights lining the parking lot. These blaze in comparison to the dimly lit gymnasium. I can't find a trash can to vomit into, so I weave toward the bushes that flank the lot. I bend over and empty the contents of my stomach, heaving and moaning as my body convulses and my mind becomes darker and cloud-ier than the sky above.

I feel a hand on my back and jump. Humiliated, I back away from the disgusting scene, its odor already filling the air. "I told you not to follow me," I mumble.

"Yeah, but you didn't mean it," comes a deep voice that doesn't belong to Peter. I try to turn my head, but Gideon has pulled my hair up into a temporary ponytail.

I scowl at the bushes but allow him to keep holding my hair. It's too early to tell if I'm done expelling my insides. "Shouldn't you be with your date?" A sardonic edge floats off my question.

"She's the one who told me you looked like you needed help." *Great.* So Gracie isn't just a pretty little damsel in distress; she's a saint.

I dry heave again, feeling slightly better afterward. Retrieving my hair from his grasp, I wobble a few feet away from where I just vomited. I sit down on the curb, straighten-ing the skirt of my short dress as best as I can.

"What are you doing, Cass?" Gideon's deep brown eyes, whose disapproval I've grown accustomed to, now reflect concern as well.

"Just having fun. This is supposed to be fun, right?" I throw him a silly face before burying my head in my dress. "Oh, that position is worse," I groan, forcing my head upright and directly into his line of sight. We exchange glances in silence until I can't hold it in anymore. "Why did you have to start going out with *her*, Giddy?"

"We're just friends. She asked me to the dance."

"You look like a lot more than *friends*."

"I could say the same about you and *my tutor*." His eyes avert to rest on the asphalt.

So he *was* watching. I should feel satisfaction. But the pain between us is too great. I can't find the words to explain any of this, so I settle on an accusatory statement: "Yeah, well, Peter isn't Melody Davenport's sister."

Gideon takes a breath. "It wasn't on purpose, becoming friends with Gracie. I just...wanted to see her. To see if she was all right. We started talking, and I felt like I needed to be around her. Like if I couldn't wind the clock back and save Melody, I could at least make sure Gracie was okay. I never told her about that day, though. I wanted to—*want* to. Being with her is nice, but you're right. It hurts." His eyes shut tightly.

I turn around to vomit again, remembering a moment too late that we had moved away from the bushes. Chunks vaguely resembling noodles splatter over the asphalt. I move farther down the parking lot, taking a seat on what appears to be a spot of clean curbside. Then, having lost all sense of timidity along with my dinner, I blurt, "Why did you kiss me on the log in ninth grade?"

Gideon lets out a faint, bitter laugh. "Come on, Cass. You really want to talk about this now? Things are so messed up. And besides—"

"Yeah, I know," I cut in. "You don't want to be with me because of Asher." I wince as my whiny voice comes to rest on my ears.

"It's not about that." He doesn't elaborate, so my mind is left to wander.

"You like her." It's a statement—one he doesn't correct.

Instead, he scoots toward me again to gently rub my arms, which are plagued with goosebumps and frozen to the touch. "How are you doing?"

"Better than I was, I guess."

"How many cups of punch did you have, anyway?"

"I don't know. Five?"

"You could give that girl from *The Exorcist* a run for her money in a puking contest." He peers down at me, biting his lip like he's trying not to laugh.

I give him my best attempt at an irritated glare. "There's the light at the end of the tunnel."

He chuckles. "No, but seriously. You look worse than the time we ate that green lunch meat we found in the back of your fridge."

I punch his arm weakly. "You were the one who said that nasty meat would be fine."

"Never thought I'd see you at a school dance."

"That makes two of us."

He shrugs. "Kinda always figured if you ever went to one, it would be with me." His eyes are distant now, perched somewhere off in the large trees bordering the school. I feel a pang in my chest. How many other hopes and dreams and firsts will pass us by while we remain stranded on opposite sides of this schism?

He pulls me to my feet and we wander away from the harsh streetlamps. He turns to face me, and in that second, beneath the faint moonlight, his eyes focus on mine the way they did on the log when we were fourteen. "Cass." His voice is soft and low.

I hold my breath, wishing. "Yeah?"

He smiles. "Stay away from the punch."

I force a smile in return, but my heart plummets. "I will. Giddy?"

"Yeah?"

"A minute ago, when you said it wasn't about Asher. What did you mean?"

"Just forget it."

"I don't want to forget it. I want..." I step toward him, reaching out to place a hand on his firm jaw.

His eyes shut as my hand moves up his scruffy cheek. "Cass, stop."

"This can work. I know it can. And I spoke to Asher—"

He pries my hand off and steps back. "Cass, it's not about Asher! It's about the fact that I can't even look at you anymore. I see you in the halls, and I can't breathe. I see you in English, and I can barely find the strength to write my name on the paper. When I look at you, I go back to the day Melody disappeared and I didn't help her. After everything that day, the way you kept things from me—from the cops, what you did to Brandon... I love you, Cass. I always will. You have this power over me. My mind isn't my own."

I don't try to contain the tears. My legs feel weak, my head impossibly heavy as Gideon continues. "I used to think that one day we would be together. But now, I know it was all a fantasy. I'm looking at a total stranger."

My vision blurs and I bend over. My heavy head sways in circles as I rest my hands on my knees. Black tears drip onto my dress. It's over. Our moment beneath the lights was just that: a moment, ephemeral and fleeting. Our old times have as much chance of returning as Melody Davenport herself. I knew turning Seth in wouldn't bring her back, but I thought it would bring back Gideon.

He puts his hands on either side of me. "Here, let me walk you inside."

"Don't touch me," I snap. "Wouldn't want you to fall under my evil spell again."

"Cass, you can barely walk."

"I'll manage. I'm going to have to get used to doing stuff without your help." I pull my head up, swallowing back the nausea, and whip around. I rush toward the side door of the gymnasium, praying I won't pass out before I make it inside the restroom.

———————

Though the queasy feeling subsides, I'm in no shape to remain at the dance. I can't face anyone in there. After briefly entertaining the idea of walking home, I think better of it, due to the difficulty of the journey and the inability to ever face Peter again if I ditch him.

After cleaning up in the restroom, I head back out to Peter.

He's no dummy, and immediately takes my hand and leads me to the exit. Judging by the glare he shoots Gideon on our way out, he also guessed who picked up the pieces during my absence. Or left me in pieces.

On the car ride home, I'm quiet. My shame and the ebbing effects of the alcohol push my now-tousled waves back against the headrest. Peter reaches over to smooth a strand of my hair. His fingers remain threaded there, tickling my ear for a moment before moving back to the steering wheel. "What happened back there?"

I shrug. "I drank the punch."

"Right." His silence is sharp and telling. I feel the need to explain myself, to try and salvage this relationship that's about to end before it started. Peter wanted to come here with me, despite the whispers that follow me everywhere. Why did I throw that away for a chance with someone I'd already lost? "I did warn you about that," he adds, playfully.

"You did." I'm an idiot. We both know it.

"It seemed like more than just the punch, though. You looked upset. Was it Gideon?" There's concern in his voice, but Gideon's name comes out like it tastes bitter.

"I'm fine." My face heats up, so I lean toward the window. I remember how Peter looked at me in the restaurant, the thrill I felt when his lips brushed mine and how, for a few seconds, I forgot about Gideon Hollander altogether.

Could I let go of Gideon and be happy with Peter? Maybe I could be content with Peter's eyes, his deep laugh, those lips. If nothing else, he's been my friend and savior since Gideon disappeared. I should try to fix this.

I twist around, an apology forming in the back of my throat. But Peter's eyes are blank and focused on the road. His hand no longer reaches out to caress my aching head.

So that's it then. Peter caught a glimpse of the real me— pathetically infatuated, hopelessly destructive. Sometimes lethal. After tonight, I'll never hear from him again. It's just as well. I doubt I could handle opening myself up to another person and getting rejected anyway.

Peter drops me off at home early enough that some of the lights are still on. I slip into my room and tumble onto the bed. I barely manage to kick off my pumps with my toes, leaving my dress and makeup untouched. Then, shutting my eyes so that the swiveling of the world around me becomes the swiveling of my own brain, I allow the darkness to take me.

That night, I dream that termites have infested the hobbit house, covering the wood walls in decay. The little creeping things made a home here in our absence. When I try to inspect the damage, my foot crashes straight through the rotted floor. The bugs crawl from their honeycombed walls toward me. My foot won't budge. Frantically, I look around for Gideon to pull me out. To help me fix this.

But he's gone.

25

The next week drags on in the wake of my Sadie Hawkins catastrophe. Emily seems shocked I even took a sip of alcohol. I don't tell her about Gideon, just that I felt experimental and everything ended awkwardly with Peter—who might never want to talk to me again.

It turns out though, Peter does want to talk to me at school. I'm not sure how or why he's forgiven my behavior. Apparently, he likes wild, vomiting, dancing wrecks. Emily's problems put things in perspective. She nearly withdrew from school, but Peter and I convinced her to press on. We help to keep the media and the bullies away.

Nothing fills the crater Gideon left behind, but having two solid friends—one who needs me desperately and one who clearly wants to be more than friends—at least cuts down its size. It permits me to slip through the days without needing to curl up into a ball in the darkness of my room.

But my mistakes are never far from my mind. News coverage of the Melody Davenport case comes at me like a blizzard. I try to avoid the television and the newspapers, which my parents always leave strewn about the kitchen table, forcing me to avert my eyes. But I still get pelted with updates and occasional visits from the detectives, leaving me anxious and restless.

Seth is facing trial. It's months away, but everyone is certain he did it. The town of Maribel can't forget how he was always lurking around, watching girls. And that hair investigators lifted from the trunk of his car and his lack of an alibi are stacked against him.

Still, I get flickers of doubt every time I remember the old Seth. I can't help wondering about Melody's necklace, and if the cops found it tangled among the books at Seth's place. Sure, he could've tossed it into the water along with her body.

But I wish I knew for certain.

Emily and Peter take my mind off these unsettling thoughts when I let them. Other times, Peter in particular is a little too perceptive.

"You must've known Melody Davenport pretty well, being in volleyball together," he says offhandedly as we sit eating our lunches in the indoor courtyard. Gideon and

Gracie just passed by and I pretended not to notice, focusing intently on my sandwich.

I shrug. "We were only on varsity together for a year. We obviously spoke. She was quite a volleyball player."

Peter nods. "What about her sister?"

I know it's unintentional, but he's getting a rise out of me. I take a deep breath. "She's nice, too. I don't really know her, though. She doesn't play volleyball. Plus, she's a grade below us."

"Right."

"Why do you ask?"

"Oh, nothing."

But he says it like he wants to say more, and is restraining himself. I know I'm in the clear with the cops. They have Seth. Still, my heart races and I can't control the nervous tapping of my feet against the concrete.

"You sure?" I anxiously squish my peanut butter and jelly sandwich between two fingers.

"Yeah." He's staring down at his cafeteria burrito. "Well, I guess I'm asking because you're always looking at her. Or is it at Gideon?"

I choke on my sandwich. The sticky peanut butter becomes lodged in my throat. I cough and then spit out, "It's no secret we're—we *were* friends, Peter."

"It's not more than that?" His narrow green eyes finally meet mine, crackling with a fervid spark.

"What are you talking about?"

"Friends don't look at each other the way you look at him."

I don't blink for a long beat. How could he presume to read my feelings? How could he know anything about me? It doesn't matter if he's dead-on about Gideon. One kiss at a dance doesn't give him the right to call me on it. I grit my teeth, fury settling into a scorching sensation in my cheeks and a pounding in my head, like nails being driven in slowly.

"You don't know how I look at my friends," I snap, standing up, "because you're not one." I wad up my half-eaten lunch and hurl it into a trash can, then bolt down the hallway in a white-hot rage in search of Emily, leaving Peter sitting stunned.

By the time I make it to the end of the hallway, regret already needles its way through the blinding wrath.

The next morning, I wake up groggy. I spent most of the night obsessing over the way I treated Peter, who's been nothing but nice to me. Before bed, Emily called to cheer me up. She said I should just apologize—that only someone who really liked me would worry about another guy.

Still, I should probably leave Peter alone. Even Emily should stay far away from me. Everyone I touch gets burned.

I enter the kitchen in a zombie state, with half-shut eyes and rigid limbs. Two steps in, I hear rustling. Asher is seated at the kitchen table, steaming mug in hand. He's reading the morning paper.

I'm slightly annoyed; I'd hoped to have a peaceful moment to let my coffee and shower work their wonders. "Morning," I mumble, and it comes out raspy. I proceed to the cabinet and reach for a mug.

"Good morning." His tone is rather perky, considering the hour.

I bury my face in my coffee mug.

"Anything interesting going on at school today?" he asks.

"No, what about you? You're up early." A couple sips of the warm drink has my voice on its way to recovery. Even my eyes are progressing toward being fully open. I sneak a glimpse at the newspaper article spread out on the table; it doesn't appear to have anything to do with Melody.

"I'm headed to the office. But after seeing this beautiful sky, I don't know if I'll be able to sit cooped up for long." He motions toward the kitchen window.

"You could go for a walk," I suggest. "It might warm up enough at some point today."

"Yeah, a walk would be good." A nostalgic expression slips onto his face and his head tilts toward the window. "The woods are real therapy for the soul."

Sadness fills my throat. *Maybe they used to be.* I get up, mug in hand, and walk to the doorway. "I think I'll take this back to my room."

Asher picks up his own mug and follows me into the hallway. I turn and raise an eyebrow at him, but he ambles mindlessly behind me. When I get to my room, he rolls right in without invitation, plunking down onto my bed. I take a seat at my desk, noticing for the first time that my doll has been returned. It rests on the shelf above the bed. "Thanks for fixing Edna."

"No problem. Like I said, it was an easy fix." He sips his coffee and looks up. "So, what's going on with this guy from Sadie Hawkins?"

I slide lower in my chair and pick at the peeling desktop veneer. "I don't know. I messed it up the way I mess up everything."

"It can't be that bad."

"Oh, with me, it's usually worse than you'd imagine."

"You must like him if there's something to mess up."

"I guess." My eyes dart about the wall above my desk, and my gaze lands on a photograph of Gideon and me. We were twelve, at summer camp. One of the girls in my cabin recognized Fire Girl, and soon everyone was talking about me. Gideon said we should probably just do our own thing, so every morning, we snuck out after breakfast in the mess hall, avoiding group activities and splashing in the sparkling green lake.

The memory sends a pang through me. Really, I should like Peter. He hasn't gotten to know the real me yet, so maybe he won't kiss me and run away.

"But you're in love with Gideon."

I freeze. Hearing this aloud is equal parts terrifying and painful. It brings back the agony from the dance, exposing me, leaving me raw. I shut my eyes, blotting out the photo.

"I take it you two still haven't made up."

I shake my head. "We're not going to. He made that extremely clear. I guess I always knew that one day he'd join the rest of the town in seeing me for what I really am." I swivel in my chair and peek at Asher.

He scowls. "What are you talking about?"

"Fire Girl. The girl who can't keep any friends. The girl who watches people die around her. Me."

"Don't be ridiculous."

"It's true. He finally sees it, and I've come to accept it."

Asher's fingers brush the pink scars on his left hand and his eyes narrow. "What did Gideon say to you?"

"Just the truth."

He stands up, jaw clenched. "I'm going to talk to him. I'm not asking your permission this time."

I shrug. "I'm telling you, it's not going to make a difference. He's done with me." A pathetic laugh escapes. "I used to worry that he didn't want to be *with* me. But he doesn't even want to be *around* me."

"Cass, I'm going to fix this for you."

"We're not broken dolls, Asher. It's too complicated. I just have to sit back and watch him be with someone else."

Asher's blue eyes are pained when he looks at me. I want to let him in, to tell him all the reasons Gideon is right about me. I have no one else to talk to. Gideon is gone, and Emily is off the list of confidants for obvious reasons.

Instead I sputter, "Things would have been better for everyone if I'd just died in that fire."

Asher's neck stiffens, but I don't let him speak. "I have to get ready for school, so..." I motion to the door. He pauses, mouth drawn. Then he gets up and walks out of my room, head slumped. My chest is heavy and my eyes sting, but I shut the door, knowing I'm right.

26

Weighed down by my thoughts, I plod through the double doors of Maribel High with my gaze on the ground. When I look up, I'm face-to-face with Peter.

Panic surges through me. He hesitates before me, hurt in his eyes, wavering between greeting me and rushing on by.

"Peter," I stammer. "I'm so sorry about yesterday. I didn't mean what I said. I just…" I sigh, mentally rebuking myself for the poor delivery. "Look, things didn't end well with Gideon—our friendship I mean. It's still painful." Peter's trademark narrow eyes are barely slivers in their skeptical state. "That's all I can say. I can't promise I won't ever talk to Gideon. But that doesn't mean I don't want *you* in my life." I reach for his hand to show my sincerity, but think better of it. "If that isn't good enough for you, I understand. And I'll stay out of your way." Peter's gaze drifts toward the lockers, and I'm certain I've lost another friend. "But I hope you can accept things the way they are, because I like spending time with you," I say, offering the words like a prayer in the dark.

Peter's face relaxes a little, its edges still guarded. "I'm not trying to tell you who to be friends with, Cass. I had no right to say what I did. I guess I was jealous."

My face grows hot. Emily said as much over the phone, but there's a difference between a friend's speculation and hearing someone as gorgeous as Peter McCallum actually say he's jealous over you. I know a few volleyball players who'd pass out from the shock; I wish I were one of them.

I lower my gaze and pick at a long thread on my shirt. "It's fine."

"Maybe one day you'll trust me enough to tell me what happened."

Never. I nod. "So, we're good?"

He takes a step closer. Then another. His breath is warm and smells like the minty toothpaste he used this morning. "Of course." He grasps my hand in his, rubbing my palm gently with his thumb. "After all, it's not every girl who asks to be your own personal mermaid."

I laugh, shaking my head. "That's not quite how it happened. Want to walk me to English?"

Maybe I never addressed his concern—the one about whether or not I see Gideon as a friend or something else. But none of that matters anymore, since Gideon doesn't see me as either.

———

At lunch, Emily and I are discussing weekend plans when Laura stops in front of me. "Cassidy, can I speak to you?" She looks at Emily. "It's a volleyball thing. I'll be quick."

I want to tell Laura to get lost, but I'm a little curious. She's captain. Maybe Coach mentioned I'm back in the starting lineup.

Or maybe I've been cut from the team. I shrug at Emily apologetically and follow Laura through the hall.

"What's up?" I ask, sounding bored.

"I need you to cover for me if I don't make it to practice."

Irritation spikes in my chest. "Why can't Stephanie or Tina cover for you?"

"Because they'll ask too many questions. No one can know where I'm headed right now." She shifts her weight and drops her voice. "Except you."

"*Me?*"

"You spoke to the cops about Melody, right?"

"Yeah," I say, drawing the word out.

"I have to talk to them too." She starts digging around in her backpack. "And if something happens to me—"

"Why would something *happen* to you?" I cut in. "Why would you need to talk to the cops?"

"Because they have the wrong guy."

My head jerks back. "No, Laura. It was Seth. They have proof."

"Yeah, well, so do I."

"What are you talking about?"

She chews on her bottom lip before letting out a resolute breath. "I was with Seth the day of the murder." She meets my doubtful look and continues. "I left right after you and Gideon did, when Coach ended practice early. Seth was at his house all day. That's where I met him. That's where we hung out until Emily was due to come home. Then we snuck off to Rosedale together until after dark."

"Wait, *why* were you with Seth all afternoon?"

She shoots me an impatient look. "We're together."

I shake my head. "No, but—*you're* his secret girlfriend?"

She nods, teeth clamped down on her lip.

"And no one knew? How?"

"I don't know, because there's something"—her words catch—"*wrong* with me. I didn't want anyone to know about Seth and me. Especially not Melody. I didn't want her to find out and scare him away like she did Brandon."

The scene from outside Gina's Diner the day Melody died flickers in my memory: Melody's raised finger, her scowl, Seth's back pressed into the wall. "But she did find out, didn't she?"

Laura nods, wiping her nose. That explains their argument that morning. Melody found out about their relationship and tried telling Seth to scram. I guess that also explains why Seth trashed Melody's yearbook photo. And the page could've been bookmarked for Laura's photo at the bottom.

"At the diner, was Seth—"

"He was there to meet me. It was supposed to be our first time together in public." She frowns. "But then Melody started in with the intimidation tactics, and I chickened out."

"He could go to jail for the rest of his life," I whisper, peeking over my shoulder. "Why didn't you tell the cops?"

"I couldn't." Her eyes dart around the hall. "The morning before they brought Seth in for questioning, someone left this for us." She pulls a flowery card halfway from her backpack, allowing me to peek. "It was on the hood of my car." The card is from the one set of stationery Carver's always has in stock, which means every household in town has a pack. There's a typewritten message in the center:

KEEP YOUR MOUTH SHUT ABOUT SETH
OR YOU'RE NEXT.

"The killer left one for Seth, too, threatening to kill me if he said anything about us. I don't know how this person knew about our relationship. He keeps leaving me these cards every couple days."

I stare, dumbfounded, as she tucks the card back inside her backpack.

"You don't have to say it," she continues. "I know, I'm a huge coward. Seth deserves better. He isn't like everyone thinks. He's sweet and funny. He didn't do any of this, and I'm not going to keep quiet about it anymore."

Sweat beads up on my forehead. "So you're going to the cops now?"

She glances toward the back doors at the end of the hall and then nods, determined.

"If this freak follows through on his threat, get Seth out of there for me." She squeezes my wrist. It's almost a thank-you, like I've agreed to help her.

But I want to call her back. I want to tell her to do anything but go to the cops. Instead, I stand here, immobile, as she strides off down the hall. Deep down, I know it doesn't matter what happens at the police station. It doesn't matter if the police believe Laura, or if they have too much evidence stacked against Seth.

Every muscle in my body freezes as the truth burrows into my mind.

If Seth and Laura were at the Greer's house during seventh period the day Melody died, he wasn't the voice from the woods.

"Laura, wait!" I call suddenly, dashing after her. When I get close enough, I whisper, "Don't say anything just yet. We'll go after practice, together. You shouldn't do it alone."

I don't know why I say it. Laura certainly hasn't earned any favors from me. But maybe it isn't some selfless whim. Maybe I want to protect Laura because the entire school knows we despise each other.

Laura hesitates, but finally, her shoulders lower. "Okay, but right after practice."

"Yes."

The words *It's okay now* turn in my mind, making me dizzy as I stare after her. One thing still doesn't make sense. If Laura was Seth's girlfriend, why did he have a photo of Melody in his desk drawer?

There's a tap on my shoulder, and I jump. "Emily, you scared me."

"Sorry. Is everything all right? What did Laura want?" Her eyes look like they might pop.

I try to breathe evenly, but it doesn't help the sick feeling in my stomach. "I have to tell you something." I pick at my fingernails. "You're not going to like it. But it's important."

She squints at me. "Ooookay."

"That day we worked on the decade project at your house, I snuck into Seth's room."

Emily's shoulders sink. A red ringlet has come loose from her ponytail to hang in front of her face. I see Peter off by the lockers, keeping an eye on me. But I can't muster a smile to show him I'm fine.

"And I found some things. Scary things. I found a photo of

Melody Davenport that was taken when she wasn't looking. At the drugstore. And"—I swallow—"Melody's yearbook photo. It had the eyes cut out." I look at Emily, but whatever I was expecting never manifests on her face.

"Did you look at the rest of the yearbook?" She stares at the floor.

"N-no," I stammer. "The page with Melody was bookmarked. I looked quickly. What was in the rest of the yearbook?"

Emily remains slouched. "My brother had a lot of tormentors. People did mean things to him. Every day. Seth never retaliated—at least, not in real life. The yearbook was where he got his revenge. He trashed all of their photos."

"What?"

"Melody's photo was nothing special. Sometimes he did worse than cutting out the eyes. It doesn't mean he *killed* any of those people."

I could hardly fault him there. It wasn't much different than scrawling my angry, irrational thoughts in that notebook. "But what about the photo from the drugstore?"

She sighs. "Melody started following Seth around the last few weeks before she died. Harassing him at work. In town. Even at the house once. I don't know why, but I saw her do it myself." She shrugs. "Ironic, isn't it? Melody loved calling my brother a stalker. Turns out she was the one stalking him. I guess he got tired of it, and took the photo to try and build a case against her. For a restraining order. I tried to tell the cops, but Seth never actually filed anything. They couldn't fathom that a beautiful girl like Melody could be anything but a victim."

I can barely hold myself up now. The hall zooms in and out of focus.

"Look, I'm not denying Seth's weirdness. He's a loner." Emily's voice is strained. "But he didn't do anything." More ringlets have sprung loose, creating a halo of curls about her head. "Melody, the rest of this school, people like you"— she jabs a finger—"made my brother what he is. Maybe he's creepy. But does it make him a murderer? I guess we both know *your* answer." She's trembling. "You're trying to tell me you turned my brother in to the cops."

"Emily, I'm so sorry. Still, there's Melody's hair in his car. I had nothing to do with that."

"No, but you and the rest of the jerks at this school made him a big, fat target, didn't you? You led the real killer straight to him." A sob escapes and she spins around.

"Emily, wait." I try to reach for her arm, but she runs off. The bell rings, and Emily disappears into the masses.

Peter emerges as students siphon off into classrooms. "Cass, what happened?"

I'm not sure I can speak. Shock and guilt combine in my throat. I cough. "I was the one who gave Seth to the cops." Peter looks surprised, but his arm wraps around me. "And now it turns out it probably wasn't him after all." My voice cracks as I push out, "Also, Emily hates me because I told her what I did."

Peter exhales against my collarbone. "Why do you think it wasn't Seth?"

"Laura says she was Seth's alibi. She's going to the cops later, so I guess everything will sort itself out. But Emily's never going to forgive me." I lean on his shoulder as my mind plays back Emily's figure racing down Hathaway Hall to get away from me.

My fears are coming true. Soon I'll have no one. And now Seth's alibi just resurrected that outrageous idea I keep trying to retire—the possibility that Melody's necklace is still missing because Brandon has it. The killer has the notebook; he has proof I wanted Melody dead. Who in the world would frame Seth when I was the obvious target?

Brandon. He knows if I go down, he goes down.

Peter places a hand on my cheek. "Cass, you can't blame yourself for Seth. That guy needs to be in prison." He tilts my chin toward his. "The cops found Melody's DNA in his car. You can't listen to Laura. You said yourself she's an evil hag demon from hell. She's probably lying."

"Why would she lie about being Seth's girlfriend? It's not exactly a coveted role."

"She wants to be the center of attention, like always. Or maybe she was in on it with Seth. Just stop worrying. You did the right thing."

Maybe she was in on it with Seth. And now she's inventing an alibi to get him released. She must've been beyond fed up with Melody always getting in the way of her relationships.

"But if I was wrong, a killer is still out there," I whisper, my mind flashing again to the flowery card Laura hid in her backpack. Peter pulls me into the crook of his arm, and together, we walk to fifth period.

27

I spend the last two classes of the day trying to make sense of everything. Laura must have left out some detail. Could Seth have slipped out for an hour? After school, I loiter in Hathaway Hall, like the answer might spill from someone's congested locker. I'm supposed to be on my way to practice, but a blond head of hair flutters by.

Change of plans. Gracie Davenport is headed to the parking lot. I follow her.

I expect her to stop in front of a car, but her willowy steps continue through the lot, to the path behind it. Of course. Gracie doesn't drive. Melody used to drop her off and pick her up. She probably has no choice but to walk now. I speed up, kicking dirt into the air as I take a shortcut across the bare patch that borders the lot. "Hey Gracie, wait up!"

Gracie spins around, a shadow crossing her face when she sees who flagged her down. "Cassidy?"

"Sorry, this is going to sound strange. I should start by saying how sorry I am about Melody."

"Thanks," she mumbles with uncertainty.

"But I-I need to ask you something. It's about the investigation."

Gracie shifts her book bag on her shoulder. "I'm not really the one you should be talking to."

"I know. I've already spoken to the detectives. I need to ask you. Was Melody seeing someone? Did she have a boyfriend?"

Gracie's soft features take on a sharpness. "Why do you want to know?"

"There's just a possibility that the cops got it wrong. Please, you don't know me well, but—"

"I know enough," she says bitingly.

What does that mean? Did Gideon tell her? Sound vanishes from the world, like the chirping birds and the whistling wind have been strangled.

"I know you hurt Gideon. He won't tell me how, though."

I exhale, relieved. "You're right. But this isn't about Gideon. This is about your sister and about making sure no one else gets hurt. Please, just tell me. Was she seeing someone?"

"I already told those detectives," she says with a sigh. "My sister went out with a guy a few times. But she never told me his name. Just that he was great, funny, smart. Nothing helpful to the cops. I didn't know Seth, but apparently he was a real bookworm. And the rest of it..." She shrugs.

I pull in a scorching breath. "That's all she said?"

"Yeah. Why? Do you know something?"

I shake my head. "No, no. If the cops say it's Seth, then it's Seth."

She looks at me warily. "That's it? Well, bye, Cassidy."

I nod, even though her back is already turned to me. She lopes down the path, tossing her hair in exasperation.

I take a frantic step back toward the parking lot, fumbling in my backpack for my keys, so I can unlock my bike. Thanks to Laura's ever-looming presence, I've spent most of high school immune to Brandon's charms. But even I'll admit I was putty in his hands the night of the party.

Maybe I'd been right when I joked about Melody crushing on him. If they hooked up, they'd both want to keep it a secret from Laura.

And knowing Brandon's obsession with Laura, he could have spotted her with Seth. What better way to get rid of your rival than to frame him for murder? Whoever took Melody out to the log had been planning it. Thoughtfully. Meticulously. And keeping his relationship a secret—from everybody—was all part of the plan. If no one knows your identity, no one can blab your name to the cops. Did I have the right killer on day one and let him slip away?

I dig deeper into the backpack, but my keys aren't turning up. Grunting, I dump the bag's contents into the dirt and plunk down alongside them. Tears drip over my books and pencils as I rummage through the pile, still not hearing the familiar jangle.

"Cass?" I look up to see Gideon. His reserved expression strikes me as completely foreign.

Then I remember we're strangers now. He said it himself.

"I can't find my keys."

"Want help?"

"Sure," I mutter, leaning away from the now-filthy heap.

He bends down to sort through the paraphernalia. A moment later, he lifts his hand, and keys dangle between his fingers.

"Thanks." I take the keys, but my hand lingers. "Giddy, I know you don't want to talk to me, but if I don't speak to someone... I just don't know what to do." My voice cracks and Gideon kneels down in the dirt beside me.

"What is it? Laura?"

"No." I shake my head. "I mean *yes*, but it's not about the fire. I wish that was it. I—can we walk? I don't want to talk about this here."

He stares at me for too long, distrustful, but nods. "Sure." He pulls me to my feet and releases my hand. We amble down the road from the school, and I kick at uneven patches of asphalt that refuse to smooth. Gideon's hands are in his pockets. "What's going on?"

My gaze flicks to the trees. The killer—whoever he is—has eyes everywhere. How else could he have known Laura and Seth were together when no one else did? "I spoke to Laura," I whisper. "Actually, she spoke to me. She said she was Seth's secret girlfriend. That she was his alibi, but she's never told anyone because the killer keeps leaving her threatening notes."

"What?" His voice is drenched in skepticism.

"That's what I thought. But why would she lie?"

"Maybe she's wrong about the timeline."

"That's the thing. She said she left right after us, during seventh period, and went straight to Seth's house."

Gideon's brows furrow. "We have to tell someone."

We've wandered off of the road and are shrouded in greenery and shadows. The occasional car zooms past. Houses stagger the opposite side of the woods, too far away to make out their shapes through the foliage. Even so, I keep my voice low. "I know, but if we do, the killer could make good on his threat. Laura says he's been putting cards on her windshield, telling her to keep quiet. He put that hair in the trunk of Seth's car."

"Does she know who it is?"

"No. Don't get mad, but I think it was Brandon. Just hear me out," I say before he can groan. "He was in love with Laura. Melody and Seth were the two people who came between them." I take his silence as a good sign. "So, I think he killed one and framed the other."

Gideon's eyes widen, and hope flickers in my chest. Maybe he'll finally open up to the possibility that I'm not some unhinged, selfish killer.

But Brandon is.

"It's not enough, Cass." My hope fizzles again. "Some cards, you thinking it was his voice. It doesn't trump the photos and the DNA evidence."

"But Seth didn't do it. He has an alibi!"

"Then we'll tell the cops. They can figure it out."

"But what about Laura? We can't just let Brandon do something to her like he did to Melody."

Gideon turns, pressing farther into the woods.

"Where are you going?" I call, following him.

"I don't know. I just...can't think clearly." He paces back and forth, rubbing his temples. "If Brandon's still in love with Laura, he wouldn't hurt her, would he?"

"To silence her? Of course he would!"

"Where is Laura?"

"Back at school. I'm supposed to be with her at practice, but I wanted to talk to Gracie."

He swivels to face me. "Did you?"

"Yeah. She said Melody was seeing someone."

Gideon's face blanches.

"I'm telling you, Giddy. It fits."

His head tilts back and his eyes close against the sunlight filtering through the treetops. A moment later, he looks at me, lips pursed. "Fine. Call Laura. Tell her to go straight home and we'll come get her. No one's going to try anything if the three of us are together."

I dial, but it goes straight to Laura's irritating voicemail. "She's not answering." I try again, with no luck. "She should be out by now. Why isn't she answering?"

"Maybe when you didn't show up for practice, she decided to go to the cops. Don't panic, Cass. I'm still not convinced Brandon would do anything to her."

We reach my street, and I breathe a sigh of relief that Asher's car is parked in our driveway. Gideon left his truck in the school parking lot, and we can't afford to waste precious time walking to Laura's house. I try Tina's number, but she doesn't answer either. I let out a growl. "We're not allowed to bring our phones into the gym. Call Peter. He was staying after school for a tutoring session. Maybe he can swing by the gym and see if practice ran late. I'll run inside and grab Asher's keys."

"Okay, but Cass." Gideon takes my hand and gives it a squeeze. "Everything's going to be fine."

It feels different from when he used to take my hand when we were kids. It feels like the time we sat together on the log. My shoulders relax.

I duck inside the house, scurrying through the foyer and down the hall. Asher's door is shut, so I pound on it.

"Coming," calls Asher's muffled voice. He opens the door and speaks through a yawn. "Hey, Cass. What's going on?"

"Nothing. Can Gideon and I borrow your car real quick? We have an errand to run, but we walked here, so—it's a long story."

Asher hoists a brow. "So then, everything's good with you two?"

I nod, too fast. "Yep. Back to normal. So, the car?"

"Yeah, that's fine. You guys wanna hang out after this *errand*?" He grins slyly.

I roll my eyes. "Stop being weird, Asher. But yes, we can meet you at Gina's later. I'll text you."

"Sounds good. Don't have too much fun."

"See you." I dash into the kitchen, grab Asher's keys from the hook, and head out the front door.

Gideon's standing on the porch. I toss him the keys and we hurry to Asher's car. "Did you get hold of Peter?"

"Yeah, but he said Laura wasn't in the gym."

"No, no, no. This isn't good. I've left her two messages and probably six texts. Why isn't she calling me back?"

"It'll be fine. Let's check her house. If she's not there, we'll go to the sheriff."

"I don't know. This is all—I just can't mess up again, Giddy. After Sara and Melody. I don't know what I'll do if I mess up again."

Gideon puts a hand on my shoulder, stopping me from getting in the car. He twists me around to face him, and I try to hide my quivering lower lip. "You're not going to mess up anything, Cass. I'm sorry I made you feel like everything was your fault. I was horrible. I know you were scared that day, and I should never have blamed Melody's death on you. Can you forgive me?"

His arms enfold me and I blink away tears, my lashes dusting his shirt as I nod.

Gideon's voice is low and frayed. "I'm not me without you. I need you back."

The words settle in my ears, wrapping around all the hurt and broken parts like bandages. "You have me," I whisper, looking up at him. His eyes melt away my fears and I straighten up, knowing my purpose for the first time in weeks. "Let's go get Laura."

My phone dings in my pocket and I dig it out. An anonymous number again.

Tell Laura to keep her mouth shut, or she's next.

My heart jolts in my rib cage. This is it—confirmation that Seth, who's locked in a cell, couldn't have done it.

The killer's still out there.

Gideon leans in. "What is it? Cass, your face. You're completely pale."

There's no point in hiding it. I shove the phone into his hands.

He lowers the phone a few seconds later. "This guy needs to be locked up," he says through his teeth.

"But if we go to the cops, he'll kill her." Tears coat my lashes.

"We have to find her and make sure she's safe."

"I'll call her again," I say, taking my phone back. I dial, but it goes to Laura's voicemail. I clamp my teeth and send a text. Call me ASAP. You're in danger.

Gideon looks at me, the corners of his eyes creased. "Do you think he already has her?"

"He must. She would've answered her phone. I'm calling Detective Sawyer."

Gideon nods. "Cass, don't worry about the notebook or any of it. All that matters is getting Laura back safely."

"I know." Gideon pulls me close to him as I dial.

Right now, getting locked up is the least of my worries.

28

We're halfway to Laura's house when my phone rings. Sheriff Henderson. "Cassidy?"

"Yes, Sheriff?"

"I'm at the Gellman place, and Laura's fine. She's sitting here watching television. Guess she didn't hear her phone."

I exhale and mouth to Gideon that she's fine. "Okay, but you can't leave her there alone."

"I'm still out front. Why don't you come by here and make a statement? The detectives are on their way, and they'll want to know exactly what's going on."

"Already on my way."

A few minutes later, Sheriff Henderson leads us inside the Gellman residence, where the detectives are waiting in the living room. Laura is seated on a cushiony beige chair, eyes large and elbows tucked in front of her. The entire house reeks of that perfume she wears.

"Go ahead and have a seat," says Detectives Reyes. "Let's start from the beginning. Miss Pratt, what gave you reason to believe that Miss Gellman here was in danger?"

"I received a threatening text message." I hand my phone to the detective. He looks over it before passing it to his partner.

Detective Sawyer shows Laura the message. "What is this in reference to? Keep her mouth shut about what?" She looks at Laura, whose shoulders slump.

Then her shoulders rise. And fall. "I have no idea, Detectives."

My eyes stretch wide open and I jump out of my seat. "Laura, tell the truth!" I turn back to Detective Sawyer. "She's lying. Look at the text."

"Honestly, it's a bit odd," she says, examining the message again. "And vague. It doesn't say what Laura is supposed to keep quiet about."

I glare at Laura again, and her lips twitch. At least, I think they do. Was this a setup? Did she purposefully not answer her phone in order to mess with me? "Someone is just trying to make me look crazy," I say as the room spins around me. "Laura, please don't do this. You're letting the real killer go free. Seth—your boyfriend—is going to jail for the rest of his life."

Laura flinches and looks to the detectives for help. "My boyfriend? Gross. Seth wasn't my boyfriend."

Or maybe I am crazy.

"Detectives," Laura continues, "I don't know what's going on here. Cassidy, as you may be aware, has a pretty sketchy past, so—"

"Shut up, Laura," I growl. "You told me not two hours ago that you were with Seth on the day of Melody's murder. That he was your secret boyfriend." At the words *secret boyfriend*, Sheriff Henderson lifts a skeptical brow. "But you couldn't tell anyone else because you were threatened! Show them the cards!"

Laura's doe eyes divert back to the detectives.

I look at Gideon. "Tell them about the cards."

"I didn't see the cards, Cass," he says, wincing. "You told me about them." I fall back into my chair with a thud. Gideon wasn't there when Laura told me about Seth.

I blink to find the white ceiling beneath me and the cream-colored carpet above. "I don't know why she's lying." I blink again, looking up to find Sheriff Henderson's eyes drifting. I can't even look at Laura, or I'll tear her to pieces right in front of the law.

"Okay, okay, Miss Pratt," Detective Reyes says, standing up. "You girls obviously don't get along, but this is a murder investigation."

"But it's—" I lob another panicked glance Gideon's way, but his eyes are on the carpet. He thinks I imagined it all.

And he might be right.

I stand up, fist curled. "This is wrong, Laura, and you know it. You really are a coward if you keep quiet now. You're letting the real killer go free."

Detective Reyes takes a few careful steps and places a hand on my shoulder. "Miss Pratt, I think you should go home and get some rest. We're confident we've got the guy who did this."

"You're wrong," I say. But my voice is timid because I'm not sure he is. I hasten out the front door and down the porch steps, Gideon close behind. At the bottom of the steps, I pause, twisting around to view the Gellman residence one last time.

No, I'm not sure anymore. The only thing I'm really sure of is an itching in my fingers. It's a familiar sensation. I rub my fingers together, but it's still there. That itch to feel the click of the lighter. The sensation squirms up through my veins, all the way to my eyes. My eyeballs are actually itching.

They're itching to see this place go up in flames.

Gideon and I get back into the car and begin the drive to my house in silence. He stares straight ahead, hands rigid over the steering wheel.

"Cass—"

"You don't have to say it," I interrupt. "I am now officially crazy."

"That's not what I was going to say. But, I do think you need to let all of this go. I don't know what's going on—"

"Come on, Gideon. Everyone else in this town gets it. My entire life I've been Fire Girl. The girl who killed Sara Leeds and almost killed her own brother. Everyone loves talking about how it wasn't really an accident. That I started the fire on purpose and I'll do it again." I breathe in, allowing my fingernails to dig into my palms. "And deep down, they were right. I might as well have killed Melody Davenport myself. I'm dangerous."

Gideon is silent.

My face crumples. My entire body crumples. "You see it now too."

He shakes his head. "No. This is Laura, like always. She's messing with you. The text message, the cards. She's having one more round of fun at your expense." One of his hands lifts from the wheel. "It's not fair that everyone targets you, Cass. This *Fire Girl*, I don't know her. I know you." He turns to me, narrowing his eyes. "But I'm worried you're letting this other girl take over your life. It's like you're becoming her."

Gideon parks in the driveway. He leans over, pressing his lips to my head and peering down at me. "Let's get you inside so you can rest. Tomorrow, we'll put all of this behind us."

I let him walk me up the porch steps and through the door. He grips my hand like I'm a small child crossing the street. Like I can't be trusted not to run into oncoming traffic.

Inside, I bat away the tears as he runs a hand over my shoulder. "I can stay if you want, but you should probably rest."

I shrug. I should try to sleep all of this off. Maybe I'll wake up to find Laura laughing with the rest of the team about how I spouted off a bunch of insane nonsense in front of two detectives and a sheriff.

"Cass, look at me." I try, but looking him in the eyes is physically painful. It makes me feel like I could just collapse onto the foyer floor and never get up again. He gives my hand a squeeze, then nudges my back. "I've known you since second grade—more than half of our lives—and you're not crazy. Get to bed. I'll tell your mom you're not feeling well. We'll sort this Laura stuff out tomorrow. If she lied to you, I won't let her get away with it."

"Thanks," I mumble, trying and failing to smile. I walk down the hall, closing my bedroom door behind me. I dive into bed and pull the covers all the way past my head. There, in the suffocating darkness, the confusion and guilt envelop me.

I rack my brain for one thing I know for certain. Any one thing I can hold on to with confidence. But there's nothing. All I have is a scenario disturbingly similar to the one written in the notebook I handed to Brandon Alvarez. And a muffled voice.

Even that has faded over time. I know the words, but the

trace of a voice is gone. I hear the rushing water, the rustling leaves, the birds.

If Laura was messing with me, then Seth is the killer. He's behind bars where he should be, and Maribel is safe.

But if she got scared off and lied to the detectives, it only means one thing.

A killer is still out there.

The feeling of being watched crawls over me and I lower the covers. My eyes dart to the shelf on the wall. There, sitting in her place as she has been the past eleven years is my porcelain doll, Edna. Her gigantic blue eyes stare straight ahead at the opposite wall, not at me.

I exhale and look at the framed photo of Sara and me beside it on the shelf. We were so small, so happy. We wore coordinating dresses with white polka dots that Sara's mom made. Mine was pink and Sara's was green. Those were the dresses we wore the day of our tea party. Sara's last day. My dress was scorched so badly my mom had to throw it away. As usual, the photo makes me achy inside.

I hear a ding and grab my phone from the nightstand. Gideon.

Cass, feel better. I'll talk to Laura in the morning. If she was telling the truth about Seth, we'll look into it together.

I text a quick Thanks and open the threat from this afternoon. I read it over and over again. These texts likely came from burner phones. Anyone could have sent this one.

Gideon's probably right. It's Laura's elaborate plan to make my life hell. Why did I take everything so seriously?

I can't trust myself. How can I know what I heard in the woods? How can I know what happened the day of the fire?

Maybe everyone's right. Maybe I meant to start that fire. I told Melody to knock it off in the portable classroom, but when the fire erupted, something inside me came alive. Something wanted to let it grow. To see it wrap its molten fingers around her.

Despite the warmth of the covers, a shiver pulses through my body.

I've grown up knowing the story of how I knocked over the candle, how Asher tried to open the door. How by the time he opened it, it was too late for Sara Leeds. But the memories have always felt distant. I see the series of events like pages in a picture book, not like pieces of my own life. My parents always batted away my questions, and eventually I knew the story so well I stopped asking.

I've never had the guts to do this, but I need to know the truth. I toss the phone back onto my nightstand. Then, I tear myself from my bed and retrieve my laptop. Nestling back against the pillows, I start a search on the one topic I've tried to erase from existence since I was seven years old.

Articles about Sara Leeds pile onto the search results. I click on one about her funeral, and close it. I scroll down, clicking and skimming articles. But I pause when a black-and-white photograph pops onto the screen. It's a little girl on a stretcher. She's wearing a mangled polka dot dress. The title of the article is "Girl Survives Fire, But Remains Eerily Silent."

The little girl is me.

I scroll through the article. The subheading "Investigators find no evidence of foul play" should be settling, but as I read further, the lines electrify the hairs on the back of my neck.

I keep reading until a knock on my door rattles me. I slam the laptop shut and slide it onto the bedside table.

"Come in," I call, lying back onto my pillow like the sick patient I'm supposed to be.

Asher steps into my room. "Hey, Cass. I heard you weren't feeling well. Just wanted to see if you needed anything." He nears the bed, squinting down at me like I might break.

"Thanks. I'm fine. I know I shouldn't keep sleeping this close to bedtime, but I can't get up."

He straightens and moves toward the light switch. "Go back to sleep. I didn't mean to bother you. Yell if you need anything."

"Okay. But Asher," I say before I can change my mind. I sit up.

"Yeah?" He drifts closer.

"I need to ask you something."

"Sure, anything." He bends over the bed.

"It's about the fire."

Asher's eyes meet mine questioningly, and then his face falls. His fingers go straight to the scars on his left hand. "Why are you asking?"

"I just thought if you told me what happened, I might remember more."

"Why would you want to do that?" He's solemn as he sits down on the edge of the bed.

"My whole life I've been told I knocked over the candle that burned down the place. But I don't remember doing it." I shut my eyes, letting the image of the playhouse crashing around me flicker in the darkness. "Maybe I'm not remembering because"—my fingers twist the edge of the bedsheet—"I did something horrible. Like everyone says."

"Cass, no. In the hospital, you did have some trouble talking about what happened. But then you told the doctors, the police, Mom and Dad. It's possible Sara knocked it over, and you were covering for her. You might've felt bad that she didn't make it, so you took the fall. But it was an accident either way. It wasn't anyone's fault."

I scrunch my lips. "Did you have to choose? Who to save, I mean."

Asher's eyes drop to my comforter. "Thankfully, no. You were closest to the door, so I got you out first. But you know all of this."

"I should've been on the other side of the table. Then you could've saved Sara."

Asher exhales forcefully. "It wouldn't have mattered, Cass. Why are you making me relive this?" He keeps rubbing the scars. "You want me to say I would've jumped over Sara's unconscious body to save you?"

I reach out to take his hand, to stop it from ripping his flesh apart. "No, no. Asher, I'm sorry. I-I'm asking because I found this." I release his hand and grab my laptop, opening it. I spin it around, showing Asher the article with my photograph at the top.

"Why are you reading about this?"

"I told you. I wanted to remember. I wanted to know why the people in this town have always treated me like a criminal, instead of like a seven-year-old would-be victim. And I guess this explains it."

His fingers move for the scars again, but he catches himself, lowering both hands carefully to his sides. "The trouble you had talking after the fire... It wasn't a little trouble."

"What do you mean?"

Asher's eyes glaze over. "When they took you to the hospital, physically you were fine, apart from some minor burns on your legs. But you weren't acting fine. You asked a couple times about your doll, but you weren't exactly lucid. And then you didn't speak again. You refused to talk about the fire." His shoulders sink. "For days. You were silent for days. You didn't cry about Sara. You wouldn't answer any questions from the cops. Not one. People started talking. It got around town, in the papers. A shrink came to see you. Mom and Dad were worried you'd get taken away." Asher's eyes veer from me to the carpet, and his voice drops. "I was outside the door to your room the night Mom and Dad fed you the story about how you knocked over the candle." He takes a breath. "Over and over again."

My fingernails dig back into my palms. Breaking the skin.

So they thought I'd done it. My family fabricated the candle story to keep me out of some mental hospital. "What do you think happened, Asher? You were the first one through the door."

"Don't ask me that, Cass."

Tiny needles prick my eyes. "I need you to tell me. Please. Something is happening to me, and I...I just need to know."

Asher takes a long breath. His lips purse tightly before he releases it. "I thought I was going to lose you—not just to the fire. To yourself."

"What?" I blink, like maybe it will restart this day. But it doesn't.

"I told the cops that the door was stuck. But Cass, you were on the other side of the door." He bites his lower lip. "You were holding it shut."

I'm sick for real now. I fight back a gagging sensation and blurt, "Why didn't anyone tell me this?"

"We were protecting you."

"What about everyone else? Didn't Mom and Dad wonder if I'd do it again?"

"We all kept a close eye on you for a long time. And eventually, you started talking again. You met Gideon and went back to normal."

I'm anything but normal.

"I didn't want to tell you."

"No, I'm glad you did. I'll be fine, really. I just need to sleep."

Asher tries to smile, but it's forced. "It was a long time ago, Cass. Whatever happened, it's best you forget it. You're not that little girl anymore." He takes the laptop from me and places it on my desk. "Get some rest." He turns the light off, shutting the door behind him.

I lie back down, letting the truth expand in my brain until it strangles every other thought. I'm capable of horrible things. Much worse than letting Melody die. Maybe when I wrote the murder plan out in that notebook, some part of me hoped it would come true. That Brandon really would work up the guts to go through with it. Or maybe I wanted to carry it out myself. Only someone else got there first.

No one should be protecting me. It's only a matter of time before I give in to that blazing impulse again.

Get it together. If I continue unraveling, my family's efforts—this decade-long charade to keep me out of a mental hospital—will have been for nothing. This is exactly what Laura wanted. To witness Fire Girl's return.

I tell myself that it was Seth Greer's face that Melody

Davenport saw before she was taken from this world. Not Brandon's. Not anyone else's. I repeat that over and over as I try desperately to sleep.

29

I wake in the morning before my alarm. The mottled light breaks through the slits in my window blinds, to bring with it a jumbled mess of emotions.

Either I'm the target of a mammoth prank or I hallucinated my encounter with Laura. And there's a third possibility: Laura was telling the truth about being Seth's alibi, and a killer is still out there. A killer whose identity was concealed beneath the sounds of rushing water.

None of these possibilities are comforting.

Thanks to a night of worrying about all three options, I'm having trouble getting out of bed. I try to wake myself up with a quick shower. Afterward, I examine my face in the vanity mirror, seeing the lack of sleep drawn in my drooping, puffy eyes. Tiny rivulets of blood web throughout the whites. My hands tremble too much for makeup, so I secure my hair into a ponytail, dab some blush on my cheeks, and shrug at my reflection.

The sound of the doorbell startles me. The clock reads 7:10 a.m. Gideon used to pick me up at 7:20 in the olden days; he must have forgotten our routine.

I open the front door, and confusion washes over me. Peter stands on my porch, wearing a shy smile.

"Peter! Hi! What are you doing here?"

"Hey, Cass. Sorry to just show up like this. My tutoring appointment this morning canceled and I don't have a first period. So I got to thinking"—he pauses, cocking a brow playfully—"maybe a certain mermaid would be willing to skip first period to come on a breakfast date?" He flashes his crooked smile, and there's a tug on my insides.

"Oh, Peter. That's really sweet. I wished you'd called. I... um, Gideon's picking me up for school in a couple minutes."

"Gideon?" Peter's forehead wrinkles.

"Yeah, we started talking again. You know, trying to work stuff out. To be friends again."

"Got it." His eyes drop to his sneakers, causing my heart to crash down along with it.

My gaze travels to the thermos in his hand. "Did you make breakfast?"

"I *bought* breakfast. If I'd had more time, I probably could've whipped you up some Pop-Tarts from scratch, but—I thought we could have a picnic. Maybe another time.

You're right, I should've called." He turns toward the steps, but stops. "I'd be surprised, though, if Gideon goes to school today. I think he's sick."

"What do you mean?" The question bursts out much too loudly.

"He was my tutoring appointment this morning. He didn't show. I texted him, but he never responded. That part wasn't a surprise. Things have been a little weird ever since…you know."

"Since what?"

"Since you and I went to the dance. He barely speaks to me during our sessions. But this is the first time he just hasn't shown up. That's why I assumed he must be sick."

"He would've at least texted if he wasn't going to pick me up." It's 7:20 now: pickup time. If Gideon does pull up in front of my house right now, things are about to get all kinds of awkward. "Let me call him."

I duck inside, remembering my phone is still on the nightstand, where I tossed it last night. I hurry down the hall to my room, surprised to see a colorful glow radiating from the screen. I grab my phone and see the text is from Gideon. Sent at 6:55. I must have missed it while I was in the shower.

Sorry, not feeling well. Can't pick you up.

I feel a stab of disappointment as I trudge back out to Peter. "I guess you're right. He's sick. Well, the plus side is I'm free to take you up on breakfast." I force a grin.

I should go by Gideon's house to check on him, but I

see Peter's face light up and push the thought aside. I send a quick text back to Gideon and grab my backpack.

Feel better. I'll come by after school.

Peter's car is still warm and filled with the sweet scent of fresh-baked bread. A brown bag rests at my feet. "Mmm. Where did you pick up breakfast?"

Peter starts the car and we head the opposite direction from town and school. "Gina's, of course. You know, if you went to your precious Daisy's Ice Cream Parlor and tried to get breakfast, you'd be waiting outside on the cold curb for like, four hours, right?" he says, grinning. "Because they're not open for breakfast, if you didn't get that."

I roll my eyes. "I got it. Thanks, but I was about to say it smells delicious."

"Oh." He pats me teasingly on the arm. "Hey, Gideon called me yesterday. Did you end up finding Laura?"

"Yeah, thanks for your help. Everything's fine."

"That's good." He pulls over to the side of the road and turns off the ignition. "Well, we're here."

I laugh. "We barely left my house."

"I know, but my secret spot happens to be near your house. Just through there." He points to the woods, thick with evergreens, where it seems the sunlight from the open road can't infiltrate.

My heart suddenly fills my throat, making it difficult to achieve a playful tone. "Where exactly is your secret spot?"

"I'll show you. I'm sure you've seen it before, since it's so close to your house. But I usually go this way because I live over on Sunnydale. It's my shortcut."

My eyes drop to my feet. "I don't suppose you'd want to just eat in here?"

"What?" Peter stops reaching for the bag to look at me. "It's such a nice morning. Finally sunny out."

Not in there. My eyes tunnel through to the dark area behind the trees. "We should probably stay out of the woods. Melody was killed in there."

"But Seth is behind bars. Besides, I'll keep you safe." He flexes a bicep.

I try to laugh, but it's useless. There has to be a way to change his mind without letting him know how much I hate his plan. I keep my eyes on the messy passenger's side floor, searching for an idea in the pile of wrappers, empty water bottles, and random articles of clothing. A ding from somewhere by my feet gives me the excuse I need. "Sorry, just a second. That might be Gideon or my mom."

I fumble through the bottom of my backpack where I stashed my phone. There's a text message from Laura, but I'm distracted by a pop of green among the books and folders. I bend over and pick up the item, a green hoodie, letting it hang from my two fingers. A memory of Gideon tugging at the strings of a green hoodie in Hathaway Hall, his eyes distant and jaw scruffy, floods my mind.

I swallow hard. "Why do you have this?"

Peter glances at the hoodie, his knuckles tightening over the steering wheel. "Oh, Gideon and I had one of our sessions at good old Gina's a couple weeks ago. He said he hadn't gotten much sleep or something and needed coffee." Peter licks his lips. "He practically collapsed onto the desk at the tutoring center. I drove. He must've left his sweatshirt in here." I follow Peter's every movement. Every twitch. "I'm surprised I never noticed it down there."

Peter's voice quavers. He wipes his palms on the steering wheel. I unlock my phone and read the text from Laura, trying to ignore the panicked thoughts swirling in my head.

I'm really sorry about yesterday. I started freaking out as soon as I told you about Seth. Then the cops showed me that threat on your phone and I couldn't do it. But I told you the truth. If the killer is sending you threats, be careful.

I close the conversation and stash the phone back in my backpack. The once-heavenly scent of bread is now suffocating. I want to crack a window or throw the bread outside. I settle for unzipping my jacket. I take a deep breath and try to blink away my dark and blurry vision. I'm going to pass out in Peter's car.

After another blink, my eyes open and settle on the brown bag with the blue writing: *Gina's Diner.* I shut my eyes again.

If Peter's a regular at Gina's, he would have seen Melody all the time. She'd been a waitress there since last June, which would've given Peter months to get to know the pretty girl behind the counter. And she must've noticed the gorgeous guy with the emerald eyes who came in twice a week to order a milkshake—or perhaps to chat up the waitress.

"I need some air," I say. Peter laughs like I made a joke. Then he shrugs and rolls down the window. The cool air rushes into the car along with the chirping of birds and sounds of the rushing creek in the distance. Gracie's words simmer in my brain: *He was a great guy, smart, funny.* Was it always Peter? And now, with his breakfast and his jealousy and guilt trips about me looking at another guy, is he grooming me to be his next victim? I'm probably right where he wants me, about to trace Melody's steps out into the woods.

"If it's air you want, we can just head out. You know, like I suggested earlier," teases Peter, who's still smiling, but squirmy.

I need to find my phone and call Gideon or someone to help. I stuff my hand back into my backpack and thrash it around in desperation.

As I do, my backpack knocks over a large binder resting at my feet. Something small and silver spills out, joining the pile on the scraggly carpeted floor.

A spiral notebook.

My body freezes. Peter pulls at my arm, trying to get me to make eye contact. Trying to trap me with his sparkling eyes—the eyes of a cat stalking its prey.

I gape at him in horror.

"Cass," he pleads. "What's wrong? It's Gideon, isn't it? Did he tell you not to hang out with me? That guy doesn't deserve your friendship. Why can't he just let you be happy?" He inches closer, the leather seat squeaking unnervingly as he reaches for my hand. His voice drops to a whisper and he bends over me, the words barely audible over the birds and the gushing stream in the background: "Come on. Forget about him for an hour. We have breakfast and we're alone."

A prickly sensation runs up my spine. Hearing the words, low and softened by the sounds of the woods, brings back the fragmented line from that day: *We're alone.* And it puts me back into the hole in the ground.

Only this time it isn't Melody who's alone with a killer.

Peter looks at me with his crooked smile, and that smile is no longer adorable; it's sinister. And it was probably the last thing Melody Davenport saw before she died.

I try to unlatch my seat belt, but it's jammed. It holds me down, strangling me while Peter's smile morphs into a confused expression. His hand reaches toward me.

"Stay away from me!" I pull my arm back and press myself against the car door.

Peter stares at me, his hand frozen in midair. "Cass," he says with a hard blink. "Are you *afraid* of me?"

"Of course I'm afraid of you!" I shout. "You killed

Melody! You did something to Gideon. And for all I know, he's dead too!"

"What are you talking about?" Peter's brow is furrowed, his mouth open, but I'm not falling for it.

I keep pressing my back farther into the door, even though the handle stabs me. "She worked at the diner. You go there twice a week. Don't pretend like you never spoke to her. Flirted with her."

"Of course I talked to her. That makes me a killer?"

"Explain this," I snap, lifting the notebook from the pile on the floor. I hold it before him with shaky fingers.

Peter's face reddens and his eyes fall. "I was going to return it. I only read a couple pages. I'm sorry." He pushes the hair off his forehead, but it sticks. "I found it a few weeks ago at the diner, and I should've given it back to you right away. But I really liked you, and you didn't know I existed. I thought I could watch some of the movies you wrote about and we'd have something to talk about." His head slumps. "But then I was too embarrassed to return it."

"You did something to Gideon," I repeat. I feel around again for my phone, keeping my eyes on him.

"That's crazy."

"I'm not *crazy*. Stay back!" I flinch. My elbow smacks the glove compartment, sending a volt of pain up my arm.

"Cass, I don't know what you're talking about. Why would I *do* something to Gideon?" My heart is pounding. My phone is still lost within the backpack. Or he must have taken it when I wasn't paying attention. I fumble with the seat belt latch again, my eyes still glued on his.

"I don't know. Because he was getting between us. Because he was helping me look into Melody's murder. Because I told him about your threats!" Where is Gideon when I need him? Finally releasing my seat belt, I search frantically for some way to distract Peter.

"Cass, I have no idea where any of this is coming from." Peter's eyes are stuck to the steering wheel.

"Prove it then. Call him! I want him to tell me he's sick!" I move my hand back against the door.

"He won't answer my call."

"Just do it!" I scream. Peter hesitates, and then gives a long sigh before scrolling—or pretending to scroll—for Gideon's number.

I don't waste a second. While his eyes are on the screen, I fling open the car door. I run in the direction of my house, straight through the forest. I can see my back gate, but a familiar sound, though faint and muffled, halts me in my tracks.

It's the theme song from *Rosemary's Baby*. Gideon's ringtone. The notes have never sounded as eerie as they do drifting toward me through the dark woods. I follow the sound of the music, hearing the snapping of sticks and the crunching of leaves as Peter pursues me.

The phone has been discarded or dropped several feet

from my backyard. Partially buried beneath the earth, its screen still glows blue after the music stops. I dig it up, turning to face Peter as I back away from him, carefully.

"Cass. Please stop running from me."

"You'd like that, wouldn't you? Make it easier for you?" My shoulder brushes against the sharp edge of a branch and I recoil.

"I don't know how the phone got there. I haven't been anywhere near here."

Gideon's screen is cracked, but the phone still works. I scroll through the messages. Our conversation from this morning is the last thing on it, but he never responded to my text. A tremor snakes its way up my core.

Why is Gideon's phone in the woods? Did Peter bring him here this morning when they were supposed to have tutoring? It would explain why Gideon never turned up at my house. My mind is a tornado of confusion, with terrifying images of Gideon lying helpless, or lifeless, at the forefront.

Shaking my head, I step back onto something white and fluffy strewn about the dirt. I take another step, and it's like walking on the clouds. I must be dreaming, or dead.

"Please don't come any closer," I whisper as Peter steps toward me, leaves crackling beneath his feet. Between his looming figure and the shadows of the evergreens that block out the morning light, I am trapped.

As my vision darkens, a thunderous crash followed by a

deep cry echoes through the woods. I meet Peter's eyes—I've never seen those eyes so big—and immediately know.

I'm wrong.

But I'm not dreaming.

I'm not dead.

And I'm not crazy.

30

Peter and I sprint toward the sounds, which become fainter with every step through the mossy, leaf-ridden ground. We near the log, where I'm certain Gideon is hurt, or worse.

We hear voices—or *a* voice—as we near the log, and this time, though still obscured beneath the sounds of rushing water, there is no mistaking it. The same voice from that day with Melody. The voice that haunts my dreams.

It hits me in the gut, knocking me off balance. *No.*

When we stop, Peter pulls my face before his, mouthing, "What's going on?"

Breathe. I whisper into his ear, "It's Asher. The killer. And he has Gideon."

I peek out from behind the tree, stifling a cry as I glimpse

Gideon's figure slumped over the log, swathed in the ethereal glow that spills through the treetops. His lifeless face is hidden beneath matted hair and dripping blood. I steady myself against the tree trunk. I'm light-headed, incapable of processing the stillness in Gideon's always-active body.

Asher stands behind the log, facing our direction. He hovers over Gideon, who suddenly manages to hold himself upright, but just barely. One of his eyes is swollen shut. His hands are bound behind his back, and his feet are tied together with thick rope.

Over Gideon's head, Asher dangles something that glimmers under the rays of light.

Melody Davenport's necklace.

"Is this what you were looking for?" Asher snarls. He clutches the golden chain in his fist and stashes it into his pocket. "I really didn't want to do this, Gideon, but you follow every idiotic command my sister gives you like a lost puppy." He makes his way toward a black canvas bag resting on the ground beside the log. A blood-coated metal wrench pokes out through the zipper. I fight back nausea.

Something else is half-concealed in the bag. Shiny ringlets of hair dangle over the side and I can make out one glassy blue eye. The rest of the face is covered by the doll's upturned dress, leaving its soft, torn belly exposed. More of the cloud-like material has spilled from its bowels and is scattered across the forest floor.

I gag, doubling over again. Asher didn't take the doll to fix it; he used it as a hiding place for the necklace. The evidence was moved to my room.

There's something else buried in the fluff: a scrap of green material with white polka dots, its edges singed black.

Asher rifles through the bag, pulling out a shiny blade, and resumes his position behind Gideon. He raises the wood carver and proceeds to lower it in front of Gideon's throat.

"No!" I shriek, stumbling from my secure location into the open woods.

At my outburst, Asher drops the tool to his side, a shocked expression washing over his face.

"Cass? What are you doing here?" He moves toward me, and I back away, expecting to shuffle straight back into Peter's firm arms. But the arms never meet me. When I turn, Peter has vanished.

I'm on my own.

As I stand, helpless and alone, the weight of my brother's crimes and my blindness come crashing down on me. My knees buckle, and I crumple to the ground, allowing him to step closer and closer. My fears, my selfishness that day in the woods, probably kept Asher out of jail, and maybe even ended Melody Davenport's life. And now my best friend's life is about to be extinguished, just like hers.

I sense Asher standing over me, and I glance up. He gazes down as though pleased to see me perfectly playing my part in whatever game he's operating. Traces of worry mark his face, but I'm focused on his eyes. Those icy cold eyes I now know match his soul. I shudder, knowing we share more than those eyes.

"Asher, please. Let Gideon go."

"You really should've gone to school today. You need to leave. Now." His voice is firm but pleading. Clearly, my presence has ruffled him. He can't go through with his plan as long as I'm here.

"I won't leave him."

"Cass, this only ends one way. Let me finish this"—he gestures to the log with the carver—"and we can go back home together."

"No!" I scream.

"You have to see that I can't let him live. Not with everything he knows."

"Asher, he won't say anything."

He sneers. "I'm sure."

I notice movement behind the log, and Peter's blond head of hair bobs up behind Gideon, fumbling around back there. A gush of hope stirs me from my paralyzed state. I have to engage Asher in conversation. I want to keep him occupied, to buy Peter time to free Gideon. But I also want to conjure up the brother I know: it couldn't all have been a lie.

"Just let me help you," I say. "The way you always help me."

"I already told you. The way you can help is by going to school."

"Did you plant the evidence in Seth's car?"

Asher's lips nearly curl. "Don't feel too bad for the guy. He was dating your nemesis, and you hate guys who do that."

"I didn't—"

"Oh, but you did. You forced my hand when you refused to let things go. The cops had no suspects. You're the one who did this to Seth. I couldn't frame Brandon because he would've pointed the finger at you. All I wanted to do was help you, Cass. By following the instructions in the notebook."

"You found the notebook? But—"

"Not *found*, exactly. I wanted to know what you and Brandon were getting so friendly about, so I snuck it out of your purse that night after the diner. What I can't quite understand is why you've been working so hard to screw everything up for us. I really thought you'd be happier with Melody gone. Now I'll probably have to get rid of Laura." He flashes a chilling half smile.

"How did you get the photo from Melody's phone?"

"I read the notebook and became extremely curious about what she had on you. So I asked her out. On our first date, I told her I wanted to take a photo of her and send it to myself." He tilts his head like he's bored. "She gave me the password, I snapped a photo of her—you might remember that one from her last Instagram post—and I sent your fiery photo to myself. I think you already know what transpired on date two."

My will is slipping. I can't hold my head up or move my legs from their contorted position amid the twigs. "What about Sara Leeds? Why do you have part of her dress?"

"Cass, I never meant for that day to plague you the way it has. If you would've just repeated what I said when I rescued you—that Sara started the fire—no one would have blamed you. Instead you had to act like a weird, fire-starting zombie child."

"Did Sara start the fire?"

Asher shakes his head. "I threw a rock at the candle."

"I don't understand." I shut my eyes and the voice from the woods repeats in my head. *Shh, it's okay now.* I've been so consumed by those words without really knowing why.

The memory comes back in a rush. Asher said those words as he stood on the other side of the playhouse door and I feverishly tried to push it open. He stood there and said them as Sara collapsed to the ground behind me and I wheezed in the smoky air until I couldn't wheeze anymore.

I believed my dreams were plagued by memories of the fire, but it wasn't really the fire that haunted me. It was the boy whose voice remained calm on the other side of the playhouse door as the flames raged around us.

"I didn't hold the door shut. You did." I grip my knees and rock, back and forth. "I thought you were trying to help me open it, but you were holding it shut. You closed the window so the smoke would suffocate us. You killed Sara. You"—I try to gulp, but my throat is too dry—"almost killed *me*."

Asher shakes his head. "The fire was never going to get anywhere near you, Cass. I made sure to get you far away in plenty of time. Of course, I couldn't let either one of us get away completely unscathed." He holds up his left wrist. "Not if Sara was going to, you know."

My mind spirals and darkens. "But why?"

"She wasn't as innocent as you remember, Cass. I heard you two in the playhouse. She was threatening to tell Mom that you broke one of her teacups. I was doing you a favor, just like I did with Melody."

"You killed my best friend." All these years, the doll— Asher's gift to me—was a hiding place for that scrap of Sara's dress.

His first trophy.

My body convulses with sobs, and I whistle in a breath. I wasn't silent after the fire because I was protecting myself. I was in shock. My brain must have erased everything to help me cope with the fact that the brother I loved murdered my friend right in front of me.

When I look at him, I still see myself cuddled up beside him on my bedroom floor as he read *Fox in Socks* over and over again. I can reason with him. He saved me that day.

However twisted, his aim has always been to help me. "Asher, you can't do this."

"See, that's where you're wrong. After the fire, I realized I can get away with anything."

Asher is still facing me, his back to the log. I steal a glance at Gideon, whose hands are now free. Peter kneels in front of him, working to untie the rope binding his feet. "I love him. Please don't."

Asher's features shift and a familiar expression creeps back onto his face. Maybe this is genuine remorse. Maybe the brother who read me stories was real, and he'll come back to me.

His face is soft as he lowers over me. I envision him helping me up, the two of us walking off through the woods together, headed to watch a classic horror flick on the sofa. "I don't want to. You have to believe me. I would never do anything to hurt you. But he gave me no choice." His face presses even closer to mine, and I notice he doesn't reach for his scars the way he always does when he worries about me. His voice doesn't quaver in concern. Instead, he whispers in a voice as smooth as the blade of the wood carver he holds inches from me, "And if you don't hurry up and get far away from here, *you'll* be leaving me no choice."

I see Asher now. The real Asher. It's the first completely honest thing he's ever said to me. It shatters whatever remnants kept my heart intact, sucking the breath from my lungs.

It also breaks the shackles that bind me to him.

"Go ahead," I say, giving up. I deserve it. Peter seems seconds from releasing Gideon. If my death can somehow help the boys escape, it's the least I can do. It won't make up for all of the hurt I caused. But it will be something. I close my eyes, ready to let the blade do its job.

A deep grunt rattles me from my state of surrender. I open my eyes to see Peter and Gideon standing in front of the log. Peter is already rifling through the black bag in the next second, pulling out the wrench while Asher stands, stunned. Gideon's body sways slightly, and I'm afraid he might collapse. But his gaze unites with mine. In that flicker from his one good eye, I know we have a plan.

I turn and take off running through the woods. My feet pound against the uneven terrain, and I know Asher has a choice to make. He can either chase after me or face the two boys and their bag of tools. Barely a second passes before I hear the sound of his body barreling through the branches.

I keep running like I never have in my life, until I reach the familiar barricade of trees. I dive into the small space at the base of the trunks, hearing Asher close on my heels. When I'm nearly through, my hair catches on a cluster of pine twigs and needles.

His footsteps hammer the earth just yards behind me, but my hair stubbornly refuses to budge. Just as Asher's fingers pounce upon the bottom of my shoe, I give one final yank of my head. I pull myself free, abandoning a large chunk of brown hair to the tree.

I drag myself the rest of the way through the trees as Asher struggles to navigate. Once free, I race to the hideout and kick the woven cover off, leaving the tarp in place. Then I sprint around to the opposite side of the hole.

Asher finally pokes his head through to find himself in what was once the magical realm of my childhood. He brushes himself off, like he can't commit his intended crime in such a disheveled state. I stand, shaking behind the blue tarp, completely exposed and defenseless. Asher holds the wood carver at his side. "It's not too late, Cass. We can get out of here together. You and me." He steps toward the tarp, squinting quizzically at the large blue piece of plastic that doesn't belong in the natural world.

He bends down to examine the tarp, but Gideon comes crashing through the wall of trees. He makes his way like a low-riding bullet on the ground, hands outstretched as he shoves my brother forward.

Asher yells as he falls into the hole, taking the tarp down into the depths with him. Gideon and I push the woven cover over him just as Peter navigates his way to us. The three of us hold down the cover as my brother continues to stab and slash through the flimsy woven contraption with his tool.

We use feet, knees, our entire bodies to keep the cover down. My body trembles with sorrow and fear, making it nearly impossible to keep my grip. My strength is slipping. I can't hold on any longer.

I'm about to let go when the merciful sound of sirens resounds through the woods. We shout at the top of our lungs until footsteps reach the outskirts of the barricade.

But Asher hasn't given up. He slices straight through the cover and into Gideon's hand, which flies upward as blood spurts over the cover. I want to rush over there, but with him down a hand, my two are even more essential. I grit my teeth and put every last ounce of strength into keeping my brother trapped.

A swarm of officers finally makes it through the trees and we back away, allowing them to cuff Asher, whose frantic efforts to escape the hole have ceased. His face resumes the composed demeanor that I know will haunt me the rest of my life.

I turn to Gideon in time to see his eyes roll back into his head. Then he collapses, as though he'd been holding on just long enough to rescue me. Screaming, I fling myself over him. I allowed myself to believe Asher's lies my entire life; now Gideon, who is more family than Asher ever was, is paying for it. I cry in short, staccato bursts, the tears pooling over Gideon's blood-caked body, until paramedics tear him away.

They let me ride with him to the hospital, and I sit, holding his hand so tightly. Peter, whose phone call to the police and heroic efforts saved our lives, is left in the woods to answer questions. I catch his eyes trailing after me, his figure becoming smaller and smaller through the back window of the ambulance.

31

My brother is secure behind bars now. For a while, my parents struggled with whether or not they should keep his senior portrait hanging in its spot on the foyer wall beside mine. I know they felt like taking it down meant he was really cast out of the family for good. Leaving it up allows them to hold on to some semblance of a family unit, however fictional.

Seeing his portrait there with those cold blue eyes and that smug, cracked smile always conjures up the memory of Asher's tear-filled breakdown in his room; I get a stab of pain remembering how I believed his performance.

I wasn't the only one who believed my brother's performance over the years. I often wonder, if we'd all been paying a little closer attention, would my parents have seen the truth about their precious prodigy? Would Gideon and I have noticed a nervous tremble run through the strong jaw of Maribel's hero?

Then again, maybe he never betrayed such a tremble. I remember a lot of things about my brother—all lies—but memories, nonetheless. I remember him happy. Sad. Angry. But now when I think of my brother, I see the utter calm, like a pristine patch of snow beneath the dappled light of dawn.

In the end, my parents decided to keep the portrait up. Of course, this meant my mom had to sacrifice her weekly coffee dates. No one wants to come to your house and drink coffee while the handsome face of a murdering psychopath watches. I doubt the decision was too difficult for my mom, though, seeing how there isn't much left to brag about where her children are concerned.

My schoolwork took an unprecedented dive in the wake of Asher's arrest. Emily eventually forgave me; however, like my mom's friends, she stays far away from my house. She doesn't need a reminder of how her daydreams within the walls of my house became the stuff of nightmares. But she stood by me even after my family and I became social pariahs. She knows better than anyone how hard it is to be the sister of a killer in Maribel. I've had to get used to a new level of seething glares. I deserve them. I soak them up in silence. My penance for all of the destruction I've caused.

One painful reminder of my destructive nature comes in

the form of an attractive blond who can't make eye contact with me anymore. Peter hasn't forgiven me for believing he was a murderer. He doesn't look at me with seething glares; he just doesn't look at me. Period. I don't deserve his forgiveness.

I don't deserve Gideon's forgiveness either. I'm part of a family that cracked his soul and his body, to the point where no one was certain he'd recover.

When I visited Gideon in the hospital, I was prepared for him to scowl at me the way he had the past few months. I feared that even though he'd survived the attack, I'd lost him forever. He'd managed to keep me at a distance for so long, maybe he finally realized he was better off without me.

Because he was.

The truth is, I *do* share something with Asher besides our crystal eyes. There is something broken in me, just like there's something broken in Asher, that lets people get hurt while I walk away unscathed.

I know now that much of my identity stems from a lie. I'm not a killer; I didn't even accidentally kill Sara Leeds. But I let myself believe the lie—the story Asher told me about myself—and it shaped every decision I made. I let those little creeping things embed themselves inside my brain, inside my very core, until they ate away at who I was. They created the hollow person who refused to help Melody. The girl who allowed Gideon's conscience to rot away so I could stay safe. The girl who let the murderer escape so no one would think

I'd killed again. The girl who made Seth into Maribel High's new target and later put him in jail.

And the thing is, Seth let the lies invade him too. He let the rumors I started push him into the shadows. He became the skulking loner the way I became Fire Girl.

But Gideon never saw Fire Girl. He believed in me and defended me starting in Mrs. Kent's second-grade class. So his reaction at the hospital should've come as no surprise. I hovered cautiously over his battered body, afraid he might open the one eye that wasn't swollen shut and scream for me to leave the room. Instead, when he saw me, he forced the corner of his cracked and bleeding mouth to lift.

Maybe it was blindness or maybe it was forgiveness. Maybe it was that perfect blend of goodness and audacity I've always loved about him. Or maybe I just managed to make my way onto Gideon's list of people who needed fixing.

Gracie came to see Gideon at the hospital, and she burst into tears when she saw how his handsome face had been dismantled. While she cried, I thought horrible things about her. How she had no reason to cry over Gideon. How she'd only known a fraction of him. How she probably even believed she loved him while she let her tears drip onto his hands—hands I should've been holding.

I'm not sure if Gracie felt my thoughts pierce through the back of her skull like lasers or if she caught Gideon's eyes periodically drift from her tear-streaked face to where I sat on a chair in the corner of the room. But she kissed his hand in that angelic way she does everything, and then she left. And I had the feeling she wouldn't be back.

Good or bad, she doesn't share what Gideon and I share.

After Gideon's release from the hospital, we didn't speak about the hobbit house. Our secret hideout occupied a dark place in my mind, along with Asher and the other horrors I felt responsible for. It made me want to stay far away from the woods, and Gideon seemed to feel the same way. It was like we'd never be able to get past what happened out there, unless we buried it once and for all.

So one day, I woke up and the sun's rays landed on my pillow, glittering the way they always did in the spring when the weather was warm enough to spend childhood days outside.

That morning I decided to return to the hobbit house. And I took Gideon with me.

By the time we crawled through the evergreen trees on hands and knees, the sun had vanished behind the clouds and a light snow began to fall over us. The hideout, which had seen even more ruin thanks to Asher's brief stay, was no longer the hobbit house of our childhood. Brown blood still smeared the ground and the torn, mangled cover. The termites I'd dreamed about had actually materialized. We could see the ugly, translucent creatures slithering over the blue cover down in the bottom. Tiny flecks of snow sprinkled the ground. Our once-serene world was now a dilapidated wonderland.

I continued to peer down into the hole, waiting for a joyful memory to emerge from the pit. Instead, I observed the devastation I'd caused.

Gideon proceeded to kick some dirt into it, watching the little bugs scamper away as the brown clods fell on them, dispersing granules of dust into the air. I kicked some more.

Then we abandoned that hole in the ground to the beastly critters.

We trudged back through the trees in silence. Gideon walked a few paces ahead of me. I noticed he wasn't leading me toward my backyard, but in the direction of the road. Shivering, I wiped off some of the crystals of snow that had swirled beneath my jacket hood and onto my face. I wondered where he was headed, but didn't want to interrupt his somber, reflective mood. I followed until we passed through the final line of fir trees, entering the narrow space beside the road.

There, as cars passed by, swerving to avoid us, we teetered on the edge of the road until Gideon took my hand and pulled me close. He lowered his head and peered into my eyes through snowflake-sprinkled lashes. I recognized his expression, and a familiar wish stirred in me along with a warmth even the chill in the air couldn't touch. I was home.

He closed his eyes, causing the small flecks of snow to

tumble onto my cheeks. And that's when our lips met, melding together the way our souls had years ago.

A driver honked while we kissed, and I held on to Gideon tighter. As I relaxed in his arms, allowing his embrace to heal so much of what was broken inside me, a chorus of catcalls sounded from a car's open window. Probably some kids from school.

But I didn't care. People could say what they wanted. Rumors and expectations were left back in the termite-laden hole in the woods.

And Fire Girl. I left her back there too.

ACKNOWLEDGMENTS

First and foremost, all gratitude and praise to my Lord and Savior. Every ounce of hope, joy, and success comes from You.

Thank you to my amazing agent, Kristy Hunter, for believing in this story. I couldn't ask for a more hardworking, enthusiastic, and dedicated champion for this book.

I owe many thanks to my brilliant editor, Eliza Swift, for loving this story and getting it in a way I never believed possible. My thanks go out to the entire Sourcebooks team: Chris Bauerle, Sarah Cardillo, Margaret Coffee, Chuck Deane, Cassie Gutman, Jessica Rozler, Sarah Kasman, Ashlyn Keil, Kelly Lawler, Danielle McNaughton, Sean Murray, Beth Oleniczak, Valerie Pierce, William Preston, Dominique

Raccah, Todd Stocke, Sierra Stovall, and Cristina Wilson. Thank you to Kerri Resnick, Tony Watson, and Nicole Hower for the fantastic cover.

Love and gratitude to my AMM family. Meeting you was truly the turning point in my journey to publication. I'm so grateful to Alexa Donne for everything you do to help aspiring authors. A million thanks to my mentor, Samantha McClanahan, for taking on this story and giving me the kick in the pants that I needed.

Thank you to the friends and critique partners who have made this book better along the way: Julie Abe, Laura Kadner, Jenny D. Williams, Madeline Dyer, Moriah Chavis, Emily Kazmierski, Katlyn Duncan, Katy Hamilton, Heidi Christopher, Jordan Kelly, and Graci Kim. A special thanks to Kit Frick for your generosity when I needed it most, and to Dana Mele for your wisdom and encouragement since the early days of this story. Love and thanks to George Kienzle, Rebecca Kienzle, and Monica Lewis for reading the very first draft of this book and not telling me to quit writing.

I'm forever grateful to my parents, George and Rebecca, for supporting my love of books and for watching my kids while I wrote. Thank you to my Ichaso family (Ann, Guillermo, Cristina, and Andrés) for your encouragement and for hanging out with my kids so I could work on this book.

Many, many thanks and sparkly unicorns to Julie Abe

and Laura Kadner for being the best writing friends a girl could have. Thank you for listening, reading, supporting, encouraging, joking, and everything else in between. You manage to brighten up even the worst of days.

Thank you to my church family for your prayers. A special thanks to Alec Kienzle, Marianne Cota, Monica Lewis, and Leah Huizar for asking me about my writing every chance you get. Your enthusiasm and support have been invaluable.

All my love and appreciation to Kaylie, Jude, and Camryn, for always listening in the wings, trying to figure out what this book is about, for constantly asking me when I was going to finish it, and for being excited to read it one day.

Thank you to my awesome husband, Matias, for suggesting I use my active imagination to write books, and for supporting me in every possible way once I took your advice.

ABOUT THE AUTHOR

Chelsea Ichaso earned her BA in English and her MA in education from Biola University. A former high school English teacher, she resides in Southern California with her husband and three children. When she isn't writing, she can be found on the soccer field. You can visit her online at chelseaichaso.com or on Twitter @chelseaichaso.